Author Note

The setting for this story is the Norman Conquest, a period that has long interested me because it was such a watershed in English history. However, the Battle of Hastings was far from being decisive in political terms. For the next six years William had to contend with numerous rebellions, which he put down with great severity. One such rising was in Northumbria. In the winter of 1069–70 the King's army exacted a terrible retribution for this. Known afterwards as The Harrying of the North, it was one of the most infamous episodes of William's reign. Contemporary chroniclers describe the region as being littered with corpses because there were not enough people left alive to bury them. One estimate puts the number of dead at 100,000. Over twenty years later, Domesday Book records much of this area as 'waste and desolation'. It is alleged that William, on his deathbed, confessed that his treatment of Northumbria had been unjust and troubled his conscience greatly.

My heroine and her family are innocent victims of these events. When their manor at Heslingfield is destroyed by the King's mercenaries, Ashlynn is alone and penniless in a dangerous land. Her troubles are compounded when she falls into the hands of Black Iain, a notorious border warlord. Haunted by the past, and driven by his thirst for revenge, Iain believes he has no time for the kind of encumbrance that Ashlynn represents.

THE LAIRD'S CAPTIVE WIFE

Joanna Fulford

MILLS & BOON

First published in Great Britain 2010
Harlequin Mills & Boon Limited,
Eton House, 18-24 Paradise Road, Richmond, Surrey TW9 1SR

© Joanna Fulford 2010

ISBN: 978 0 263 87595 9

Harlequin Mills & Boon policy is to use papers that are natural, renewable and recyclable products and made from wood grown in sustainable forests. The logging and manufacturing process conform to the legal environmental regulations of the country of origin.

Printed and bound in Spain
by Litografia Rosés, S.A., Barcelona

Joanna Fulford is a compulsive scribbler, with a passion for literature and history, both of which she has studied to postgraduate level. Other countries and cultures have always exerted a fascination, and she has travelled widely, living and working abroad for many years. However, her roots are in England, and are now firmly established in the Peak District, where she lives with her husband, Brian. When not pressing a hot keyboard she likes to be out on the hills, either walking or on horseback. However, these days equestrian activity is confined to sedate hacking rather than riding at high speed towards solid obstacles.

Recent novels by the same author:

THE VIKING'S DEFIANT BRIDE
    (part of the *Mills & Boon Presents...*
    anthology, featuring talented new authors)
THE WAYWARD GOVERNESS

For Helen,
who shared so many childhood adventures.

**Praise for
Joanna Fulford's
debut novel**

THE VIKING'S DEFIANT BRIDE

'Fulford's story of lust and love
set in the Dark Ages is reminiscent of Woodiwiss's
The Flame and the Flower.'
—*RT Book Reviews*

Prologue

The Scottish laird rested a moment on his sword, letting his gaze range the length of the defile where his men were now searching the bodies of the slain. Though the ambush had been successful the exhilaration of the fight was underlain by frustration as he realised the one he sought was not there. Surveying the scene now, his dark gaze hardened. Before he left he would find out what he wanted to know. Not all the men lying here were dead.

As the laird's shadow fell across him, the wounded Norman mercenary glanced up quickly, taking in the naked sword and the uncompromising expression of the man who held it. Then he spat. The Scot's gaze never wavered.

'Where's Fitzurse?'

The Norman returned him a cold stare but made no reply. A moment later the point of a blade was pressed against his throat.

'I'll ask you just once more,' said the quiet voice. 'Where is he?'

'We're dead men anyway. Why should I tell you?'

'Tell me and you can take your chance with the kites and the ravens. Refuse and I'll cut your throat and ask someone else.'

The man swallowed. 'Fitzurse rides north with the rest of his force.'

'Where?'

'Durham.'

'You're certain of this?'

'We're in his pay.'

'Paid to destroy everything for miles around?'

'Aye, for sixty miles around. On King William's orders.'

Recalling the devastation he had seen on the journey north, the laird felt his gorge rise. Once upon a time, in a past life, French society had been dear to his heart. At fourteen the world had been new and green, a place full of exciting possibilities of which France had been one. At the time it had seemed like a dream come true, a welcome chance to escape the cheerless confines of Dark Mount and his father's enmity. Back then the castle at Vaucourt had been the warm centre of his universe; the military training it afforded the highest peak of achievement. At Vaucourt he had grown to manhood. At Vaucourt he had first met Eloise…

That recollection inspired others less welcome. All the dead faces he had seen in the past days blurred and merged until he saw just one, the one that had been all to him. Time dulled the pain of loss but it did nothing to extinguish anger—or hatred. Both burned brighter for being cold.

'Why are you so anxious to find Fitzurse anyway?'

The prisoner's voice drew the laird back to the present. 'That's my business,' he replied.

'Suit yourself. It's nothing to me.' The other paused. 'I doubt if Fitzurse will care either.'

'Oh, he'll care all right when *I* catch up to him.'

'And who are *you* exactly?'

'My name is Iain McAlpin.'

The Norman's eyes widened slightly in recognition and with it the first flicker of fear.

'I have heard of you, my lord.'

'You're like to hear more, assuming I let you live of course.'

The other licked dry lips. 'I've told you what you wanted to know.'

'You can have your life, you Norman scum. I'll not soil my sword with you.' With that the laird sheathed the blade and walked away.

He headed back to the edge of the path where his men were wait-ing with the loot taken from the Normans.

'Well?' he asked.

His lieutenant shook his head. 'Not a lot, my lord. We found only copper coin and a little silver. Hardly worth their effort to get it.'

'Loot is only their secondary aim, Dougal. The first is revenge for the death of an earl.'

'De Comyn was a fool.'

'True, but he was also William's chosen man and Northumbria will pay the blood price.'

He had found out early in life about the abuses of power, first at his father's hands and later from other men. They were lessons well learned. Only when you were strong and feared could you protect yourself and others. His reputation might have come too late to help Eloise, but it now served well to protect all those for whom he was responsible.

Dougal eyed him quizzically.

'What now, my lord?'

'Tell the men to mount up. We ride for Durham.'

The other lowered his voice. 'Is that wise?'

'Wise? Aye, if I am to find Fitzurse.'

'Have a care, my lord. The man has the king's favour.'

'That will not save him,' replied the laird. 'I have waited eight years for the chance to get him within my sword's length.'

'Aye, and you have just cause to seek him out. I know that if any man does.'

'And your point is?'

Undaunted by that hawk-like stare his companion met and held it. 'I'm only asking if Durham is the right place to meet him. The area is like to be swarming with William's men. Fitzurse will be well protected.'

'Not well enough to save him from me.'

'Cut the bastard's throat with my blessing, but what of your mission and your oath to Malcolm?'

'Both will be honoured. He'll get the intelligence he seeks at the appointed place and time.' Retrieving the reins of a dapple grey stallion, the laird swung easily into the high saddle. 'But come what may I shall have my revenge.'

Chapter One

'Keep your guard high, Ashlynn. Like this.' Ban held his own sword aloft in demonstration. 'That's it. Now let's try those moves again.'

Nothing loath Ashlynn closed in to attack, trying to remember everything her brother had taught her over these last weeks, her whole attention focused on the two blades. The clash of metal rang in the frosty air. Ban parried dextrously and for a moment or two she had the satisfaction of seeing him forced back several paces.

'Ha! Take that!'

He returned the grin. 'You grow cocky, little sister.'

Ashlynn redoubled her efforts, laying on with a will, and saw him give ground again. Exultant she laughed. Laughter turned to a yelp as a blow beneath the hilt sent the blade flying out of her grasp and he tripped her neatly, sending her sprawling on her back, his sword point coming to rest against her throat.

'Do you yield?'

She sighed. 'I yield…*again*.'

'Don't be disheartened.' He put up his blade and extended a hand, pulling her to her feet. 'That was much better.'

'Not good enough.'

'It takes time, Ash, and you've made real progress.'

His praise heightened the flush of colour in her cheeks. At nineteen Ban was a year her senior and had already established his fighting credentials, his career having been founded at Stamford Bridge and Hastings three years earlier.

'Progress of a kind,' she replied. 'Yet I think my skills would not long withstand those of a seasoned mercenary.'

'God send you never need to put them to the test.'

'God send none of us does.' She shot him a shrewd glance. 'And yet you think it may come to that, don't you?'

'William will not suffer resistance lightly.'

She knew the words for truth. In recent days the manor at Heslingfield had seen a steady stream of people fleeing north from Durham ahead of the approaching army. None would willingly stay to face the Conqueror's wrath, knowing it would be terrible indeed, for the slaying of the Earl of Northumbria would be avenged with interest.

'De Comyn should have listened to Bishop Aegelwine. If he had he might be living still. Commandeering men's homes and womenfolk was never going to win him friends.'

It was an understatement and they both knew it. What had followed the arrival of the new Earl of Northumbria was an orgy of violence and cruelty. Provoked beyond endurance, the people of Durham had risen up in the night and slain the hated invaders, almost to a man. The streets of the city had run with blood. De Comyn had been burned alive when the mob set fire to the house where he and some of his men tried to make their last stand. Of the original force of seven hundred Norman soldiers only two had lived to tell the tale.

Ban shook his head in disgust. 'The Normans are arrogant brutes and heed none when their minds are set on blood and conquest.'

'William will find the city empty when he comes.'

'Then his wrath will fall elsewhere.'

It was the reason he had begun to teach his sister the rudiments of swordsmanship. Women were vulnerable in these unsettled times, even those possessed of courage and spirit.

'Surely he would not punish the innocent, Ban?'

'A man like William won't bother with such distinctions. Why, he even burned his own men at York.'

'He could not have intended it. No commander in his right mind would destroy his own troops. 'Twas only that the fire burned out of control.'

'He seemed to find it an acceptable level of loss all the same. The man holds life cheap.'

She shivered, feeling the cold for the first time. By tacit consent they sheathed the swords and retrieved their cloaks from the foot of a tall oak. Then they began to retrace their steps towards the manor. Beneath their feet the snow, already ankle deep, scrunched with each step. It had come early this year and above them a lowering sky gave promise of more.

As they left the shelter of the trees they paused,

seeing movement on the road in the distance. Roused
from her thoughts, Ashlynn saw a small group of people
heading that way.

'More fugitives from Durham, would you say?'

Her brother nodded. 'Aye, most likely.'

The bitter weather must surely have rendered any
journey unthinkable that was not undertaken from strict-
est necessity. It was a measure of their desperation that
the people came anyway. As they drew closer she could
see they numbered a dozen in all, men, women and
children, their frightened faces pinched with cold. A few
pitiful bundles contained all that they had been able to
carry when they fled the city. Ashlynn's compassion
woke and, exchanging a swift glance with her brother,
she saw the same thought reflected in his expression.

'I'll take them to the kitchen house,' she said.
'They'll need hot food before continuing their journey.'

'No, I'll go. You'd best change your clothes before
Father sees you.'

Ashlynn nodded, knowing very well that he was
right. She watched for a moment as he went to meet the
refugees and then hurried off towards the women's
bower. She had only just reached her chamber when a
servant arrived with a message.

'Your father desires your presence, my lady.'

Ashlynn grimaced, more than ever aware of her unorthodox appearance. Having dismissed the servant,
she swiftly divested herself of leggings and tunic, and
dressed again in her blue wool gown. Pausing only to
tidy her hair and throw a mantle over her shoulders
against the chill she made her way to the hall.

Lord Cyneric had been sitting in his accustomed

chair by the fire but hearing her step he looked up, his shrewd blue gaze appraising, surveying her in silence. Then he inclined his head.

'Sit down, Ashlynn.'

Obediently she took the offered chair opposite and waited, wondering what this meant. For a moment or two he said nothing, his weathered face thoughtful. Almost it was as though he were seeking the right words. His expression was more sombre than usual and for the first time she felt the vague stirrings of unease. Had he found out about the sword practices with Ban? Was she about to be rebuked again for unladylike behaviour? Would her brother get into trouble too? It wouldn't be the first time, of course. As long as she could remember, their escapades had landed them deep in the mire. Her mind, following that track, was quite unprepared for what came next.

'It is time you were married, Ashlynn.'

For a moment she was rendered speechless and could only stare at him.

'We live in dangerous times,' Cyneric continued. 'For your own protection you must have a husband, and one well able to defend you.'

She swallowed hard. 'But I am under your protection, my lord.'

'It may not be enough. The situation is dangerous and getting worse.' He paused. 'I would see you safely settled. Heaven knows you've had suitors enough. Yet at eight and ten you are unmarried still.'

Her face grew hot. It was true. By rights she should have been married long since. 'I never met a man I liked well enough.'

'You have had plenty of time to choose, but you have not done so. Now the circumstances force me to choose for you.'

Her heart lurched. 'My lord?'

'The Thane of Burford has asked me for your hand several times already and—'

'Burford!'

The name brought her out of her chair. In her mind's eye she could see the man for they had met several times during the celebratory gatherings for Yule and Beltane. Older than her by ten years he was of average height with a stocky frame and, like many Saxons, his colouring was fair. He was unfailingly attentive and courteous yet nothing about that homely, bearded face attracted her in the least.

Her father fixed her with a piercing gaze. 'He is much smitten with you, Ashlynn, and it's my belief he will make you a good husband.'

She shook her head. 'I do not love him, my lord.'

'It is not necessary to love your future partner in life, only to respect him. The rest will come later when you know him better.' He paused. 'You are a pretty wench, enough to twist any man around your little finger if you wished to.'

Ashlynn took a deep breath, fighting panic. 'I don't want to twist Athelstan round my little finger. I don't want to get to know him better!'

She had only ever behaved towards him with the requisite good manners though his interest in her had been clear from the first. She had never encouraged it knowing she could not return the sentiment. The thought of receiving much closer attentions from him was inconceivable.

'Ashlynn, listen to me—'

'No! I am not some chattel to be handed over thus.'

'I would not give you lightly to any man. Athelstan is worthy and he has been most constant in his affection for you. He will treat you well.'

'I will not agree to this.'

'My word is given. You will be married at Yule.'

The blue eyes widened. Yule was only a few weeks away. 'No!'

Lord Cyneric's jaw tightened but he held his temper in check. 'There is no time to be lost. Burford's lands lie further off some five days' ride, and he has at his command a large force of men under arms. He will protect you.'

'But I—'

'No more argument, Ashlynn. You will marry him and there's an end. This year our accustomed Yuletide feast will be to celebrate your wedding. Afterwards you will leave with your new husband.'

'My lord, please…'

'Enough. I am the head of this household and I shall be obeyed.'

If the tone had not been enough to convince her of the futility of further argument one look at that implacable expression was. Ashlynn turned on her heel and ran from the room, ignoring the exclamation that would have demanded her return. Half-blinded by angry tears she had no real idea of where she was going, only of a need to be alone for a while. In the event, her precipitate flight brought her to the stables and she slipped inside, pausing a moment on the threshold to look around. Mercifully the place was devoid of human company. Dashing the tears

away with a shaking hand she made her way along the
stalls until she came to Steorra's. The chestnut mare heard
her step and turned to look, whickering softly in recognition and presenting the white star on her forehead for
which she was named. Ashlynn stroked the velvet muzzle
for a moment or two. Then she buried her face in the
horse's mane and wept.

It was late when she returned to the hall. The evening
meal was preparing though in truth she had little appetite
for it. A group of people was gathered near the fire, among
them her father and brothers. Ethelred was deep in conversation with his parent but Ban saw her come in and
smiled. Then the smile faded a little and his eyes
narrowed, taking in her altered appearance, for although
she had sluiced her face with cold water before rejoining
the company, her eyes were still suspiciously pink-
rimmed, her face unwontedly pale. However, one warning
glance held him silent and he merely watched as she
turned away, extending her hands towards the blaze.

Letting the conversation wash around her Ashlynn
kept her gaze on the fire, though in truth she saw
nothing. All she could think of just then was being tied
for life to a man she did not love, and being taken from
her home and everything that was familiar to live in a
distant place among strangers. Her father used the
excuse of the troubled times but both of them knew it
was more than that. Whenever he looked at her he saw
her mother, the beloved wife he had lost just days after
Ashlynn's birth. Though he tried to hide his resentment
afterwards he had never quite succeeded. With this
marriage she would be gone and the reminders with her.

In due course they took their places at table but Ashlynn's appetite had deserted her and she ate little. Around her the conversation continued, still very much focused on the political threat that hung like a pall over all their lives.

'Will Heslingfield remain safe from the Conqueror's anger?' said Gytha.

Her sister-in-law's voice penetrated Ashlynn's consciousness and she glanced up, her attention caught in spite of her sombre mood.

'We have done nothing to provoke it,' Ban replied. The tone was even enough but Ashlynn detected the criticism beneath. Her brother had been much in favour of the rebellion and their father's refusal to allow his kin any involvement had rankled with him. Lord Cyneric threw him a shrewd glance.

'Be thankful for it.' He frowned. 'All the same we shall be ready to defend ourselves if the need arises.'

'Against an army?' replied Ethelred.

'William will hold the city and use it as a base to consolidate his position as he has with York. Besides, the weather is on our side too. He will seek winter quarters for his men. We may perhaps see forays for food and supplies but little more, I think. We shall be secure enough until the spring.'

'If William finds none to punish within the city he will look elsewhere. Heslingfield may not be as safe as you think, my lord.'

Lord Cyneric frowned but he did not immediately reply, pondering his son's words. Though they did not always see eye to eye on every issue, Ashlynn knew her elder brother's opinion carried weight with their father.

At three and twenty Ethelred had much of the look of his parent, being tall and well made and with the tawny hair and blue eyes that were a family characteristic.

'He is right, my lord.' Ban threw his brother a swift glance. 'It may not be safe to stay.'

'The women should be moved to a place of safety,' Ethelred went on, 'though heaven knows those are precious few these days.'

'We shall consider Gytha's situation in due course,' their father replied. 'Ashlynn is to marry Burford at Yuletide. Her future safety is assured.'

The news fell like a thunderbolt and for several seconds there followed a deep silence in which all eyes went from Cyneric to his daughter. Ashlynn felt her face grow warm as resentment rose like a tide.

'Ashlynn to wed Burford?' said Ban. 'Since when?'

She could hear disbelief in his tone. The same incredulity was registered in his face.

'Since this morning,' she replied.

He threw her a penetrating look. 'I didn't know you cared for him.'

'Why should she not?' replied Ethelred. 'He is a worthy man in every way.' He smiled at his sister. 'Congratulations. I wish you happy, Ashlynn.'

As the others hastened to add their felicitations Ashlynn bit her tongue forcing back the angry denial that would otherwise have burst from her. Inside, her heart felt like lead.

'You will be safe enough with Burford,' Ethelred continued. 'Would I could say the same about Gytha. The only way to go is north and the border country is dangerous enough.'

'Aye,' said Ban, 'and always will be while men like Black Iain of Glengarron ride unchecked.'

''Tis said he's a friend of Malcolm Canmore, so he's not likely to be checked, is he? Besides, the man commands a small army and raids with impunity deep into English territory. No doubt the rogue will use the current situation to his further advantage. If William is busy hereabouts he'll not be able to see off the Scots as well.'

'Black Iain or no Black Iain 'tis a risk plenty of folk are prepared to take.'

'Belike he would not bother with refugees anyway. They are too poor to tempt him.'

'Let's hope so for all those wretched souls fleeing the Norman wrath,' Ethelred replied. 'He has been known to seize much more than gold and cattle. The tales of his deeds are legion.'

Lord Cyneric snorted. 'Tales grow with the telling. The man would have to be at least ninety just to have had the time to carry out all the exploits attributed to him.'

'Even if only half are true his reputation has been well earned, and I would not have my wife fall into his clutches.' Ethelred threw another thoughtful glance at the two women. 'But may not Gytha go with Ashlynn after Yule? I am sure that Burford would readily offer her his protection too, until such time as the situation becomes clearer.'

Ashlynn's heart thumped. With every passing moment it seemed that this loathed marriage was becoming more real.

'The idea has much merit,' replied Cyneric. 'I will speak to Burford on the matter as soon as may be.'

Gytha's brown eyes revealed her anxiety more than

words. The prospect of a lengthy journey in the depths of winter, with a young child to boot, did not appeal. Ashlynn could well understand it. However, she also knew that Gytha would do whatever was necessary to protect her son.

She was fond of her sister-in-law whose pretty plumpness and placid nature were enhanced by her gentleness. Sometimes she wished she could be more like her; wished she had the same sweet patience and outward serenity. Ashlynn promised herself that one day she too would comport herself with the same ladylike demeanour and good humour for Gytha surely was the model of a perfect wife. She loved Ethelred and her child and put their needs above her own with a degree of selflessness that Ashlynn wondered if she could ever emulate. For a start her tongue was too ready with quip or argument to admit of her ever being so completely under a man's thumb. Yet Gytha did not seem to mind. Ethelred's every word was law to her, even on those occasions when, in Ashlynn's view, she would have done better to hit him rather than humour him. Yet Ethelred was a good husband in his way and the marriage was a success.

Ashlynn's hands clenched in her lap. She accepted that she must marry one day and have a husband and family of her own. But not like this, she thought, not like this. Had she still been free to choose, the man she married would be very different from either Athelstan or her brother. Both had their good qualities: they were steady and hard-working and honest; kind enough too in their way, but they lacked vital passion somehow, passion and fire. And something more that was harder to define: a certain dangerous edge that should set the pulse and heart racing. Ashlynn acknowledged to herself that she had never met such a man. Now she never would.

Sleep proved elusive that night. Her mind was racing with thoughts of the Norman retribution and of her proposed marriage. Unless something happened to change her father's mind, then in a matter of weeks she would be Athelstan's wife. The duties of the role were familiar to her: she had been tutored in them since childhood. It was not the thought of running his household that filled her with foreboding. Visualising her future husband, she swallowed hard. How was it that the good qualities he undoubtedly possessed could not render him any more attractive?

The new day dawned without bringing her any closer to an answer. Wanting to be alone Ashlynn avoided the hall and made her way to the stables. There she told the groom to saddle Steorra. Five minutes later he led the horse out.

'Do you wish to be accompanied, my lady?'

'No, Oswin, I'll ride alone today.'

He held her stirrup and watched her mount. She smiled her thanks and headed the chestnut away from the buildings, following the path across the fields towards the wood about a league distant. She kept the pace gentle for the ground was hard and the snow tended to ball in the mare's hoofs causing her to stumble. However, when they reached the wood the covering was less and they made better progress. Despite a warm gown and thick cloak Ashlynn could feel the aching cold in her hands and feet and face, felt it parch her throat and lungs with each breath. Above her grey clouds massed against the blue. More snow was certainly on its way.

She continued on to the edge of the trees as planned, intending to ride a wide loop around the wood before turning home. It was good to be alone for a while. The quiet countryside and fresh air were soothing, but nothing could detract from the fact that Yule was fast approaching. Ordinarily she would have looked forward to the celebrations. Heslingfield was renowned for its hospitality and the season was associated in her mind with joy and laughter and good fellowship. This year it would all be very different. Her throat tightened. Unwilling to think about it until she had to, Ashlynn nudged the horse with her heels. At once the mare broke into a canter. The swifter pace and the rushing air blew away some of the gloom and Ashlynn found herself smiling again in spite of everything.

She had almost reached the road before she saw the clouds of thick dark smoke rising into the sky. The wind brought with it the smell of burning. Ashlynn's smile faded and she reined the horse in, staring at the billowing plume with a deepening sense of disquiet. Her mind turned over the possibility of a hearth fire but rejected it; the smoke was too high and too dense. She also knew it originated in the direction of Heslingfield. Instinct told her to get back there and soon.

Pushing Steorra to a swifter pace she rode for a mile or so before drawing rein again. The feeling of uneasiness intensified for the smell of burning was much stronger now. Moving forward with more caution she came to the top of the rise above the manor and looked down on a sight of horror: Heslingfield was ablaze, hall, barn, stable and byre sending great tongues of flame shooting skyward. Above the sound of the fire could be heard the dying screams of trapped animals. All around human forms lay crumpled on snow reddened with blood and trampled by the hooves of many horses. Ashlynn could only stare in disbelief, her face ashen, while fear closed like an icy fist around her heart. Then she screamed.

'Nooooo!' The word echoed across the winter landscape in a protracted and desperate cry of denial. Then she was spurring forward, her mount plunging down the slope towards the burning manor.

The roar of the fire was much louder now and the acrid stench of burning choked the air. The mare slid to a stop on her haunches, wild eyed with fear from the din and the hideous oily reek. Ashlynn could feel the heat of the flames on her face, see the sprawled bodies. Tears of rage and grief stung her eyes. By the shattered gate lay her father's mangled form and near it Ethelred. Ban was nowhere to be seen but all around lay many others, retainers and servants, men, women and children, their eyes staring in sightless terror. None had been spared. Of Gytha and her child there was no sign either. Ashlynn looked around wildly and her horrified gaze came to rest at last on the burning hall and the women's bower, and in a final leap of understanding she knew where they were. The image splintered in her tears as, leaning down the side of the horse, she vomited repeatedly until her stomach was empty.

Then, turning the animal's head she guided it away from the scene of devastation, coming to a halt on the edge of the pasture hard by. With a shaking hand Ashlynn dashed the tears from her cheek even as her mind struggled with the enormity of what had happened. With the knowledge came guilt. She should have been there. She should have stayed. Yet if she had, her blood would be staining the snow like theirs. What malign fate had chosen to spare her and destroy all she held dear?

Just then Steorra threw up her head and snorted. Instinctively Ashlynn looked up too, her gaze following that of the mare. The movement was followed by a sharp intake of breath and her heart lurched to see the mounted group not a quarter of a mile away across the fields. The cold light glinted on helmet and mail. Her jaw clenched. Normans! Had they seen her? All other thought fled before the knowledge that she couldn't stay to find out. If they caught her she would be as dead as the rest.

She urged the horse away and nothing loath the beast leapt forward, eager to be gone from the scene of carnage and blood. From somewhere behind her Ashlynn heard men shout. One glance over her shoulder assured her she had been seen. Spurring Steorra to a gallop she sped across the snowy fields towards the distant wood. If she could reach the trees it might be possible to throw her pursuers off the trail.

They retraced the route to the wood, hearing behind the muffled thunder of pursuit. Ashlynn estimated perhaps twenty armed men. Fear vied with rage in her heart and a determination not to meet her end here in the icy fields. Ahead she could see the wood and felt a small spark of hope for it covered a large area and she knew it well, having ridden over it since childhood. Soon enough she reached the edge of the trees and hurtled down the track, bent low on the horse's neck to avoid the overhanging branches that tore at her clothing and threatened to sweep her from the saddle. The snow was not so deep here but she saw with sinking heart that there was enough to leave a clear trail. The Normans couldn't fail to see it.

Ashlynn followed the path until it came to a fork and then branched off left. She knew the way would emerge from the trees close to the north road. After that she would be in the open for a while and the more vulnerable. However, her horse was swift and fresh and not carrying anything like the weight of her pursuers' mounts. It might give her the advantage and tip the balance.

At the edge of the trees she stopped briefly, scanning the open space before her. Her gaze lit on the copse hard by and seeing it the germ of an idea grew into being. Touching the mare with her heels once more she gave the horse its head. The game little beast flew along the road, her tracks mingling with those of other traffic, and then Ashlynn turned off into the trees again. The snow was sparser here and the dry leaves left no sign of their passage. Set back off the road and hidden among the trees was a rocky outcrop and she made for it now, knowing that on the far side was a shallow cave. She would stay there until her pursuers had gone past, then double back. If she made a circle through the fields she could rejoin the road further on. By the time the Normans realised what had happened she would be long gone.

She reached the outcrop in question and found the cave. There she dismounted and waited. In the distance thudding hoof beats announced the rapid approach of the Norman troops. Ashlynn put a hand over Steorra's muzzle, willing her to silence, holding her own breath as the riders drew nearer. The noise grew louder and louder still, drumming like the blood in her ears. Presently the thunder of hooves was so near it seemed she must see soldiers appear at any moment. In her imagination she could hear their triumphant shouts and see the grinning faces as they closed in for the kill. Then, just as quickly, the sound of hoof beats began to diminish. Ashlynn leaned against the mare's neck in undisguised relief. It had worked. They were gone.

She rode until the light failed and found an old barn by an abandoned homestead. The place had been deserted for years. Part of the roof was gone but the rest would provide some shelter for the night for her and for the horse. Exhausted and cold Ashlynn fought back tears. They would not help anything now. With an effort of will she unsaddled the mare and then set about finding something with which to make a fire. That part wasn't difficult for the fallen roof provided wood and there was enough old straw lying around to start it. With cold fingers she drew the flint and tinder from the pouch on her belt. It took a while and several false starts but at length a spark fell on the tinder and glowed into life. Blowing gently she coaxed the spark to flame and fed it the old straw. Then she added small pieces of wood and gradually built up the fire to a size where it would at least afford some warmth. She had no food but just then it didn't matter; she could not have eaten it anyway. Somewhere in the darkness an owl cried. An omen of death. Hers perhaps. Ashlynn trembled. At one stroke everything she had known and held dear was gone. Heslingfield was reduced to ashes and her kin were slain. She felt tears spring to her eyes anew as the memory of that terrible hour returned. As long as she lived she would see the flames, hear the dying screams of living creatures burning to death, see the bodies scattered on the bloody snow.

She was a homeless, penniless fugitive. Fleeing where and to what? If she eluded the Normans she might find herself prey to robbers on the road, or to cold and hunger. She had nothing beyond the clothes she stood up in and the horse she rode. Perhaps later Steorra could be sold—if they both survived the journey, if the weather and hunger didn't account for them first. Suddenly the balance of survival hung on an awful lot of ifs. In that moment it occurred to her that death might not be so very bad.

Pushing the thought away, Ashlynn considered her options. They were precious few. Her only recourse was to keep heading north. If she could somehow reach the Scottish court at Dunfermline she would throw herself on the Princess Margaret's mercy. Since that lady was about to become Malcolm's new queen and was known to be a pious and good woman, she might take her into service in the royal household. However, Dunfermline was a long way off and a vast tract of dangerous territory lay between her and it. The reputation of the local warlords was well deserved—men like Black Iain of Glengarron, ruthless and dangerous. She shuddered, thinking that cold and starvation might be the least of her worries. In comparison, sleep seemed to offer a tempting oblivion, albeit only a temporary one. Wrapping herself in her cloak she lay down on a pile of rotting straw and closed her eyes.

* * *

In spite of her weariness she only dozed intermittently and awoke just after dawn. For some time she lay quite still, trying to recall where she was. Then she saw the lightening sky through the jagged roof of the barn and memory returned with a sickening jolt. Shivering she glanced at the fire but it was now a pile of comfortless dark ash and she got to her feet, trying to ignore the aching stiffness in her muscles. For a second or two she thought about remaining where she was but just as quickly rejected the notion. It was too dangerous to linger. She must ride for the border. It would not be quick or easy but it was her only hope now.

In her mind's eye she could already see the long road stretching ahead and feel the aching cold of nights spent in the open, for how often would she be able to find shelter and food? As she saddled her horse she knew the poor brute was hungry too. Heaven only knew how she was to find fodder enough on the journey north, but without the horse her plight would be desperate indeed. Resolutely pushing such negative thoughts away she pulled the girth tight. She was alive and she had the mare. There was that much to be thankful for at least. Even so it was hard to dispel the leaden feeling in her stomach.

She led the horse from the barn but had not gone half a dozen paces before Steorra threw up her head and whinnied. Ashlynn looked up quickly and froze to see the circle of armed horsemen not a hundred yards away. In the pale light of the breaking dawn she could see their mail and helmets.

'Dear God,' she murmured.

How had they found her? What evil chance had led

them here? Were they the same men who had followed her before? Then she realised it didn't matter. They were Normans. If they caught her she was dead anyway. The thought awoke fierce resentment. If she was going to die she would at least give these scavengers a run for their money. Quickly she gathered the reins and mounted.

As she did so the riders began to advance at a walk, closing in on their quarry. Ashlynn took a deep breath and spurred the horse forward, moving from a standing start to a canter, heading for the gap between the nearest horsemen. Her only chance was to try and barge through them. However, they anticipated it, moving swiftly to intercept her, narrowing the space, cutting off the escape route. Ashlynn reined and the mare wheeled round. Then seeing another gap she drove forward again. For one brief moment she saw the open ground beyond their horses and thought she might reach it. Then they closed on her and a strong hand seized her reins and yanked hard, bringing her mount to a plunging halt. She could see the wolfish smiles on the faces all around her. For a moment she closed her eyes, fighting the threatening faintness. When she opened them it was to see a mounted Norman knight in front of her. The cold eyes raked her from head to toe and she saw him smile before turning to his nearest companion.

'A pretty wench, De Vardes.' The words were spoken in the Saxon tongue though heavily accented.

'Yes, my lord.'

'Well worth the chase, wouldn't you say?'

'Indeed, my lord.'

Ashlynn kicked her mount forward in one last futile attempt to break free. The animal plunged but the grip on the bridle held firm. The Norman surveyed the proceedings with evident amusement.

'Whither away, wench? Surely you would not deprive us of your company so soon?'

She looked around in mounting panic at the ring of grinning faces.

'Get her off the horse.'

Men moved to obey. In spite of her resistance strong hands dragged her from the saddle. With pounding heart Ashlynn watched the knight dismount and move towards her. All her instinct was to flee but the two soldiers on either side held her fast. Then she was face to face with her captor.

'Did you really think to escape?' A mocking smile twisted his lips as he ran his gaze over her. 'Of course you did. You couldn't know that Waldemar de Fitzurse never loses his quarry.'

Ashlynn's eyes blazed with rage and hatred. 'Murderers! Norman brutes!'

The words ended in a gasp for he hit her hard, a stinging blow that brought the water to her eyes. Warm blood trickled from her lip.

'These rebellious northern swine must be taught better manners.' The words were quietly spoken but the tone sent a chill through her.

'Shall I kill her now, my lord?' The man called De Vardes stepped forward with a drawn dagger.

Ashlynn felt a hand in her hair yanking her head back and then the icy point at her throat, but her eyes never left Fitzurse. He would give the word now and all this would end with one welcome thrust of the blade.

'Not yet,' he replied. 'I am minded to have her first.'

His hand casually brushed across the front of her gown. Ashlynn glared at him. The Norman's smile widened. 'I detect defiance here that would be humbled. The rest of you may take your turns when I'm done. If she's still alive after that then she's all yours, De Vardes.'

Ashlynn's stomach lurched. The swift death she had hoped for would not come. They intended to make her long for it instead. She saw Fitzurse glance over his shoulder towards the barn.

'Take her in there and strip her.'

Chapter Two

As they dragged her back towards the ruined building Ashlynn began to shout and fight like one possessed, her screams shattering the still morning air. It availed her nothing. If anything it seemed only to add to the enjoyment of the men who held her. They reached the barn and, kicking the door open, strode inside with Fitzurse following at leisure a few paces behind. Dry mouthed with horror Ashlynn struggled harder but in vain for they held her with ease. One man pinioned her arms while the other unfastened her cloak and let it fall, his hand moving across her breast with coarse and deliberate slowness. She shivered as he stepped in closer and gripped the neck of her gown. For one moment her gaze met his and saw the mocking smile before he ripped the cloth apart in one sharp downward jerk. Never taking his eyes off her face he did the like with the kirtle beneath pulling the material wide to reveal her breasts. Only then did he glance lower and the cold eyes glinted in evident appreciation. He was not alone.

'Well, now, a very pretty little chicken,' said Fitzurse. 'I would see more, Duchesne.'

His henchman grinned. 'As you wish, my lord.'

Ashlynn trembled as his hands reached for the fabric of her gown.

Outside among the trees at the top of the sloping pasture another group of horsemen drew rein in obedience to their leader's command. Mounted on a dapple grey stallion he held the powerful horse in check with one gauntleted hand while his keen gaze swept the scene taking in the barn and the group below. Then he glanced at the man beside him.

'It seems our information was correct, Dougal.'

'Aye,' replied his lieutenant. 'It has to be them.'

'It's them all right. That blue roan destrier down yonder belongs to De Vardes. The cur never strays far from Fitzurse's heel. In any case they've left a trail of devastation that a four-year-old child could follow.'

'Aye, Reedham, Welbourne, Heslingfield.' The other shook his head in disgust. 'The cowardly dogs attack women and children because they like the certainty of winning, my lord.'

'Let's shorten the odds and find out how they greet our Scottish steel. We'll hit them fast and hard. Pass the word back.'

As the latter hastened to do his bidding the rider on the grey horse never let his gaze shift from the scene in front of him. A few moments later he heard the soft scraping sound that accompanied the drawing of many swords. Then Dougal returned, blade at the ready, a gleam of anticipation in his eyes.

'Just say the word, my lord, and let us at them.'

His laird nodded. 'Kill as many as you can. We'll take no Norman prisoners. But remember…'

'Aye, I know. Fitzurse is yours.'

'That he is. The bastard little dreams this day is his last.'

Lifting his sword arm he touched the grey with his spurs and called the charge. Quivering with excitement the big horse leapt forward, hearing behind the echoing battle cry as fifty riders burst from cover and hurtled down the slope toward the foe.

Taken completely by surprise the Normans could at first only stare at the advancing tide of horsemen. Then, as they awakened to the impending danger, the instinct for self-preservation returned. Amid shouting and confusion they scrambled to remount, turning then to face the enemy with scant time to draw their swords before the Scottish vanguard was upon them in a deadly wave of steel.

The laird's blade cleaved its first skull and came back for a wicked lunge into the next opponent. He heard the death scream and was aware of the rider toppling sideways even as a third opponent closed in. Since both hands were engaged with sword and shield he used his seat and legs to guide the powerful horse beneath him. At the given signal the grey reared, striking out at the enemy with its iron-shod hooves. Thrown off balance by the attack the bay destrier screamed and staggered, its rider crying out in agony as half a ton of targeted power drove downward, cracking bone and driving steel links through leather and padding into the flesh beneath. Grey-faced and swaying in the saddle the rider swore at the pain in his ruined knee. Before he could regain his balance the Scottish sword slashed across his breast.

Saved by the mail hauberk he looked down, scrabbling for the reins in an attempt to wheel the horse away from the danger for the injured leg was useless. That moment's inattention cost him dear and with a savage thrust the Scot drove his blade into his enemy's ribs. The man's face held a look of shocked disbelief. Then the Norman's sword fell from nerveless fingers and he toppled sideways from the saddle to lie still in the snow amid a widening pool of red.

Reining in the grey, the Scottish warlord surveyed the field. Everywhere the churned snow was stained red and scattered with the fallen. The Norman numbers were dwindling fast as he knew they must but his gaze still sought one man. Rage burned anew as he discovered no sign of his quarry. Where the hell was Fitzurse?

Ashlynn heard from without the spine-prickling war cry from fifty throats followed by a warning shout in French and the sound of thudding hooves, then more shouts and the clash of steel. Fitzurse frowned. For a moment he was quite still, listening intently. The din without intensified and his men released their hold on her. Fitzurse's hand went to the sword at his side and in cold terror Ashlynn saw him unsheathe the blade. Seeing her expression he bared his teeth in a smile.

'Never fear, chicken, I'll be back and we shall continue where we left off. Waiting will only make the pleasure all the sweeter.'

With that he turned and strode to the door: then with one last glance at his prisoner he was gone.

For some moments after Fitzurse left Ashlynn remained where she was, weak with relief, her body trembling with horror and revulsion, still unable to believe the narrowness of her escape. Outside she could hear the unmistakable sounds of battle, the clash of arms and neighing horses and shouting voices. Her heart leapt. She had no idea who the new combatants were and cared even less, but while men slaughtered each other she might be able to make good her escape. If they saw her they would kill her but it could not be worse than remaining. Just a small taste of what Fitzurse had planned for her made a swift end at the point of a sword seem infinitely preferable. Even if the French did not survive the fighting the victors might well decide to investigate the barn. If they did they would find her and there was no guarantee their behaviour would be any different. On top of that she might just freeze to death for the cold was biting.

Shaking violently she pulled up the rent gown and looked about for her cloak. It had been slung aside when Fitzurse's men had begun to strip her. After a frantic search she located it at last and threw it about her shoulders, holding it together over her torn clothing. Then she crept towards the door.

Peeping through a crack in the woodwork Ashlynn watched the pitched battle without. A large mounted group of dark-clad and wild-looking warriors were falling with evident enthusiasm upon the Norman mercenaries who were putting up a fierce resistance. However, there appeared to be far more of the newcomers than there were of the French and several bodies littered the ground already. It meant the fight would be over all too soon. She must use the confusion to make good her escape. Taking a deep breath she opened the door a little way and slipped out, darting looks left and right. An area of open ground surrounded the ancient barn but beyond it was a copse that might afford cover. Summoning all her remaining courage she edged along the wall to the rear of the barn until at length it was between her and any observers. Then she ran.

She was barely halfway to the trees when she heard the sound of muffled hoof beats behind and then a shout. A glance over her shoulder revealed the approaching Norman horseman, and her heart leapt towards her throat. Without staying to see more she fled. The sound of hoof falls grew louder and then Ashlynn was jerked off her feet. Suddenly vision became limited to galloping hooves and flung snow and a horse's shoulder, every bone in her body jarred by the swift pace. The saddle pommel pressed into her stomach making it harder to breathe.

After what seemed an eternity the horse slowed and she had a confused impression of trees and the sound of flowing water. A large gauntleted fist dragged her upright and a mailed arm closed about her waist. Chain mail links dug into her back. Chill air met bare flesh beneath her torn gown. Ashlynn glanced up and with sick horror saw that her captor was Fitzurse.

However, his attention was not on her just then but rather on the mounted figure who had reined in some thirty yards away. Automatically she followed his gaze and drew in a sharp breath as her startled mind registered a powerful dapple grey stallion almost seventeen hands at the shoulder. The beast was impressive enough but it was the rider who commanded every ounce of her attention. Flowing black hair framed a rugged, clean-shaven face that was arresting for the angular planes of cheek and jaw. It spoke of a man in his late twenties perhaps, but otherwise gave nothing away. Its very lack of expression sent a shiver to the core of her being. Boots, breeches, tunic and gauntlets were all of leather as dark as his hair and a great fur-lined cloak was thrown about a pair of powerful shoulders. He emanated an aura of dangerous strength, an impression enhanced by the wicked-looking dagger thrust in his belt and the great blood-stained sword casually held across the saddle bow.

For the space of several heartbeats neither man moved. Then her captor laughed softly.

'Well, well, I little thought to have the pleasure of meeting you again.'

'Everything comes to him who waits,' replied the other, 'and I have waited long for this moment.'

Fitzurse bared his teeth in a mocking smile. 'Ah, the aggrieved Scot. Not still smarting surely?'

''Tis you will smart, Fitzurse.'

'No, I shall have your head on a spear.'

The laird lifted his sword. 'This shall determine that.' Then the dark gaze flicked to Ashlynn. 'I see you're still in the habit of carrying off defenceless women.'

Fitzurse glanced down at his captive and his smile widened. 'Do you like her? I'll give her to you—by way of recompense.'

As he spoke his hand pulled aside the torn edge of her gown to reveal what lay beneath, ignoring her efforts to prevent it. The laird's dark gaze took in every intimate detail and lingered. In spite of the cold Ashlynn's flesh burned. Crimson-cheeked, she glared at the man on the grey but still that impassive face gave nothing away. Eventually his attention returned to her captor and when he spoke his voice was perfectly level.

'The only recompense I'll accept this day, Fitzurse, is your head.'

'Attack me and the girl dies.'

'Perhaps,' replied the other, 'but then so will you.'

Ashlynn watched as the stranger brandished the great sword aloft. The blade glinted in the cold light. With hammering heart she saw him nudge the grey stallion into a walk. She expected Fitzurse to advance and meet it, and could only pray that death would be swift when it came. However, instead of advancing, her captor reined back some ten yards and brought his horse parallel to the stream hard by. Swollen with rain and snow the stream was wide and twice its usual depth, the current swift and strong. Feeling his hold alter, Ashlynn's eyes widened as an unpleasant implication dawned. Surely he would not... The thought ended on a shriek as he lifted her clear of the saddle and flung her into the swirling water.

Fitzurse called to his opponent. 'If you want her, McAlpin, you'll have to pull her out.'

Stopped in his tracks for a moment the Scottish laird swore softly, his hand clenched round the hilt of the sword. The other held in the curvetting stallion. He glanced once toward the stream, saw the woman catch hold of an overhanging branch and smiled grimly. Then he spurred forward to meet his enemy.

Ashlynn surfaced with a choking gasp for the shock of the icy water drove all the breath from her body. Dragged along with the powerful current she fought instinctively to keep her head above water. It was instinct too that made her grab for the overhanging branch. It arrested her progress but the water dragged relentlessly at her clothing and with each passing moment the cold sapped her strength. If she didn't get out and soon, she was going to die. Somewhere in the background she heard the clash of swords. A frantic glance took in the fighting figures on the bank. Her clutching hands inched along the branch. As she shifted her weight the wood cracked like a whip. Ashlynn screamed and fell back into the water. It swept her headlong on its course for another hundred yards before slamming her against a large rock. Her icy fingers clutched desperately at the slippery surface for the force of the current threatened to sweep her away again at any moment. Mentally she wondered how long she could hold on. Another minute? Two? A voice inside her head said it didn't matter. If she did not drown the cold would kill her and then it would all be over. She closed her eyes.

The exchange of blows was fierce and evenly matched at first with neither man gaining the advantage until the Scot's blade cracked against his enemy's head in a savage back-handed slash. Had it not been for the helm the blow would have severed the top of Fitzurse's skull. The Norman reeled in the saddle, temporarily stunned. Iain wheeled the grey round to go in for the kill. Then, from somewhere behind him, he heard the woman scream. Involuntarily he glanced over his shoulder to where she had been. The branch was gone and she too. He frowned. That moment's diversion proved expensive for when he looked back Fitzurse was bent low on his horse's neck, spurring away through the trees. A hundred yards away three other riders in helmet and mail appeared. Seeing Fitzurse they reined in and waited. As soon as he had joined them, all four rode away at a gallop. The Scot glared after them then back at the stream. Just then the woman screamed again and, hearing it, he swore fluently.

Ashlynn could no longer feel her hands, only the drag of the water against her body. Soon she would have to let go and it would take her. Then, through the numbing cold, a voice penetrated her consciousness.

'Give me your hand, lass.'

She had a brief impression of a horse's neck and shoulder and a man's reaching arm. It towed her out and lowered her on to the bank. For a moment or two she lay there, gasping, unable to take it in, aware only of the cold, bitter, numbing and heart deep. Locked in its grip her body shook uncontrollably. Saddle leather creaked and then a pair of boots appeared in her line of vision. Her gaze followed them upward and came to rest on a face that was vaguely familiar. Memory began to return.

For a moment the Scottish laird was quite still, his gaze held by eyes the colour of cornflowers. They were the only colour in her face. The flesh on the delicate bones was deathly pale. He shuddered inwardly, reminded suddenly of another face and another time. This one would die too unless she got some warmth very soon.

'Come, stand up, lass.'

In response to that firm command Ashlynn struggled on to her knees. However, when she tried to rise, the sodden gown tangled itself round her legs and she staggered. Strong hands dragged her upright. She didn't see the swift appraising glance that took in every detail of her shivering form.

'I wager you'll live, but we need to get you out of those wet things.'

For a moment the words made no sense. Then, as the implication dawned, her hands clutched protectively at the torn edges of her gown.

'No.'

'Dinna be a fool. You'll catch your death.'

He reached for the front of her gown. Seeing his intent she turned to run but staggered again and almost fell, prevented only by the arm about her waist. Ashlynn shrieked, struggling to free herself from his hold but it was like doing battle with oak. The arm yielded not a whit. It swung her round instead bringing her eyes level with a broad chest. Panicking now she struck out with clenched fists. They might as well have been bird wings and, as they had relinquished their grip on her clothing, her garments fell open affording him an uninterrupted view of what lay beneath. He caught his breath. The reality close to only served to reinforce his earlier impression.

'Well now, not just a pretty face then.'

As soon as the words were spoken he regretted them, realising they were hardly calculated to reassure, but his temper just then was not of the best. Thanks to her his quarry was away and free. Just why he hadn't left the wench to drown was a mystery. Right now he half-wished he had.

'Be still, you little hellcat!'

'Let go of me!'

'I said be still,' he growled.

For answer Ashlynn kicked out and felt the blow connect. He gritted his teeth but his grip yielded not at all.

'All right, have it your way, you contrary little vixen.'

Without warning his hands closed on the edges of her gown and dragged it down over her shoulders. Ashlynn began to fight like a cornered wildcat. In her panic she saw only Fitzurse's men, felt their hands on her, restraining her while they did their will. It was all happening again. She wanted to scream but her throat was dry and suddenly it was harder to breathe for it was as though there was an iron band around her chest. The stranger's face loomed over hers. Then all colour drained from her cheeks and she was vaguely aware of him catching her before she fell into a dead faint.

She had no idea how long she was unconscious but when she came round it was to an awareness of voices, of men and horses. She was cold, her body shaking violently. Then something was supporting her shoulders and a hand was forcing a cup between her lips. She heard a man's voice.

'Drink this.'

The tone brooked no refusal. Hot sweet liquid carved a path down her throat and all the way to her stomach. Ashlynn gasped. He made her drink it all, but slowly, and by degrees the heat spread and began to warm the cold core within, enough for the shaking to subside a little. Becoming more aware she realised that she was swathed from head to foot in a huge fur-lined cloak.

Looking up for the first time she saw a black leather tunic. Above it was long dark hair and a face whose rugged good looks were only too familiar. Dark eyes met and held hers for a moment before turning their attention to someone opposite, out of her line of vision.

'We'll leave presently, Dougal. We've delayed long enough as it is and I want to reach Hexham tonight. Besides, the injured need tending.' He glanced up at the sky. 'We need to be back at Dark Mount before the weather closes in.'

'Aye, my lord.' Dougal paused. 'What about the lass?'

'We'll take her with us for the time being.'

'I can see your reasoning. For a drowned rat she's no so bad-looking. Dry, she'd be a welcome addition in any man's bed.'

Ashlynn's heart lurched. The man beside her glanced down briefly, his expression sour.

'This one would turn your bed to a couch of thorns.'

'Well then,' Dougal continued, 'sell her. She'd likely fetch a good price were ye minded to get one. Or ye could ransom her, did she have kin.'

He frowned. ' I'll decide later. In the meantime, where are the things I asked for? Where the devil is Archie?'

As if on cue another man hastened forward and handed over a bundle of cloth. 'Beg pardon, my lord. I'd a problem with the size.'

The laird looked down at Ashlynn again and then at the bundle he was holding.

'You'll be needing this.'

For a moment she stared at it and then back at him. Then, slowly, her dulled wits began to understand the significance of the great cloak around her and the immediacy of the soft fur against her skin. Her cheeks, so pale before, turned scarlet.

If she could have hit him she would have but both

hands were imprisoned beneath the folds of the heavy cloak. 'How dare you treat me like this!'

'Dare had nothing to do with it, you wee fool,' he replied. 'Your clothes were soaking and little better than rags anyway. If you'd kept them on you'd have gone down with a fatal ague for certain.'

'Is that your excuse?'

'It needed no excuse. 'Twas a matter of common sense.'

Bereft of speech she looked away. The man neither appeared nor sounded even remotely apologetic. Instead he drew her to her feet and taking a firm hold on her arm led her aside to a clump of bushes. Then he thrust the bundle of clothing at her.

'Put these on. They're not the most feminine of garments, but they're all that's available and they do at least have the advantage of being intact.'

Ashlynn glared at him. The dark eyes grew flinty.

'Perhaps you'd like my help, lass?'

'No.'

'Then dress and make haste or by heaven I'll finish the task myself.'

Her jaw clenched but she took the offering without further comment and retreated a few yards behind a small clump of bushes. Bare of leaves, they were not ideal to the task but provided a degree of privacy from prying eyes. A glance over her shoulder revealed that her large companion hadn't moved. Indignation surged: the brute had no shame at all! Then she reflected that it scarcely mattered; there was nothing for him to see now that he had not already seen before.

Giving her attention to the bundle she found it comprised a cloak in which were wrapped shirt, tunic, belt, trews and hose all clean and of strong and serviceable material. With them was a pair of leather boots. With no little relief she hurriedly pulled on the hose and trews and dragged the shirt over her head before divesting herself of the big cloak. Finally she pulled the tunic on. Like the shirt it was decidedly roomy but, she reasoned, it would allow for greater freedom of movement. It would be a lot warmer too. She fastened the belt but even on the last hole it still hung loose on her waist. The boots completed the outfit. Like everything else they were too big but better than going barefoot. Finally she threw the cloak round her shoulders and fastened it. Then, having retrieved the borrowed fur she rejoined her companion.

He watched her come, observing the transformation wrought in one comprehensive look. His expression gave nothing away but under that penetrating gaze she felt her anger mount again. With an effort she controlled it. The knowledge that she was beholden to the rogue didn't make things any better. Trying to gather a few protective shreds of dignity she drew in a deep breath.

'I suppose I should thank you for pulling me out of the water.'

'Aye, you should. If it hadn't been for you, Fitzurse would never have escaped.'

'I'm sorry he did.'

'So am I.'

'Why did you want to kill him?'

'That need not concern you.'

His wrath was almost palpable. That she should have been in part responsible only made matters worse. In a more diffident tone she said, 'I am grateful for what you did back there.'

The reply was a snort that might have been com-pounded of anger or disgust, or both. It brought her chin up at once.

'You could have left me to drown. Why didn't you?'

'Believe me, lass, I was tempted.'

With that quelling reply the conversation died, for Ashlynn could think of nothing to say and her taciturn companion clearly had no wish to pursue it further. Instead he took his cloak from her and put it on. Then, resuming his grip on her arm, he led her towards a shaggy bay gelding that stood among the waiting horses.

'Get on.'

There was nothing for it but to obey. He watched her gather the reins and swing into the saddle. Then he mounted his own horse and drew it alongside. A few moments later the whole cavalcade set off.

They rode in silence for some considerable time. The stranger made no attempt to break into her thoughts and in truth she had no inclination for speech either. In her mind she saw Heslingfield in flames and the bodies of the slain all around. Her jaw tightened. She would never see any of her loved ones again. There had not been a chance to bury them either or say a mass for their souls. They lay unshriven on the cold earth for the crows and the foxes to pick the flesh from their bones, or else their ashes lay in the blackened ruins of the hall. They were memories too bitter for tears. Once she had imagined that an arranged marriage was the worst fate possible. How naïve she had been to think so.

It wasn't until noon that the cavalcade stopped to rest. The landscape had changed as they progressed, wood and pasture giving place to rolling hills and open heath strewn with boulders and dead bracken. A few scrubby trees leaned to the prevailing wind and, hard by, a brook tumbled over a rocky bed. The riders turned off the road and dismounted. Ashlynn watched the stranger step down.

'We'll stop here awhile,' he said. 'The horses need a rest and the men too.'

Glancing around she realised with a start that there were perhaps fifty of them all told, mostly long-haired and bearded and variously dressed in stout leather tunics and cloaked like their leader, and every one of them fully armed. Remembering that they had defeated the Norman mercenaries she shivered a little. Unaware of her regard the men opened saddlebags and drew out bread and cheese and pieces of dried meat. It was then she remembered that she had eaten nothing since the previous morning and precious little then. The stranger threw her a shrewd glance.

'Come.'

He steered her to a boulder nearby that was a convenient height to sit on. Then he opened his own saddle-bag and drew out the food inside. When he offered her a piece of bread she took it and fell to devouring it at once. Observing this he passed over a chunk of cheese as well before falling to himself. The solid fare was coarse and plain enough but it lined the stomach and took the edge off the clawing pains she had felt before. They ate in silence and only when they had finished did he bend his gaze on her again.

'Tell me, how did you fall foul of the Normans, lass?'

She looked away. It was a painful subject and she had no wish to discuss it. He made no attempt to push her.

Instead he let the silence draw out and waited, though the quiet gaze never left her. Ashlynn forced herself to meet it and drew in a deep breath. He had saved her life after all so she supposed he was owed an explanation.

'They burned my home and slew my family. I was the only survivor.'

'How came you to escape?'

'I wasn't there. I'd gone out for a ride and when I returned…when I returned the rest were dead.'

'I see.' He paused. 'Where was your home?'

'At Heslingfield.'

'Heslingfield!'

'You know it?'

Recalling only too vividly what he had seen there, he could understand her earlier reticence. He would not revisit the nightmare now. 'I know *of* it. Lord Cyneric was its thane, I think.'

'Yes. He was my father.'

'I never met him but his reputation went before him: a brave fighter by all accounts. He had two sons I heard tell.'

She nodded and blinked back treacherous tears. 'They died trying to defend our home. Ethelred fell beside my father. I didn't see Ban's body and there was no time to look.'

'How did the Normans find you?'

'They had not gone far by the time I returned. When they saw me they gave chase. I thought they would kill me too at first but Fitzurse…Fitzurse had me taken to the barn and stripped. He meant to take his pleasure and afterwards let his men take theirs.' She drew in another ragged breath remembering every detail of the ordeal at the Norman's hands, the fear and the humiliation and the impending horror. The stranger was silent, waiting. Ashlynn's gaze was on the ground and she missed the expression of pity and anger in his eyes. 'Before he could do what he intended, your men arrived and launched their attack. In the confusion I tried to run away. The rest you know.'

'Where were you heading before the Normans found you?'

'North, over the border.'

'You have kin there perhaps?'

'No. I'd hoped to reach the court at Dunfermline and perhaps enter service there, but I didn't exactly have time to make a detailed plan.'

He did not miss the ironic edge to the tone but let it go.

'The border country is wild and dangerous; too dangerous by far for a woman alone.'

'There was no other choice.'

'No, I suppose not.' He paused. 'You never told me your name.'

'You never asked.'

One dark brow lifted. 'I'm asking now.'

'Ashlynn.'

'A pretty name and most apt, I find.'

As he spoke he knew the words for truth. Dougal was right: most men would find her a welcome addition to their bed. Unbidden his mind went back to the scene by the river and relived it with startling clarity. He indulged the memory for a moment and then pushed it away. That kind of distraction had no place in his scheme of things.

Unable to follow his thought and uneasy beneath that apparently dispassionate gaze Ashlynn forced herself to meet his eye.

'You still have all the advantage.'

'Aye, I believe I do.'

'Is your identity such a closely guarded secret that I may not know it?'

This time irony was underlain by a hint of impudence. Moreover, there was an expression in those blue eyes that was almost provocative as though she were testing the boundaries. It was tempting to show her just how close those were, but again he let it ride. His turn was coming.

'No secret, my lady,' he replied. 'I am Iain McAlpin.'

The name seemed strangely familiar somehow though it resisted precise identification. It niggled like a bad tooth. Earlier she had heard him say they would stay at Hexham that night. Where exactly? Surely no inn could cater for so large a party. Had he friends then who would give them shelter? His men called him lord. Lord of what? Where was Dark Mount? The missing pieces of the puzzle plagued her. Rather than labour over it she decided to ask. The answer was given readily enough.

'Dark Mount is a fortress at the head of Glengarron.'

'Glengarron!'

'Aye.'

She was suddenly very still as, in one moment of total comprehension, the last pieces of the puzzle fell into place.

'You are the Laird of Glengarron?'

'That's right.'

Ashlynn felt her stomach knot. In her relief at having escaped the hands of the Normans she had put herself into others every bit as dangerous, for who in the north of England had not heard of Glengarron or the man they dubbed Black Iain? It was small comfort to think she had no gold, nothing with which to trade for her freedom, in short nothing to tempt him at all. Then she remembered his earlier conversation with Dougal and her cheeks paled.

'What are you going to do with me?'

'I haven't decided yet, but you'll come with us as far as Jedborough at least.'

'Jedborough?'

'Aye, I've business there. When it's concluded I'll make my decision.'

She drew in a deep breath and tried to get her voice under control. 'You could leave me at Hexham.'

'I could, but I won't.'

'Why not?'

'It doesn't accord with my plans.'

Incredulous she glared at him but the gaze that met hers was unwavering and utterly disconcerting. Indignation swelled like a tide.

'Why should I co-operate with you?'

'Because you won't like the consequences if you don't.'

The threat was thinly veiled despite the mild tone with which it was delivered and, for a moment, it hung there between them. Given his previous experience of her, he was half expecting an outburst of rage. It never materialised, though her chin lifted at a defiant angle. In spite of himself he was amused and oddly touched. With somewhat grudging admiration he acknowledged that the lass had spirit as well as looks.

'Why are you doing this?' she demanded. 'My future can be of no interest or importance to you.'

'It isn't.'

'Then the only reason for holding me is concerned with profit.'

'Good enough reason, in my view.'

Ashlynn strove against rising panic. 'Leave me at Hexham.'

'I have just said I will not. The matter is closed.'

'I cannot…I will not go with you further.'

The dark gaze met and held hers but now there was no discernible trace of humour in it.

'You can, my lass, and you will.'

Chapter Three

The question of how to free herself from her captor exercised Ashlynn strongly now. What she would do after effecting an escape was uncertain; the important thing was to get away and find somewhere to hide. Somewhere he wouldn't think of looking. When he failed to find her he would perhaps give up for all his efforts seemed to be directed towards reaching Scotland. What was his business in Jedburgh? Who was he meeting there? *'After that I'll make my decision.'* Since she had no close kin who might ransom her, there was only one other way for her captor to profit. The Scots frequently seized prisoners on their raids across the border. Slaves were a valuable commodity. She shivered. Was this what the brute intended? The more she thought about it, the more likely it seemed. That being so, the more necessary it was to prevent it.

The first stars had appeared before they reached the outskirts of Hexham and already frost glittered in the blue twilight. The frozen breath of men and horses hung in the still air as the group drew rein and dismounted before an imposing walled manor. Ashlynn looked around her, taking in the house and the courtyard with its outbuildings and churned snow, while the men led the horses off towards a big barn. Then Iain took hold of her arm and guided her towards the house, a large rambling affair of timber and stone. A servant hastened to open the door and the laird strode into a large hall, drawing his captive with him. It was dimly lit and passages led off it. She was conducted down one of these and thence to a door off to the right which the servant opened. It gave on to a small bedchamber. The man set down the candle on the table and then withdrew.

Ashlynn cast a furtive glance around. The chamber was clean but sparsely furnished. There was a window, now shuttered fast, and a fire burning in the hearth. By its light she took in table and chair, a stand with a basin and ewer on it and, most prominently, a bed on the far side by the wall. With calmness she was far from feeling she turned to face Iain. The confines of the room served only to emphasise that powerful presence, and he was watching her now with an unnervingly penetrating gaze. Her chin tilted a little and, forcing herself to return that steady regard, she waited.

'You will sleep here this night,' he said then. 'I will have food sent to you shortly.'

'Whose house is this?'

'Does it matter?'

The tone brought a tinge of colour to her cheeks. 'No.'

'There are things it is better not to know.' He paused. 'You should try and get some rest. We have another long ride ahead of us tomorrow.' With that he turned to go.

At those words all her earlier desperation revived and she caught hold of his arm. 'Why will you not leave me here? Surely the price of one more slave matters little to you.'

'I told you that the matter is not open to further discussion.'

'I disagree.'

His hands closed on her shoulders, drawing her closer. The dark gaze bored into hers. 'Your opinion on the subject is irrelevant. I am the law here and you'll do as you're told.'

Ashlynn bit back the angry denial that sprang to her lips. He *was* the law here, every last arrogant inch of him. He was also very strong and much too close for comfort. She could feel the warmth of his hands through her clothing and the curbed anger behind his gaze. His face came much nearer to hers. Dangerously near. If he bent his head their lips would touch. The realisation both shocked and excited.

'Do you understand me?'

'I…yes.'.

'I hope for your sake that you do, lass.'

Unable to think of anything to say Ashlynn remained silent. He had half-expected her to argue further but when she did not the anger faded from his eyes and was replaced by something else entirely, something she could not name but which sent a shiver through her that had nothing to do with winter cold. Iain leaned closer, breathing the smell of wool and sweet air from her clothing and beneath it, the scent of the woman, subtle and arousing. The response caught him unawares and he drew a deep breath, mentally upbraiding himself. There could be no dalliance here, however tempting the thought might be. Slowly he pulled away from her.

'I must leave you now for I have other matters to attend to,' he said then. 'Get some rest, Ashlynn.'

His hands relinquished their hold and she was free. She remained quite still, watching him cross the room. He paused a moment on the threshold.

'If you require anything else let the servant know.'

As the door closed behind him she heard the sound of a key turning in the lock. She tried the latch anyway. The door didn't budge. For a moment she leaned against it, listening to the sound of his departing footsteps. When at length they died away she moved slowly back to the hearth and warmed herself before the fire, staring down into the flames, her thoughts in chaos.

Some time later the servant reappeared with a tray of food: good white bread and a large earthen pot of a fragrant meaty stew. She ate all of it for the long ride had sharpened her appetite. The food did a great deal to banish the chill and restore her spirits. By the time she had finished it was full dark and the edges of the room were blurred in shadow. She glanced at the bed. There seemed little else to do save sleep but at least it would be a welcome oblivion. Removing her cloak she undressed to her shirt and then curled up beneath the fur coverlets.

Having left Ashlynn's chamber Iain was heading for his own quarters when he met Dougal.

'Are the men settled?'

'Aye, my lord.'

'And the injured?'

'They too.'

'What of the lad we found at Heslingfield?'

'In poor case. If it hadn't been for the cold slowing the blood loss, he'd have died long before we found him.' Dougal paused. 'Have you told her?'

'No. She believes that all her kin were slain.'

'You really think he is kin? He might be just a servant.'

'They're related all right,' Iain replied. 'The likeness is too pronounced.'

'Well then, perhaps it is better she believes him dead like the others. Frankly, I doubt he'll survive and then she'd only have to go through it all again.'

Visualising the destruction he had witnessed at Heslingfield when they rode by, Iain nodded. 'She's been through enough just now. Let's wait on events. He might survive after all.'

'Aye, perhaps. If he does, it'll come as a happy surprise to her, won't it? Happy for us too were you inclined to sell him on later.'

'Keep me informed, Dougal, but say nothing to the lass. Tell the men to keep their mouths shut too. I'll tell her when the time is right.'

Having bidden the other goodnight Iain retired, but sleep did not come easily. On reflection, he wondered whether silence was the best course of action with regard to the injured Saxon youth. The resemblance to the girl was striking. It had been apparent at once. He could see Dougal's point and knew the advice was well intentioned, but at the same time was aware of a vague twinge of guilt. Was he right to keep her in ignorance? The lad's injuries were serious and there was a long way yet to travel. He was still unconscious which, given his other wounds, was probably just as well.

Then there was Ashlynn herself, spirited and rebellious too judging from her response to his plans. Recalling the scene that evening he frowned. Whether she liked it or not she was going along. There was no other viable alternative: to do anything else would take time. That would run counter to his plans and he couldn't afford to let it happen. Too much lay in the balance. Iain thumped the pillow hard: he was as far as ever from having his revenge, the work of months lost. By the time he completed his mission and was free to start hunting again the Norman might be anywhere.

The recollection of his enemy brought other related images: that first brief startling glimpse of the lass afforded him by Fitzurse *'Do you like her? I'll give her to you.'* That was swiftly followed by the memory of dragging her from the stream. In truth his sole intention in removing her clothing had been to restore some warmth to her body and quickly too. Yet when he'd stripped off the torn and sodden gown he had been unprepared for the beauty of what lay beneath or for the way the image would linger in his imagination. She had been understandably angry with him about that but, while he regretted the circumstances he could not for the life of him regret the memory of her naked body. Was that why he had been tempted this evening? His anger returned, this time directed at himself. Temptation was something he couldn't afford. In the years since Eloise there had been women, occasionally; women willing enough to satisfy his physical need. Those brief encounters were ideal: both parties benefited in their different ways and then parted. There were no complications, no entanglements, nothing to deflect a man from his sworn purpose. He thumped the pillow again. Once he was free of his obligations at Jedburgh then he'd decide what to do with the girl.

The next thing Ashlynn knew it was dawn. With the light returned all the detail of the strange room and the consciousness of her current precarious situation. As she recalled how it had come about her immediate dread was submerged by much keener sensations of sorrow and loss. For several minutes she didn't move until, with an effort, she had forced back the negative emotions. They wouldn't help her. She must help herself now.

Climbing from the bed she dressed quickly, trying to marshal her thoughts. Whatever happened she would not allow herself to be taken to Jedburgh or, God forbid, Glengarron. Having made her feelings clear on that score, she knew he would keep a close eye on her now so it behoved her to be careful, to make it seem as though she had bowed to his will. Having lulled him into a sense of false security she would await her opportunity to escape.

Presently a servant appeared with a platter of food and Ashlynn broke her fast. She had only just finished when the door opened again. Her heart skipped a beat to see the familiar figure standing there.

'In good time, lass. We need to move.' He glanced at the bed across the room. 'I trust you slept well.'

'Thank you, yes.'

'Good. There's a long ride ahead.'

'You have no right to make me come along.'

'Right has nothing to do with it. You'll come along because it's expedient.'

'Not to me it isn't. I don't wish to go.'

'But then we're not discussing your wishes.'

If he was aware of her anger it was not evident, for his expression remained maddeningly unperturbed. Her fists clenched at her sides as she fought the urge to hit him.

'I won't go.'

'You'll go, lass—one way or another.'

The threat was plain and she knew it was not idle. He had the power to compel obedience. The expression in those dark eyes was deeply disquieting and she turned away from him, heart thumping, trying to think. Once across the border escape would become harder which meant she must get away before they reached it. In the meantime argument was futile and she would not bandy further words with him, but if Lord Bloody Iain thought she would tamely submit to his will he had another think coming.

Almost as if he heard the thought Iain's voice broke in. 'Dinna think of trying to run, Ashlynn. I'd find you again very quickly and then you might find my temper unpleasant.'

'What difference would that make? Your temper is always unpleasant.'

The words were out before she was aware and drew down on her a look that caused her heart to miss a beat.

'Put the matter to the test,' he replied, 'and you'll discover a great deal of difference, I promise you.'

With that he took hold of her wrist in a vice-like grip and led her out to the courtyard. The cold air hit her for there had been a hard frost in the night and everything was rimed with silver. Around them men were already mounting. Robbie approached leading his own horse and a pretty chestnut mare.

'Dougal told me to bring this for the lady,' he explained.

Ashlynn wasn't listening, her whole attention focused on the horse.

'Steorra!'

Hearing her name the mare turned her head and whinnied softly. With tears in her eyes Ashlynn went forward to greet her, stroking the furry neck, utterly relieved that the horse had taken no hurt from her recent adventures.

Iain regarded them keenly. 'I see you two know each other.'

For a moment all her resentment was forgotten. 'Where did you find her?'

'I didn't,' he replied. 'My men found her wandering loose after the battle and brought her along with the horses we took from the Normans.'

'I see.'

'Will you mount, Ashlynn, or do you need my help?'

The bland tone didn't deceive her for a minute, nor was the implication lost. Biting back the pithy retort that sprang to mind she lifted her chin.

'That won't be necessary.'

He watched her gather the reins and swing easily into the saddle. Then he mounted his own horse.

'Let's go.'

They rode at a steady pace and soon Hexham was far behind. To her relief Iain rode on ahead with Dougal and left her to the charge of the young man called Robbie. Though he cast sidelong glances at her from time to time, conversation was minimal. However, Ashlynn had no desire for it, her mind on other things. With every stride of the horse beneath her the feeling of desperation grew. Soon they would reach the border. Soon she would be lost. She could not allow herself to be sold into slavery or worse. Death would be preferable. Escape was a risk but a calculated one. All she needed was the opportunity.

It was a relief when the column stopped at noon and she could dismount and stretch her legs for already they felt stiff from the unwonted hours in the saddle. She wondered at these men that they showed no signs of the weariness she felt, or the cold either. As they led the horses to drink at the stream Ashlynn did the same, bending to scoop a handful of water. It was icy but it slaked her thirst. She was occupied thus when she heard a man shout. At once the cry was taken up and, straightening quickly, she looked round.

Half-a-dozen riders had just appeared round a bend in the road and almost ridden into the Scottish force. There followed a con-fused impression of helmets and mail and then startled voices and the clash of weapons. Moments later a small section of the Scottish vanguard was heavily engaged in combat and being cheered on by their companions who seemed to think it quite unnecessary to become involved. Recalling the fighting skill of the Scottish warriors, Ashlynn thought they were probably right. Far from showing any concern about the unexpected confrontation they appeared to be treating it as an amusing diversion. Certainly all their attention was focused on the scene. In that realisation she saw her chance. A furtive look around confirmed it. Ducking swiftly under the mare's neck she grabbed the reins and vaulted astride. Moments later the horse was across the stream and cantering up the slope on the far side.

The fight was fierce and intense. Taken by surprise, the Normans were immediately at a disadvantage and, although they fought for their lives, were no match for the skill of their opponents. It had been an easy victory but it also raised other questions. Dougal came over to join Iain who stood surveying the slain mercenaries.

'A small raiding party or scouts for a larger force?' he asked.

'Probably the latter,' Iain replied. 'The question is how large a force?'

Before the other could say any more, Robbie's voice broke in abruptly. 'My lord!'

Hearing the tone of alarm Iain turned quickly, his hand moving automatically to the hilt of his sword. Seeing no immediate threat he relaxed a little. Then his gaze went past Robbie and caught sight of Ashlynn's retreating figure. He swore softly. Crimson with embarrassment, the young man bit his lip.

'I'm sorry, my lord. I only turned my back for a moment.'

'Damn it, lad,' said Dougal, 'could ye no keep control over a wee slip of a lass?'

'I'll go after her.'

Iain shook his head. 'No, you stay with the rest. I'll fetch her back.'

'Aye, and give her a good hiding into the bargain,' growled Dougal. 'The wee fool deserves no less.'

'I'll deal with her,' said Iain. 'Meanwhile, get the men

away. There's no telling how big the rest of the Norman force might be and I can't take a chance that would jeopardise our mission. Make for Jedburgh as planned. I'll catch up with you later.'

'Will you no take some men with you, my lord?' the other replied. 'It'll be dark in another hour and there's no telling how many more are out there, or where they are.'

'I'll be faster alone.'

'Aye, perhaps.'

'I'll take good care.'

'See you do.'

Iain turned and whistled for his mount. A few moments after that, he had guided the stallion across the stream and was heading the horse up the slope at a gallop.

Ashlynn reached the top of the hill and slowed a little, glancing over her shoulder. For a moment or two she could see no sign of pursuit. Then her heart missed a beat to see the rider on the dapple grey heading in her direction. It needed no lengthy study to work out who he was. Turning the mare's head she urged her on. The land above the summit was open and dangerous for that reason: the grey was bigger and faster and in this terrain would overtake them soon enough. Looking swiftly round she spied some trees in the distance and headed for them.

By the time she reached the wood the grey was closing the gap rapidly. She needed somewhere to hide and soon. The path through the trees was narrow but though there was thicket on either side it was leafless and afforded no concealing cover at this season. Even as she took the information in the track forked. Forced to choose she went left. A hundred yards further on she realised it had been a serious error for the path ended abruptly in a narrow defile bordered on three sides by walls of rock.

Ashlynn turned Steorra and retraced her route but as she neared the main track it was to see Iain's horse not a hundred yards off and closing fast. In a last desperate effort she urged her mount forward, conscious of the hoof beats behind thudding like her own heartbeat. However, though the mare was game her speed was no match for the bigger horse. Worse, the trees ended suddenly and the track came out into open land once more. Two minutes later the grey drew level and a strong hand grabbed the rein, drawing her horse to a gradual halt. Before a word could be spoken Ashlynn kicked free of the stirrups and leapt from the saddle. Then she ran, heading back for the cover of the trees in a last desperate bid for freedom. She had covered only fifty yards before a powerful arm swooped down. Moments later it drew her up on to the front of the saddle and locked around her. She fought the hold, struggling wildly. Reining the horse to a halt, Iain glowered at her.

'Be still, you little hellion!' Then, as the words had no effect. 'Stop this now, Ashlynn.'

'Let me go!'

'You know damned well I won't.'

Ashlynn twisted and slapped him hard. His jaw tightened and the dark eyes took on an expression that caused her stomach to turn over. Too late she realised that some unspecified line had been crossed and she was now in real trouble. Without another word he dismounted, dragging her off the horse after him. Ashlynn kicked and fought, cursing him roundly, managing only to deliver another ringing slap before she was thrown to the ground and pinned her there with a knee in her back. Iain glared down at his writhing captive.

'By God, I'll teach you to obey me, you little wildcat.'

'Get your hands off me, you Scottish bastard!'

'Scottish bastard is it?' Iain drew a length of cord from the leather pouch on his belt. 'Well then, I may as well live up to my reputation.'

Moments later she was bound hand and foot. Beside herself with fury, Ashlynn fought the rope even as she delivered a lengthy and blistering assessment of his character. Iain paused a moment and regarded his captive keenly.

'It seems to me that you're in no position to deliver insults, lass.'

'You deserve every one, you black-hearted villain.'

'Keep it up and I promise I'll warm your backside with my belt, you contrary little besom.'

It had been on the tip of her tongue to say he wouldn't dare but she choked the words off. The brute would not only do it but would enjoy it too. He had no sense of shame. Too late she was beginning to understand how he had earned his name. It was perhaps fortunate that she did not see the satisfied smirk that accompanied her sudden silence. A large hand hauled her upright. Then, adding insult to injury, he tucked her effortlessly under one arm and carried her to her horse. Moments later she was slung across the saddle like a sack of meal and tied there securely. After that he remounted and, having re-trieved her horse's reins, set off again. Incandescent with rage now, Ashlynn tested her bonds, but to no avail. They weren't cruelly tight but they were fast. The brute had known exactly what he was about. The final humiliation would be returning thus to his waiting men. Almost she could hear their laughter.

However, Iain made no effort to retrace their earlier route but continued on his present course for another hour or so. To Ashlynn he spoke not at all, or she to him. For a while hot temper and a strong sense of grievance kept her from noticing the discomfort of her position. However, as the time wore on it made itself felt, and she began to repent of her earlier actions. Her bound limbs ached; the saddle pressed hard against her midriff and the chill was more apparent. More than anything she wanted to be freed from her bonds. If he would just cut her loose she would agree to ride anywhere he wished. Only pride kept her silent.

The light was going when at last the horses came to a halt before a small farmhouse. A man came out and, from his ready greeting, it was clear that Iain was no stranger to him. To Ashlynn he paid no heed at all. The two men exchanged a few words and, having directed his visitor to the barn, the farmer went indoors again. As Iain dismounted and led the horses toward the designated shelter, Ashlynn craned her neck to take a quick look around, now keenly aware of their isolated position and the fading light. Was this where he meant to rendezvous with his men? As yet she could see no sign of them and for the first time missed their presence. For all sorts of reasons she was aware of the old proverb about safety in numbers. Moreover, she was tired, sore and cold for with the approach of darkness the wintry bite in the air was pronounced.

When they reached the barn Iain led the horses to their stalls. Then he paused, surveying his captive. Ashlynn waited, silently willing him to cut her free, though still she could not bring herself to plead. He waited a moment more, then smiled faintly and untied the rope that held her to the saddle. Having done that, he untied her ankles and let her slide down. She stifled a gasp as her cold feet jarred on the hard ground and felt her legs buckle. Had it not been for his arm she would have fallen. It kept her upright while he dragged her across to some upturned barrels by the wall.

'Sit down there and don't stir.'

The tone implied that to do anything else would be a serious mistake. Ashlynn said nothing. In fact she had no intention of disobeying him, all thought of rebellion long gone. Apparently satisfied by her chastened demeanour he turned his attention to the horses. From her vantage point she watched as he unsaddled and rubbed them down, noting with reluctant approval the sure methodical way in which he performed each task. Having done what was necessary he fed them some grain and filled the hay racks. Only when the horses were settled and comfortable did he turn his attention back to his prisoner, surveying her with a cool speculative eye.

'If I untie your hands will you give me your word not to try and escape again?'

She nodded dumbly, too cold and tired to contemplate a further attempt now. He knelt beside her, his strong fingers working the knots until they slackened. Then, blessedly, the rope loosened and she was free. Flexing her wrists she began to massage the aching flesh.

'Where are we?' she asked then.

'Among friends. We'll stay here tonight.'

'But what of your men?'

'We'll catch up with them later. It's almost dark now and the countryside is crawling with Norman mercenaries. It's too dangerous to continue.'

Ashlynn shivered, knowing it was true. Along with that realisation came the first stirrings of guilt that it was she who had put them in this position. As the possible consequences dawned she began to see the extent of her folly and the reason for his anger. It occurred to her that, had he wished to, he could have followed his earlier inclination and thrashed her soundly. She swallowed hard. Knowing his strength she was devoutly thankful that he had restrained the urge. The only thing he'd bruised was her pride.

She was drawn from these thoughts by the return of the farmer. Again he glanced once at Ashlynn and then ignored her, speaking quietly with Iain before setting down a wooden tray on one of the barrels nearby. From under the cloth covering she could smell the savoury aroma of stew and realised suddenly that she was famished. Then she glanced at Iain. He had not beaten her but he could still punish her by withholding food. If he did it would be a long time before the next meal. She bit her lip, trying to ignore the growling in her stomach. Whatever happened she would not beg.

However, it seemed that such was not his plan for he handed her a bowl of the steaming concoction and a hunk of bread.

'Here. Eat.'

Rather shyly she took the bowl. As she did so her fingers brushed his. The touch sent an unexpected *frisson* along her skin. Avoiding his eye she focused her attention on the food and, unable to resist, fell to. The stew was thick with meat and vegetables and, after a day in the open air, quite delicious. For a moment Iain surveyed her in silence, then sat down and ate his own. They washed the food down with a beaker of ale.

By the time they had finished it was dark save for the small pool of light from the lamp. Ashlynn was beginning to feel better now for the food had restored some inner warmth and, even though the barn was chilly, it was better by far than being out in the bitter night air. She drew her cloak closer, keenly aware of the man beside her. She watched him gather the bowls and beakers and return them to the tray. Then he took the lamp from its hook.

'Come.'

She rose somewhat reluctantly from her makeshift seat. 'Where are we going?'

He guided her to the foot of a wooden ladder. 'Up there.'

'The hayloft?'

'Aye.'

Apprehension reawakened and she hesitated, looking from the ladder to him, more than ever aware of the darkness, the remote place and his physical proximity.

'Where are you going to sleep?'

'In the same place.'

'You will not!'

One dark brow arched a little. 'Are you going up that ladder, Ashlynn, or am I going to carry you?'

The mild tone didn't deceive her for a moment. He wouldn't hesitate. Glaring at him in impotent wrath she knew there was no choice but to obey and with thumping heart began to climb, conscious that he observed every step. He smiled sardonically; then followed her up and lifted the lantern, illuminating piles of sweet-smelling hay.

'It's likely not what you're used to, lass, but it's dry and a lot warmer than sleeping in the open.'

Ashlynn said nothing. It wasn't the thought of sleeping in a hay barn that disturbed her.

'We've a long ride ahead tomorrow,' he went on, 'so get some sleep while you can.'

The tone was gentler than the one he'd used earlier but still Ashlynn made no move to comply. She watched him hang the lantern on a nail by the ladder. Immediately the loft was plunged into shadow for most of the light fell below. Apparently unaware of her gaze, he divested himself of his sword belt and then he lay down beside it and stretched out, wrapping himself in the fur-lined cloak. Only then did he glance at his companion.

'Goodnight, lass. Sleep well.'

Seeing he made no move to touch her, Ashlynn felt slightly less anxious. Besides, after the rigours of the day, she was suddenly bone weary. Selecting a spot as far from him as possible, she too lay down and drew her cloak protectively around her. For a while she was quite still, ears straining to detect any movement from her companion, but none came. She could hear only the sound of the beasts munching hay in the stalls below. Outside in the distance a fox barked. She shivered and curled up beneath the cloak. The sense of loneliness intensified bringing tears welling behind her eyelids, and for a while she wept silently into the folds of the cloth.

Not for anything would she have let her sobs be heard or given utterance to the grief that weighed upon her heart like lead.

However, in the quiet of the loft even the smallest sounds carried clearly. From where he lay, Iain heard the pain and sorrow underlying those stifled sobs, and with that all her aching vulnerability. All vestiges of his earlier anger evaporated on the heel of that realisation and he was unexpectedly touched, more so perhaps than if she had wept openly. For a moment he was tempted to go to her but then checked the impulse. Given all that had passed between them she'd likely not welcome the intrusion. Besides, what could he say that would in any way diminish the loss she felt? Grief needed an outlet. Better to let her have her cry out no matter how hard it was to hear it.

Sleep came for her eventually but with it troubling dreams of burning buildings and mounted men all in chain mail with the light glinting on their helmets. Like devils they rode through the flames striking down any who tried to flee. The air rang with screams of pain and terror. She could see her father and Ethelred locked in a desperate fight against overwhelming odds. Then Ban was there, shouting at her to flee. She tried to obey but her horse's legs were moving too slowly and the Normans closed in. She saw her brother fall, saw his face as he went down beneath their swords. Then she was being dragged from the saddle and the soldiers closed round her, their leering faces filled with hideous intent. Their hands reached out for her and she began to fight. Somewhere she could hear a woman screaming…

She awoke wide-eyed and panting with terror, struggling against the strong hands that held her.

'Hush, lass, it's all right. It's all right.'

Through her tears Ashlynn became aware of lamplight and the man beside her. With a jolt she recognised the face bending over hers and, involuntarily, her hands clutched hold of him.

'But I saw them…Norman soldiers and Heslingfield burning…the bodies in the snow…and blood, blood everywhere.'

As he listened Iain's expression hardened, but his voice was gentle. 'It was just a bad dream, lass. Nothing more.'

With that, some of the terror began to ebb though her body was still shaking with reaction.

'It was so real.'

He drew her close, speaking softly, his hand stroking her hair. 'The Normans canna hurt you any more, Ashlynn.'

He continued to speak to her in the same gentle tone, as he might have spoken to a child. Gradually she grew calmer for his nearness was reassuring now, not threatening, and his strength comforting, like the smell of wool and leather and wood smoke from his clothing, smells that seemed familiar and soothing. Involuntarily she relaxed a little, letting her head rest against his breast. She could feel the steady thud of the heart within, beating like the blood in her ears. His arms tightened around her and she felt him drop a kiss on her hair. The touch was light but it sent a flush of warmth through her entire being. Ashlynn caught her breath and looked up, meeting his gaze and seeing there an expression whose intensity both excited and alarmed her. It aroused a feeling unlike anything in her life before. She felt his lips brush her temple and cheek, kissing away the tears they found there. Then his mouth sought her lips. The pressure increased, gently, until her mouth opened beneath his, yielding to a more intimate embrace that awakened other pleasurable sensations that she had not known existed: sensations that thrilled and appalled sending a delicious shiver through her entire being.

Iain's heartbeat quickened as he felt that sudden tremor and with a sense of shock he felt his own hardening response, unanticipated and undeniable. The kiss grew more passionate as memory stripped her clothing away. The fire leapt and, unable to contain it, he crushed her closer, hungry now, wanting her, every particle of his being aroused by the taste and scent of her, the feel of her body in his arms again. He lowered her onto the hay and followed her down.

Unfastening her belt he pushed the tunic aside, sliding his hands beneath the fabric of her shirt, gently caressing, relearning with touch all the soft curves that his eyes had shown him before. The rediscovery sent a charge through the length of his body, a sensation of delight he had almost forgotten. Imagination outpaced him, turning his blood to flame.

He reached for the lacing of her trews. Seeing that hot devouring gaze Ashlynn felt her heart lurch and without warning she was suddenly transported back to the ruined barn and her mind filled with flooding panic. Instinctively she began to struggle, her hands pushing him away, her voice catching on a sob.

'No, no…please, I beg you, don't!'

The words acted on him like a bucket of cold water.

Looking into her face he saw fear and reluctance and with that sight desire ebbed. He rolled aside and drew a deep breath, trying to calm the wild thumping of his heart, trying to quell the riot of his thoughts. When he took her in his arms he had intended only to comfort her. He had not reckoned on that kiss. Innocent and sensual in equal measure, it aroused and disturbed, awakening memories he had thought safely buried. For all manner of reasons he could not afford the indulgence. How the hell had he let things get so far out of hand?

Aloud he said, 'It's all right, lass. I willna hurt you. There's nothing to be afraid of. Nothing's going to happen.'

'I shouldn't have…I didn't mean to…'

'Shhh.' He laid a finger gently on her lips. 'I think neither of us meant to.' He drew her cloak over her again and tucked it around her. 'Go back to sleep, Ashlynn, and sweeter dreams this time.'

With that he returned to his own side of the loft and flung himself down on his cloak. Those quiet words of reassurance might have satisfied her but he could no longer fool himself. Something had awoken inside him that he thought dead. The knowledge shook him to the core of his being and with it came a resurgence of anger for letting it happen. That was the first and last time. For both their sakes it mustn't happen again. He took another deep breath and let it out slowly. Then he wrapped the cloak around himself and shut his eyes. It was a long time before sleep came.

Chapter Four

Ashlynn was awoken by a hand shaking her shoulder.

'Time to move, lass.'

She came to with a start but, on recognising her companion, relaxed a little. Grey dawn light revealed the details of the hay loft and awoke the memory of the previous evening. With it came profound embarrassment and regret. What a fool she had been! What must he think of her? Yesterday it would not have mattered but now… A covert glance at her companion revealed nothing of his thoughts for he had moved away and was buckling on his sword belt. Ashlynn bit her lip.

'Iain, about what happened last night…'

His hands paused in their task and the dark eyes met hers. 'Nothing happened last night, lass.'

'I know.' She paused awkwardly. 'Thank you.'

Just for a second it took him aback. However, his tone was perfectly even when he spoke. 'I've never forced a woman yet, and I'm not about to start with you.' He finished buckling the sword belt and then moved to the ladder, pausing briefly to glance in her direction. 'Now we've established that, we'll get on our way.'

Having broken their fast on cheese and oatcakes they saddled the horses. Iain said nothing until they led the beasts from the barn. Then he paused, regarding her with a steady gaze.

'Will there be any need for me to tie you on your horse, lass?'

Under that piercing look she felt herself redden. 'No.'

'Do I have your word on that?'

'Yes.'

'Good. We'll be going then.'

With that he swung into the grey's saddle and waited for her to mount the mare. Then they set off. They rode in silence for some way, he seeming indisposed to talk and she not caring to intrude on his thought. From time to time she threw him a sideways glance but, as was habitual with him, his expression revealed nothing.

In fact his attention was on the countryside around them, looking for any sign of movement that might betoken a mounted force. Nothing stirred, save a few sheep grazing on the hillside. Detecting no immediate threat he relaxed a little, turning his attention to the girl at his side. She rode well, controlling the spirited little mare with ease. Once again he found himself curious.

'She's a fine horse,' he observed. 'A gift perhaps?'

'From my father.'

'He had a good eye for a mount.'

'Yes, he did.' The memory brought others that were unwelcome and she changed the subject. 'The grey is a fine animal too. What do you call him?'

'Stormwind.'

'It suits him. Did you train him yourself?'

He nodded. 'Aye, I did. A wild beast he was too when he was younger.'

Looking at the grey Ashlynn could believe it, and yet the rapport between horse and rider was pronounced. Having watched her father and brothers handling young stock she knew that such a sympathetic partnership had been forged out of skill and patience, not the use of the whip. Again it presented another facet of the man.

'I own to surprise,' he went on. 'About the mare, I mean.'

'Why so?'

'I expected to hear the word husband in connection with gift, not father.'

Ashlynn's gaze remained determinedly between the horse's ears. 'Did you?'

He paused, framing his next question with care but needing to know. 'Was your husband among those slain at Heslingfield, perhaps?'

'No.'

'Then…'

'I have no husband.'

'Why not?'

With an effort she kept her voice level. 'That is none of your business.'

'None at all,' he replied. 'I asked out of curiosity only. You are of age and you canna have lacked for suitors.'

Upon the word Athelstan flashed into her mind and, with his image, the knowledge that they would never marry now. The realisation brought both relief and guilt. And then, for no good reason, his face dissolved and Iain's took its place. Almost at once it raised a wry smile; he was the last man on earth her father would ever have chosen to be her husband. And yet, the thought persisted, what if he had? Would she have objected so strenuously to the match then? Would the thought of sharing his bed repel her? The answer was instant and shocking. Shocking because of who he was and shocking because, in spite of that, he was an attractive man. Worse, he engendered feelings that both disturbed and excited in equal measure.

Iain watched her closely, wondering at the thoughts behind that smooth brow. 'You make no reply.'

'There were suitors, only none I would marry.'

'Ah. You are hard to please.'

'Since marriage is for life should one not be careful about the choice of partner?'

'A fair point,' he conceded, 'but surely your father sought to guide your choice.'

'Yes, he did, but one cannot see through another's eyes.'

It was a partial truth only but it would have to suffice. As things stood she wasn't about to confide in him and, as she had said, it was none of his business anyway.

'True enough,' he replied. 'So tell me, what manner of man would you have then, lass?'

The directness of the question took her aback, but only for a moment.

'I'll know him when I see him.'

With that she touched the mare with her heels and cantered on ahead. Iain's lips twitched. Then he nudged the grey to a swifter pace, catching up a few moments later. Ashlynn spared him no more than a glance, keeping her attention resolutely on the way ahead. His question had unsettled her more than she cared to admit.

What matter if she did meet the man of her dreams? She had no kin, no land, no wealth; nothing to call her own save the horse she rode. It was hardly an attractive dowry. In tales of high romance the lover would care nothing for such mundane concerns as his lady's wealth: in real life things were different. Even if she had gone to Dunfermline and thrown herself on the queen's mercy, what then? She might have been given a lowly position of some sort, probably little more than a servant. Dunfermline seemed unlikely now. More probable was his disposing of her at Jedburgh. If not, would he take her to Glengarron instead? His power over her was total. He could do with her whatever he liked. She threw another swift glance at her companion and suddenly the possibility didn't seem so remote. She bit her lip. No matter how she regarded it, the future looked increasingly bleak and without hope of remedy.

They rode in silence again after that and Iain made no attempt to probe further. For the most part they held the horses to a steady pace putting more miles between them and the farm on the moors. It occurred to Ashlynn that the next night's accommodation might be very different from the relative comfort of a hay loft and, while it would not be the first time she had slept under the stars, it would certainly be the first in the depths of winter. It wasn't an enticing prospect. Now more than ever she pitied the plight of all those who had fled Durham.

At noon they stopped briefly to rest and eat before pressing on again. She noticed that Iain was keeping to tracks that skirted the hillsides, avoiding the open skyline where they would be visible for miles around.

Now, like her companion, she kept a watchful eye on the land ahead but still could see no sign of any living thing other than sheep and birds. Once again it was borne upon her that her actions the previous day had been foolish in the extreme and she would have given much to see the rest of the Scottish force once more.

She was jerked from these reflections by the sudden glint of light on metal among the rocks up ahead. Instinctively she shot a glance at Iain.

'Did you see that?'

His eyes never left the path. 'Aye, lass, I did.'

'Normans?'

'Doubtful. Robbers most likely.'

'Can we not—?'

Before she could finish, the rocks erupted with armed figures, four rough-looking men and all wielding wicked blades. Their expressions reminded her of nothing so much as a pack of hungry wolves.

Iain unsheathed his sword. 'Stay behind me, Ashlynn.'

With that the grey stallion leapt forward. She heard a scream as Iain's blade found its first victim. Almost simultaneously the big horse reared, striking out with iron-shod hoofs and a second man fell like a stone and lay still. Seeing the fate of their companions the others parted, closing in on either side so that Iain was forced to defend himself on two fronts. Ashlynn's heart leapt towards her throat. Another scream rent the air and a man fell, clutching his arm. A savage backhanded thrust opened his companion's throat.

Ashlynn exulted silently. Then exultation turned to fear as three more men emerged from concealment among the rocks behind him. She cried out a warning.

The grey wheeled in response but not quite fast enough. Hands reached up to drag the rider from the saddle. Instead of resisting Iain flung himself sideways, knocking his assailant off balance and the two men hit the ground. He rolled clear, coming to his feet in one fluid movement and leaving his attacker half-stunned in the dirt. The other two closed in.

Ashlynn glanced over her shoulder, half-expecting to see more assailants behind, but the way was empty. All she had to do was turn the mare and ride away to freedom. Even as the thought occurred, she saw the third man pick himself up and retrieve his sword, moving in on Iain's undefended back. She swallowed hard. Kicking her feet free of the stirrups she leapt from the saddle, dropping into a crouching run toward the nearest abandoned blade. As her fingers closed on the hilt she heard her brother's voice: *'Take your opponent by surprise if you can, and hurt him with the first blow. You may not get a second chance.'* As the robber raised his sword to strike, she swung at him. The edge bit deep. He cried out and staggered, clutching the wound, reeling round to face his unexpected assailant, his expression registering shock and rage. A second later it became malice and in one last deadly effort he lunged at her like a striking snake. Ashlynn leapt aside as the blade hissed past, bringing her guard up for the next assault. It never came. Her attacker collapsed in the dirt, blood pumping from the gash in his neck.

With pounding heart she threw a swift look over her shoulder; Iain was still hard pressed. Without stopping to think she launched herself at the nearest foe. He saw the movement just a second too late, crying out as the sword thrust through his ribs. For a moment he hung there, then slowly slumped and fell. She had a vague impression of the last man going down under Iain's blade a few moments later. Then it was over. Trembling with reaction, she drew in a deep breath, her gaze moving involuntarily toward her companion.

'Are you all right?'

He was breathing hard but standing yet, and now regarding her with an expression she had not seen before.

'Aye, lass, thanks to you.'

'It was thanks to me that this happened at all,' she replied.

'You couldn't have known yon scum would attack us.'

'No, but it *is* my fault we were separated from your men.' She swallowed hard. 'Iain, I'm so sorry.'

For the second time in five minutes he was completely taken aback for there was no mistaking the sincerity in her voice.

'Dinna fret yourself, lass. We'll meet up with them again soon enough.' She watched him wipe the blood from his sword and sheathe it again. 'In the meantime we need to get out of here.'

'You think there may be more of them?'

'No. If there were we'd know it by now, but there are plenty more like them hereabouts. Time is getting on and we've a way to ride before we reach shelter. I'd as soon do it in daylight.'

Ashlynn nodded. The thought of travelling through this country after dark had no appeal at all.

They retrieved the horses and for a while rode fast, putting distance between themselves and the scene of the recent ambush. However, they saw no one else.

* * *

It was dusk when they came to the farmhouse. Like the place they had stayed in before it was remote and again it seemed that Iain was known here for he was greeted with words of welcome before being directed to the stables. The latter was a long low building constructed of stone and thatch, but it was weatherproof and would afford shelter for the beasts and for themselves.

Ashlynn unsaddled Steorra and rubbed her down while Iain dealt with his own mount. Then she fetched grain from the nearby bin and fed the two horses while he filled the hay racks. When the animals were settled Iain removed the heavy cloak and sword belt and then eased off his tunic. Her startled gaze fell on the torn and bloody sleeve beneath.

'You're hurt!'

'A scratch only.'

'It needs tending. I'll go and beg some clean cloths. The farmer's wife may have some honey and wound-wort salve too.'

Iain didn't argue. Nor did he follow her from the stable. A few minutes later she returned with the necessary items and a bowl of clean water. Seeing this he unfastened his belt and eased off his tunic. Ashlynn stepped closer and rolled back the sleeve of his shirt the better to inspect the wound. It was a long shallow gash, vivid against the paler flesh of his arm. It had bled profusely and she knew it must hurt. However, Iain made no complaint, merely observing her in silence. Keenly aware of that penetrating gaze and the proximity of the man, Ashlynn tried to concentrate on the task.

'I need to clean this but it may sting a little.'

He returned a non-committal grunt. She dipped a cloth and carefully wiped away the dried blood. For a moment or two he watched the deft movements of her hands before letting his gaze move higher. It lingered a little on the soft hollow of her throat before travelling to her face, a face whose delicate contours were as familiar to him now as his own hand. The ride and the cool air had brought fresh colour to her cheeks and loosened tendrils of hair from her braid. The effect was strangely beguiling.

'It would have been a lot worse if you hadn't been watching my back today,' he replied. 'Where did you learn to use a sword?'

As her eyes met his, the cornflower blue deepened with inner emotion. 'Ban…my brother…taught me a few basic skills.'

'He taught you well I'd say.'

She shook her head. 'I got away with it because I took my opponents by surprise. There wasn't much skill involved, believe me.'

'Skill enough for the task, lass,' he replied. 'It took courage too.'

Something in his tone and look caused her heart to skip a beat. To hide her confusion she bent more assiduously to her work.

'You had the chance to run back there,' he continued. 'Why didn't you?'

It was a good question, she thought, and hard to answer. Yet in that split second when the choice was offered she could not leave this man to die. 'Let's just say I owed you one.'

'Maybe so, but this doesna make us quits.'

Ashlynn's hands paused in their task. 'By that you mean Fitzurse.'

'Aye.'

'For what it's worth, I'm truly sorry he escaped.'

'Ach, well...I'll meet up with him again.'

'To settle that score you mentioned?'

'That's right.'

She hesitated a little. Then, 'May I ask what manner of score?'

'That need not concern you.'

The sudden coldness in his tone was jarring. 'I beg your pardon; I didn't mean to pry.'

Iain frowned, annoyed with himself for snapping like that but somehow the words had just come out. A verbal reflex, he thought ruefully. Even to his ears it had sounded boorish. He gritted his teeth. 'Forget it.'

It was as close to an apology as she was going to get. Ashlynn kept her face determinedly neutral while her hands spread salve on the wound. 'I cannot. It was thanks to me he escaped.'

He sighed and when he spoke this time the sharp edge was gone. 'It wasna your fault, lass. What happened that day was typical of the man.'

She laid a clean pad over the cut. 'I have never met anyone more evil.'

'Pray you never do.'

He watched as she began to bandage the arm. Once or twice her fingers touched his skin, a pleasing touch that was both gentle and unexpectedly sensual and sent his thoughts in forbidden directions. With an effort he brought them back.

When she finished tying the bandage he flexed the

arm experimentally. 'You've done a good job.' He glanced down at the pot of salve. 'Allow me to return the favour.'

Drawing nearer he reached out and brushed the stray wisps of hair from her face in a gesture that was both casual and oddly intimate, like the warm musky smell of his skin. In an instant it evoked the memory of the hayloft and that sudden startling kiss and her breathing quickened.

With great care he applied a little of the soothing balm to her bruised cheek, smoothing it lightly across the bone. Thence he moved to the cut on her lip, his touch as delicate as a butterfly wing. Having applied the balm he scrutinised his handiwork.

'That will suffice I think. In a few more days the marks will fade.'

Before she could reply their host appeared with a tray of food and Iain stepped away from her to greet him. Glad of the distraction she replaced the lid on the salve and tossed away the dirty water. When Iain turned back again she had herself under better control.

'Time to eat, lass.'

The food was simple fare, bread and vegetable pottage, but it lined the stomach and warmed the body. By the time they had done it was dark and the only thing to do was retire. Iain spread a thick layer of clean straw in the only empty stall and then turned to Ashlynn.

'Again, I regret the basic nature of the arrangements.'

She shook her head. 'It doesn't matter.'

True enough, she thought, it really didn't. One place was much like another now. Wrapping herself in her cloak she lay down. Iain retrieved his sword and unsheathed the blade. Then he too stretched out, laying the naked weapon beside him, the hilt by his hand. Having done that, he glanced across the intervening space and bade her goodnight.

He heard her reply and then the rustling of straw as she turned on her side. He had noticed that she always slept on her side. Drawing his cloak tighter he turned over too, taking care not to jar his injured arm. In truth he hardly felt it now. She had done a good job in tending him. More than that, he thought, but for her timely intervention today he'd likely have been food for the crows. No question but the lass had courage. She could have left him to die and seized the chance of freedom. Why hadn't she? After his treatment of her thus far he could hardly have blamed her. Then he'd almost bitten her head off when she asked about Fitzurse. His jaw tightened. He should have dealt with it better but her question had taken him unawares and he was not used to sharing his thoughts with a woman. In truth it was not a subject he wanted to discuss at all. The memories it evoked were too bitter.

In spite of her weariness Ashlynn found sleep elusive for her mind was crowded with thoughts. What was Iain's connection with Fitzurse? Some quarrel existed between them, but of what nature? Recalling his earlier response, she knew she wouldn't dare ask again. He kept his secrets close. For a while that day it had seemed as though the barrier between them had been lowered a little, but she was wrong. It was still firmly in place. Why that should have mattered was unclear, but somehow it did. Suddenly she wanted to know what drove this man. What events in his past had made him who he was? Had Fitzurse had a hand in that? Likely she would never know for their present relationship would be of short duration.

For the first time Ashlynn thought ruefully of her masculine attire. She could not recall the last time she had washed or combed her hair or looked in a mirror. Self-consciously she raised a hand to the bruise on her cheek. It was tender to the touch and no doubt an ugly colour into the bargain. Hardly a face or form to charm a man. Almost at once she smiled in self-mockery. If Iain had wanted her before it was merely because she was there, the only possible choice, and darkness hid all defects anyway. Men had different needs, she had been told, and would satisfy them where they could. The thought was sobering. More than ever now she was glad that she had not yielded in a moment of madness. To be considered by any man as an easy victory would have been anathema, but for this man to think so would have been even worse somehow.

Much to Ashlynn's relief the remainder of the journey passed uneventfully and they reached Jedburgh without further incident. At a fortified manor house about a mile from the town they made the rendezvous with Iain's men. As they rode through the gateway and into the courtyard Dougal hastened forward to greet the returning chief, his weather-beaten face creasing in a smile. Iain returned it, stepping down from the horse and handing the reins to a groom. Ashlynn followed suit, watching as the two men shook hands.

'It's good to see you back, my lord. We've been looking out for your return these last two days.'

His gaze flicked to Ashlynn and in that brief glance she saw contained anger and disapproval. The same expression was evident on the faces of the men nearby. She swallowed hard, knowing their anger was merited. Her actions might have caused her death and Iain's too, and while she could not suppose that hers would trouble them overmuch, their chief was a different matter.

If Iain was aware of the strained atmosphere he gave no sign of it.

'It's good to be back, Dougal.'

'Did you encounter any Normans on the road, my lord?'

'No, none.'

Ashlynn shot him a swift sideways glance. The answer was true as far as it went. Would he tell them of the encounter with the robber band? She dreaded to think how his men might react if they knew how close they had come to being leaderless. The knowledge of her folly returned with force. However, he made no reference to the incident and merely inquired of Dougal if all was well with the men. On receiving a reply in the affirmative he nodded.

'Well, then, shall we go in?'

He steered her towards the house, his hand warm and strong under her elbow. Not so long ago she would have considered that touch intrusive. Now it felt strangely reassuring. Once inside she was escorted to a chamber not unlike the one at Hexham. Her grateful glance around took in a cheerful fire and, blessedly, a bed. Tonight at least she would not have to sleep in a draughty stable. Iain paused on the threshold and for a short space they surveyed each other in silence.

'Is there anything you need, lass?'

Ashlynn glanced down at her clothes. Then, somewhat tentatively, she said, 'I'd like to wash. Perhaps borrow a comb.'

'I'll see what I can do.'

When he had gone she unfastened her cloak and laid it over a chair. The thought of being clean was suddenly very appealing. In the enclosed space she was keenly aware of the smell of horse and leather emanating from her clothing. Every part of her felt grubby. How much she would have given for an hour in the bath house at Heslingfield. Unbidden tears pricked her eyelids and she forced them back, swallowing hard. No use to think of it. Heslingfield was gone, part of a past life.

The arrival of the maid was a welcome distraction and in a short time Ashlynn was provided with a large basin, a jug of hot water, soap, comb and linen towels. She regarded them with real pleasure and in moments had stripped off. Washing had to be done in parts but she scrubbed herself as well as she was able, starting with her hair and working downwards. It took a while but eventually every inch of her was clean and glowing. Then, wrapping a dry towel round her, she sat down before the fire and combed out her hair, easing out the numerous small tangles until it slid freely through the comb. Then she let the heat of the fire dry it. That done, she combed it again. Restored now to its normal lustre it fell in soft waves down her back. Rather anxiously she lifted the polished metal mirror from the table and examined her appearance. The cut lip was healing but a dark bruise marred the left cheekbone. Then she reflected that it would fade, in time. The bruise would be gone at least, if not the memory.

* * *

While Ashlynn had been busy thus, Iain had been checking on the disposition of men and horses. Later he rejoined Dougal and received a more detailed report of what had passed in his absence. He listened without interruption, and then nodded.

'It is well. What of the injured?'

'Making good progress, most of them.'

'The Saxon youth?'

'Still with us,' said Dougal. 'He's a fighter, that's for sure.'

'Like sister like brother.'

'The wench is spirited, I grant you, but she's a head-strong troublesome little jade for all that. Did ye take your belt to her, 'twould be no more than her deserts.'

'Dinna think I wasna tempted, but that same trouble-some little jade saved my life two days since.'

Dougal stared at him. 'Saved your life? How so?'

Iain furnished him with a brief account of what had happened during the robbers' attack. The other heard him with mounting incredulity.

'Well, I'm damned. With a sword, ye say?'

'Aye, just so.'

The idea clearly appealed to the laird's companion and he permitted himself a grudging smile. 'A rare wench—for a Sassenach.'

'That she is.'

'Will she come with us to Glengarron?'

'It depends.'

'On what?'

'The king's will.'

'You'll discuss her case with Malcolm?'

'Aye. The lass originally intended to go to Dunfermline. If the king wills it, she may yet.'

Even as he spoke, the thought jarred though he could not have said precisely why.

'You'll no sell her then?' said Dougal.

'No.'

'Ach, well, whatever you say.'

Iain left his lieutenant a few minutes later and made his way back to the chamber where he had left Ashlynn. There were things they needed to discuss.

Ashlynn heard the knock and, having assumed it was the maid returning, bade the girl enter. It was a very different figure who stepped into the room. The sight brought her to her feet with a sharp intake of breath.

Iain checked abruptly, his smile fading as he stared at the figure standing by the hearth. Every vestige of boyish appearance was gone, to be replaced by a feminine vision that caused his heart to miss a beat. She was clad only in a thin linen sheet. It stopped short at breast and knee and, in between, the damp cloth had moulded itself to the curves of her body. Unbidden his imagination stripped it away and reminded him of what lay beneath, only mantled now with tawny hair that hung in a soft curling mass to her waist. Huge blue eyes met his.

'My lord?'

She had never called him by that title before and it took him by surprise, not least because of the thoughts it engendered. Involuntarily he glanced at the bed across the room. Her lord? Hardly that, but, by God, if he were… Recollecting himself he cleared his throat and forced his thoughts back into line.

'I beg your pardon, lass. I came to discuss something with you but it can wait awhile.' He paused. 'Do you have all you require for now?'

'Thank you, yes.'

Ashlynn was aware that her face was glowing now with a lot more than the effects of soap and water; aware too of her present state of undress, and the disturbing nearness of the man. Nor could she fail to misinterpret the expression in the dark eyes. To her chagrin she saw him smile, a slow disconcerting smile that, though rare enough, did nothing to dispel her embarrassment. Clearly the rogue felt no such emotion. On the contrary, he seemed to be enjoying himself. With that realisation annoyance woke.

'Are you going to stand there all day?'

'It's a tempting prospect, lass. You clean up rather well if I may say so.'

Ashlynn glared at him. His enjoyment grew. Under other circumstances he'd have seen that unspoken challenge well met. He indulged the fantasy another moment or two, and then reluctantly retraced his steps to the door. When he reached it he paused a moment on the threshold.

'We dine in the hall with my men this evening. Until then, Ashlynn.'

With considerable relief she watched the door close behind him and then heard the sound of his retreating footsteps. With indignant haste she dressed again, heedless now whether her borrowed masculine attire smelled of horses or not. It occurred to her that it might be a good thing if it did. No man was likely to find that remotely attractive.

* * *

Iain made no mention of the incident when they met later, a fact for which she was grateful. However, when at length he had finished his meal and his cup was replenished, he leaned back in his chair and turned his attention towards her. Under that steady scrutiny the blood leapt in her veins.

'We need to talk, lass.'

Recalling his earlier words she took a shrewd guess. 'Business?'

'Just so.'

'Will yours keep you in Jedburgh long?'

'No, another day only.'

For some reason she had not been expecting that. Managing to keep her voice steady she said, 'And afterwards you will return to Glengarron.'

'Aye. The weather will close in soon and I want to be back before it does. Besides, my men are keen to see their wives and families again.'

'I see.'

'You spoke once of wishing to go to Dunfermline,' he said. 'Is that still the case?'

Ashlynn's heart beat a little faster. Now it was presented to her she was by no means certain it was what she wanted. However, to say so would make her sound indecisive and anyway there was no viable alternative plan.

'I must get my living somehow and can think of no other way,' she replied.

'Then I will speak to the king on the matter.'

'The king?'

'Aye. 'Tis he whom I've come to meet.'

Her surprise was unfeigned. 'When?'

'Tomorrow.'

She stared at him, her mind struggling to assimilate the information. If the king agreed to the request then tomorrow would bring a parting of the ways with Iain. In all likelihood she would not see him again. Once that thought would have gladdened her beyond measure. Now several different emotions vied for supremacy as she considered the ramifications. Underlying them all was something harder to identify. However, he was watching her closely now, waiting for her answer. Taking a deep breath she nodded.

'Very well.'

'So be it,' he replied. 'Of course, the king may refuse.'

'And if he does?'

'Then you'll come with us to Glengarron.'

'Oh.' It was a lame response and she knew it, but could think of no words that would have described her feeling just then. If Iain took her to Glengarron it could have only one ultimate outcome. To suppose anything else was naïve in the extreme. To think she had once regarded marriage as a problem!

Misinterpreting that reply entirely, he frowned. 'Whatever is meant to be will be, lass, whether you want it to happen or not.'

They left for the rendezvous at dawn accompanied by an escort of six men. The cold was biting and grey mist curled in wreaths above the fields. Every branch and blade of grass was furred with hoar frost. Ashlynn did not ask where they were going; that would become clear soon enough. She had slept ill the previous night, her mind in turmoil, no longer certain of anything.

Once or twice she glanced at the man beside her but his expression revealed nothing of his thought. Was he hoping that the king might grant her wish and take her to Dunfermline? Hoping that he might be rid of her for good? When she considered the trouble she had caused him already it would hardly be surprising. Once she would not have cared two straws for his opinion. Now, the thought of his disapproval was strangely discomforting.

The journey was short, little more than a mile, and ended outside a house hard by a small stone church. Half-a-dozen horses were tethered nearby, guarded by two armed men. Iain greeted the latter briefly, receiving a like greeting in return, and dismounted. Ashlynn followed suit. They went together into the house where a servant showed them into a small, sparsely furnished chamber. It was clean however, and a cheerful fire burned in the hearth. For a moment neither one said anything. As usual Iain's expression was unreadable.

'Wait for me here, lass.'

With that he left, closing the door after him. Ashlynn crossed the room and put her ear to the wood, listening intently. She heard a few murmured words beyond and knew then that there was a guard outside. The windows were high and barred with iron. Clearly she wasn't going anywhere. He fully intended that his parting instruction should be kept. An unnecessary precaution as she had no wish to leave just then anyway. She sighed and turned away to warm herself by the fire, trying to ignore the knot of apprehension in her stomach and wishing she could hear the conversation taking place elsewhere.

* * *

Malcolm listened carefully while Iain delivered his report on the military situation in England. As ever it was clear and precise. Moreover, it favoured his plans entirely.

'This falls out better than I had hoped.'

'William's forces are divided in dealing with several different rebellions, my liege; not only in Northumbria but also along the Welsh Marches and in the east, in the Fen country.'

'Then he'll be too busy to deal with Scottish incursions across the border,' Malcolm replied. Clapping his companion on the shoulder he poured two cups of whisky from the jug on the table. 'Let us drink to his confusion.'

Recalling the destruction he had witnessed on his journey north, Iain nodded. 'Right gladly.'

When the toast was drunk they fell into companionable silence. Iain gathered himself to broach the next subject. The king eyed his companion shrewdly.

'There is something else on your mind, I think.'

'Your Majesty reads my thoughts.'

'We've known each other a long time you and I. We've hunted and caroused together and fought side by side in battle. You have watched my back and risked your life to save mine, my friend. So, if it pleases you, will you not tell me?'

Iain explained then about Ashlynn, or at least related the essential facts. Malcolm listened with close attention, his penetrating gaze never leaving the other man's face. He had not lied when he spoke about friendship. Iain McAlpin was one of the few men he liked and trusted. That liking was mutual and, in consequence, Malcolm had learned something of his friend's past, a confidence he had never broken. Moreover, kingship had taught him early about the need to read men accurately, and what he saw here surprised him greatly. Had his companion known how much this spare account was revealing to his listener, he might have been much surprised in his turn.

'A bad business,' Malcolm commented when the tale ended. 'The maid is lucky to be alive. She has no kin who could take her in?'

'None, my liege.'

'Had she been a commoner I'd have suggested you sell her to the highest bidder. I suppose you still could as she has no kin to pay a ransom for her.'

Iain's brow drew together. Now that the matter was so baldly stated it seemed strangely unwelcome.

'Is she fair?' the king went on.

'Aye, she is.'

'Well, that's something. Of what temperament is she?'

'Spirited, my liege.'

'Unfortunate, but it would soon be beaten out of her I have no doubt.'

Iain frowned. That had not occurred to him before but now he admitted the truth of it. The life of a slave was one of drudgery and unquestioning obedience. For a woman it had other connotations too, especially if she was attractive. He remembered the first time he had set eyes on Ashlynn, remembered her torn dress and Fitzurse's mailed fist pulling the cloth apart. The memory was accompanied by a surge of anger, for it was but a short step to imagining what else would have

happened had the brute been allowed to follow his inclination. Could he be responsible for selling the girl
into such a fate? It took but a second to know the answer.

'I'll not sell her, my liege.' He hesitated. 'I wondered
if some place might be found for her at court.'

Malcolm shook his head. 'The court is no place for a
girl alone. Nor has she any dowry that would attract a
suitor. 'Twould only be a matter of time before she attracted the attentions of a very different kind of protector.'

Again Iain was forced to recognise the truth of that
statement and with it a fresh twinge of guilt. Perhaps he
should have left the girl in Hexham after all. Yet if he
had, what would she have done? Her fate there might
have been no different.

'Since you will not sell her and she cannot go to Dunfermline, there is only one other honourable solution,'
Malcolm continued. 'You must take her to wife.'

Iain's cup paused halfway to his lips as the ramifications dawned. Mentally recoiling, he was shocked into
temporary silence. Then he shook his head.

'I have no mind to marry again, my liege.'

'Your loyalty to your wife's memory does you much
credit, but you cannot live in the past.'

'I know it. Eloise is gone and there's naught can
change it.'

'Yet you are a man for all that, and you have a
man's needs.'

'When I want female company I can find it.'

'Of course. Nothing wrong with that, but you cannot
get heirs thus.'

It was an aspect of the matter that Iain had not chosen
to dwell on, but now that the topic had been raised he

confronted it. 'I'll marry again and breed sons, but not until I have destroyed Fitzurse.'

'I understand your desire for revenge and know you have good cause, but this quest has dominated your life these last eight years,' the king replied. 'A man needs more than hatred to sustain him. He needs the healing touch of a woman. You have been a widower long enough, my friend. 'Tis time to put the past behind you and move on.'

'I cannot move on knowing that my enemy lives and thrives, and a woman cannot help me there.'

'Marriage will show you the way as it has shown me.'

The king's regard for his newly affianced bride was well known and Iain forced a smile. 'Fortune has favoured your Majesty.'

'I would that all men might be so blessed.'

'It is a state to be hoped for rather than attained, by the majority at least.'

'Perhaps, and yet having attained it once do you not seek it again?'

'There seems little point in seeking what may not be found, my liege.'

'And yet I sense you are not entirely indifferent to this girl.'

It was a shrewd shot. Recalling what had happened in the hayloft Iain knew he could not deny it. However, wanting a woman was one thing, marriage quite another. Seeing his companion made no reply, Malcolm seized the initiative.

'If it is God's will, you may yet meet Fitzurse in combat. In the meantime you must look to those areas of your life that you have neglected. You must get sons to carry on your line.' The king eyed him with a level gaze. 'Besides, you have in some sort become the maid's protector already. Make it permanent.'

Nothing could have been more genial than his expression or his tone but Iain knew better than to think the words a suggestion only. His heart turned over as he saw the precipice looming. The king intended to be rid of the problem and with the least possible inconvenience to himself. Belatedly Iain realised he should have foreseen this and mentally cursed his own stupidity. Malcolm was nothing if not cunning.

'You must take her to wife,' he repeated. 'It is the only logical step.'

'My liege, I—'

'You must take the girl in marriage and there's an end.' The words were quietly spoken but the tone was as inflexible as steel.

Iain took a deep breath and gave the only possible answer. He wished now that he'd kept his mouth shut and never mentioned the subject at all. This was a damnable complication, one he didn't need or want. Nor did he imagine for an instant that Ashlynn would welcome it either. However, to disregard a royal command was out of the question. He had to get her consent. God knew it was going to take all his powers of persuasion. Then he reflected that once he had her safe at Glengarron there would be time to spare; time for them both to get used to the idea. Malcolm's next words undeceived him.

'Excellent. You shall wed the girl this day and I myself shall stand witness.' He gave his companion a beaming smile. 'Go, fetch the bride, and bring her to the kirk. Let the matter be settled once and for all.'

The interview was over. For a moment Iain was rooted to the spot before he recollected himself enough to make obeisance to the king and withdraw. Once outside the door he swore softly, needing that temporary vent for his feelings even though, just then, he wasn't quite sure what they were.

Ashlynn stared at him, dumbfounded. He had to be joking. Yet nothing about his expression suggested that he was anything other than deadly serious. With that look came the first stirrings of unease. Mingled with it was another feeling she didn't want to examine too closely.

'Malcolm has no right to do this.'

'He is the king, Ashlynn.'

'Not my king. I owe him no obedience.'

'But I do, and may not disregard a royal command.'

'Then let the fault in this be mine, not yours.'

'It's no use, lass. Face the facts. Even if the king were to take you to Dunfermline it would be to place you in a position of lowly servitude. It would only be a matter of time before some swaggering young buck took you to his bed.'

'I would not so demean myself.'

'Do you really think you'd be given any choice?'

She swallowed hard, having the unpleasant suspicion that he was right. He read her silence correctly and nodded.

'The only option left you now is marriage.'

An inexorable tide was sweeping her further and further out of her depth but Ashlynn fought the current anyway.

'I will not let your king treat me like a chattel.'

'We are in Scotland now. My king may do as he wills.'

It was the truth and she knew it though it did nothing

to lessen her present consternation. Nominally at least marriage did afford an honourable alternative to her predicament, but it was also irrevocable. The idea had been bad enough when it involved an unattractive man. Now it was infinitely worse.

'And what is your will in all of this?' she asked then.

'In this matter my will is the king's.'

'Damn your will and his too!'

She would have turned away but he prevented it, taking her shoulders in a firm grip.

'You will bend to it, lass, I promise you.' His gaze locked with hers. 'You can do nothing else.'

That also was the unpalatable truth, a fact acknowledged in strained silence. Unable to bear that intense scrutiny she lowered her gaze. It was capitulation and they both knew it.

'Better the devil you know, lass.' His hand closed round her arm. 'Come.'

'Where are we going?'

'To the kirk.'

'The kirk! Now?'

'There's no time like the present. Besides, the king is waiting.'

He drew her with him to the door. Ashlynn hung back, fighting panic. The hold tightened.

'It's no use, my sweet. There's no escape now—for either of us.'

Chapter Five

The church was freezing and empty at this hour, save for the waiting priest and the figure beside him. Malcolm was a physically impressive man with the powerful build of the warrior. Ashlynn had an impression of brown hair and a weathered face with shrewd appraising eyes. She could imagine that in battle they would look without pity on the enemy. They took in every detail of her unorthodox appearance but gave no clue as to the thoughts it engendered. No doubt all the circumstances had been explained anyway. The priest, however, was regarding her with cold disfavour. Women were not welcome in churches here, never mind a woman so outrageously clad. If he said nothing it was due to the exalted nature of the company.

The king glanced towards him and nodded. 'Let's get on with it.'

Ashlynn drew in a sharp breath. Then Iain's hand pulled her on to her knees beside him. In that moment she knew only a desperate and irrational urge to flee.

She knew it was irrational because there was nowhere to run. In any case half-a-dozen of Malcolm's men stood by the door. Her fate had been decided. Tears and pleas would avail her nothing, even if pride had not forbidden their utterance. Through the chaos of her thoughts she was aware of the priest intoning the words of the marriage ceremony. The whole scene was like something from a bad dream, except it wasn't a dream and she would not wake to find it all untrue.

As one in a daze she heard Iain repeat all the requisite words. And then it was her turn. When it came to the key question she hesitated, wanting to shout her defiance at the Scottish king, to say no, and to consign him and Iain McAlpin both to a place of great heat. The temptation was almost overwhelming. Almost. The silence drew out and grew louder. Though the man beside her didn't move she sensed the sudden tension in every line of him as he waited. Ashlynn swallowed hard, then made her answer, hearing the softly exhaled breath when she uttered the words.

Why had she? Certainly not from fear of his king, though she could hardly have forgotten the power of the silent royal presence just behind them, but rather what Iain had said before: *'Better the devil you know.'* The choice was stark: take him or accept a fate that would likely be much worse. No choice at all. She knew it and so did he. Yet there was more to it than that, as she now admitted. What she resented here was the method not the man. Toward him what she felt was not indifference and she could no longer pretend to herself that it was, and that made everything so much more complicated.

Since there had been no time to provide a ring Iain

improvised with the one he wore on his thumb. It was ludicrously big but served its turn. When the words were all spoken and the ring on her finger he kissed her, a gentle kiss on the mouth which burned none the less and set her pulse racing. Understated and subtle it was underlain with a deeper promise whose implications quickened every fibre of her being.

Then the king moved forward to offer his congratulations, bowing over her hand. Ashlynn lowered her eyes, her face an expressionless mask. Malcolm regarded her keenly for a moment and then looked at Iain.

'You spoke true, Glengarron. Your lady is most fair. Guard her well.'

'I intend to, my liege.'

Iain took her hand then and raised it to his lips. For an instant their eyes met but, as so often, his face gave little away. Did he share the resentment she felt? This marriage had been forced upon him too. Given the choice he would never have entered into this bargain. From the outset he had regarded her as an encumbrance. What possible argument could have persuaded him to agree to this? She lowered her gaze quickly, this time to hide her confusion. Then she handed him back the thumb ring.

'For safe keeping,' she said. 'It would be too easily lost.'

He returned her a wry smile and slipped it back on his hand. 'I promise you a proper wedding ring, lass, as soon as occasion permits.'

They went out to the horses and Iain took leave of his king. As the royal party rode away, he turned back to Ashlynn.

'Come, my wife.'

The use of that title and all it implied sent another wave of heat the length of her body. Not so long ago the notion of a forced match with Burford had filled her with anger and abhorrence. Now a very different husband claimed her. Soon enough he would take her to his bed and make his possession complete. Powerlessness kept her anger very much alive. Yet in the entire chaotic pantheon of emotions at that moment, abhorrence was conspicuously absent. With an effort she kept her voice level. 'Where are we going?'

'Home—to Glengarron.'

The journey that day was long and cold, but Ashlynn was scarcely aware of physical discomfort. Her thoughts had turned inward, trying to come to terms with what had happened, trying not to contemplate the future too closely. For the most part they rode in silence, the swift pace not being conducive to conversation. However, when they did stop to rest the horses at noon it quickly became apparent that news of the laird's marriage had spread. Dougal took it upon himself to issue each man with a dram of whisky from the keg on the wagon, and proposed the toast to the newly married couple. A loud cheer rent the air.

Iain looked down at his bride and smiled wryly. 'It seems they approve, my lady.'

Ashlynn shot him a swift glance but remained silent, not knowing what to say. In truth the press of grinning faces was a little daunting, though oddly she could see none of their former antipathy now. Rather than show any apprehension she forced herself to an outward display of calm.

'Will ye no kiss the bride, my lord?' called a wag from the crowd.

A roar of approval greeted this, followed by the chant of *'Kiss! Kiss! Kiss!'* Iain handed his cup to Dougal. Then he took Ashlynn in his arms, crushing her against him and bringing his mouth down on hers in a searing embrace. Another roar erupted around them. Ashlynn scarcely heard it, aware only of a rush of warmth deep within, like the sudden rekindling of a flame. The flame leapt and became fire. Unable to help herself she yielded to it, her body melting against him, her mouth opening to his.

In that moment of unexpected surrender he felt his own desire quicken and imagination tantalised, offering another glimpse of something he had thought was lost. If they had been alone… The thought stopped him in his tracks: this was a union undertaken out of duress, not love, and they had an audience besides. Ashlynn only kissed him now because she could do no other. Reluctantly he drew back a little, letting the general noise wash over them, his gaze burning into hers.

'By God, lass,' he murmured, 'you play the game well.'

Her cheeks turned pink, much to the delight of the spectators for though they had not heard the words they thought they could guess the import. She took refuge in their noisy enthusiasm, trying to calm her thumping heart, overwhelmed by the sudden knowledge within it. She darted another glance at Iain but the look in his eyes did nothing to restore a tranquil mind. Did he really think this was some game to her?

It was no small relief when the column mounted up again and set off. The pace was steadier now but the cold no less for that. As they rode, the hills closed in around them, a barren snow-clad waste of rock and heath and dead bracken that vanished into mist above. Ashlynn shifted her weight in the saddle, aching with the chill and the long hours spent on horseback and longing for nothing so much as a warm fire and hot food, wherever they might be found. However, not for anything would she have uttered a word of complaint. These men already regarded her as a liability and, although their manner appeared to have softened a little today, she would not give them any cause to despise her further. Nor would she have them think the less of their chief for wedding a soft Sassenach wench. Pride kept her chin up and her tongue silent but, as the afternoon wore on, the effort became greater.

Iain, riding alongside, saw her pallor with concern and could well understand the cause. The journey was hard enough, never mind all that had gone before. Had it been any other woman he would have expected tears at least by this, but then, he acknowledged, Ashlynn wasn't just any woman. Experience had shown him her courage; he could only guess at the will-power that kept her going when others would have cracked. By rights she should have after all that she had endured of late. Her silence touched him more than any words could have done and seeing her composure now he felt the first stirrings of pride.

The afternoon was wearing on when they came at last to the head of a narrow valley. Seeing the sudden lightening of spirit in the faces of the men nearby, Ashlynn glanced at Iain. Interpreting that look aright he nodded.

'This is Glengarron.'

She should have felt relief to hear those words but now her stomach knotted instead. This was the lion's den, the place from which there was no escape. The cavalcade rode into the misty glen in single file for the way was narrow with trees on one side and the peaty waters of a racing burn on the other. On either side the hills rose into the low cloud and marked their passing with the muffled echo of the horses' hooves. After about half a mile the glen widened out and through the snow the muted outlines of houses were just visible in the distance. However, it was not the houses that held Ashlynn's attention for there, dead ahead, a great granite outcrop thrust up from the ground and, brooding over the whole scene, a fortress that might have grown from the rock itself.

The horsemen made straight for it and then she discerned a huge wooden gate, studded and banded with iron and seeming to lead straight into the hillside. Someone called a cheery greeting which was returned and the gate swung open to reveal a narrow defile between sheer walls of rock. Wide enough to take two horsemen abreast, it wound upwards to another gate. This too swung open and they emerged into a large walled courtyard with various buildings along its sides, all overshadowed by a great tower of wood and stone. Iain glanced at his wife.

'Welcome to Dark Mount, lass.'

Ashlynn said nothing, being temporarily incapable of speech and fighting to control a rising sense of dread. Iain dismounted. Seeing there was nothing else to be done, Ashlynn slid reluctantly from Steorra's saddle. Standing there among the throng of horses and men she felt suddenly very small, and the feeling of isolation and vulnerability increased. Then she became aware that Iain was watching her. Not for a bag of gold would she have displayed the fear that gripped her now and so she lifted her chin and forced herself to meet his gaze. His expression was unreadable.

'Come.'

He guided her towards a great iron-clamped door. The space beyond was subdivided and, as her eyes adjusted to the relative dimness she had an impression of store-rooms and pantries. The smell of food suggested the presence of kitchens. They bore left towards a stout oaken staircase. It led up to the great hall. Glancing round apprehensively she had an impression of a large, stone-walled chamber with high and narrow windows. However, most of the light came from the wall brackets and the candles set on huge circular iron chandeliers. Greasy trestle tables, littered with the stale remains of a meal, ran along three sides of the room. Its wooden floor was begrimed with mud and strewn with old straw whose musty smell mingled with ancient food odours and burning tallow. Shields and weapons adorned the walls along with huge and dusty racks of antlers. Wolf and fox masks snarled from among thick cobwebs. One wall was dominated by a great stone hearth where several big logs blazed, the sole source of comfort in the place.

As Ashlynn surveyed the scene cold dread settled like a lump in her stomach. Was this gloomy lair to be her home from now on? It hardly deserved to be dignified with the word home. Prison seemed more accurate somehow. Unwilling to contemplate it longer she turned away towards the fire.

Though she had spoken no word her expression was more eloquent and Iain frowned. As a stronghold Dark Mount had served him well but, he admitted, it could not pretend to cosiness or comfort. It had lacked a ruling female presence for too long. His mother was the last woman to leave her stamp upon the place, a stamp that time and absence had almost obliterated. He shot a sideways glance at Ashlynn. Her courage was not in doubt, but whether she had the skills to follow in his mother's footsteps remained to be seen. The memory brought back others far more bitter, memories better left buried. To banish them he summoned a servant and rattled off a string of orders. The man hurried off and presently several others could be seen scurrying about. One brought food and hot possets. Others hastened to the stairs carrying brooms and logs and other items less obvious to the casual glance.

'The servants will prepare a chamber, lass. In the meantime come and take some food.'

She followed him to the table and sat in the chair he indicated though in truth nerves had driven her appetite away. Unwilling to let him see it she forced herself to eat some bread and a little salted beef and then drank the posset. Its fragrant spicy warmth put some heart into her. Iain leaned back in his chair, surveying her shrewdly, sensing the tension and the fear beneath that outward calm. The thought recurred that most women in her situation would have gone to pieces by now. The lass had courage all right.

A little later the servant returned to say that the room was prepared. She saw her husband rise and hold out a hand to her. For a second she hesitated but common sense decreed there was no other choice than to go with him. Reluctantly she accompanied him to the stairs. There proved to be another two floors above the hall, variously divided into living quarters. On the topmost of these he stopped before a stout wooden door and, pushing it open, stood aside for her to pass. Beyond it was a moderate-sized room. Its stone walls were stark and free of ornament but the bare floor was clean enough. The sole furnishings were a small table and two chairs and, on the far side, a bed strewn with furs. A fire burned in the hearth but, being only recently lit, had not yet taken the chill off the air or dispelled the faint odour of mustiness and damp. On the table an oil lamp was burning for the window was shuttered fast against the cold. Ashlynn shivered inwardly.

'If you need anything Morag here will attend you,' he said.

The serving woman, buxom in thick homespun, might have been any age between forty and sixty. Her grey eyes regarded Ashlynn with frank curiosity. However, their expression was not unkind and when Ashlynn smiled it was returned. Iain glanced at the servant and jerked his head towards the door.

'Wait outside.'

The woman bobbed a curtsy and withdrew. For a moment husband and wife faced each other. In spite of the chill Ashlynn felt sweat start on her palms for she was keenly aware that the servant's restraining presence was gone and there was a large bed just across the room. Not only that, her husband was a head and shoulders taller than she, weighed roughly eighty pounds more, and was much too close for comfort. The dark eyes held a disquieting expression and were focused on her face. In confusion she looked away. In fact he guessed her thoughts with shrewd accuracy but just then had no intention of following up his advantage.

'The accommodation is rough and ready at present,' he observed, 'but no doubt you'll amend it to your liking in due course.'

Not knowing quite what to say Ashlynn remained silent.

'Is there anything more you require just now?'

She shook her head. 'Nothing more.'

He moved towards the door. 'Until later then, Ashlynn.'

Weak-kneed with relief she watched the door close behind him, then sank down on one of the chairs. It took her a moment or two to recover her self-possession. She was recalled by Morag's return.

'Do you require anything, my lady?'

'Yes. I would wash after my journey. I would also like a change of clothes if that can somehow be arranged.'

'I'll see what I can do.'

When Morag had left, Ashlynn took another glance round the room and shivered, instinctively moving closer to the fire, seeking some comfort from its warmth. However, it did little to dispel the sensation of sick dread that sat like lead in the pit of her stomach.

Some time later the woman returned with a jug of hot water, soap, towels and a comb. Over her arm she carried a clean shift and a gown of brown woollen cloth. With them were woollen stockings and a pair of sturdy leather shoes.

'These are as near to your size as I could guess, my lady.'

Ashlynn thanked her. Then, as the servant poured water into the basin and laid the towels ready, she unfastened her cloak and tossed it on to the bed before divesting herself of belt and tunic. Since the cold did not encourage her to strip off she contented herself with bathing her hands and face. With Morag's help she combed and braided her hair and then pulled on the clean shift, stockings and gown. The latter was too big but not unduly so, and they contrived to disguise the fact with the aid of a girdle. Ashlynn glanced down at herself, smoothing the skirt with her hand. The cloth was warm and serviceable, the colour practical, but the garments had no pretensions to beauty or elegance. They could hardly have been more different from the ones she had worn hitherto. However, beggars couldn't be choosers. Morag handed her the cloak and she put it on, glad of the additional layer.

'Will there be anything else, my lady?'

'No. I thank you.'

The servant withdrew then and Ashlynn was left alone. Once more her sombre gaze took in the details of the room and for the first time noticed the door, partially concealed by shadow, in the side wall. When she tried the handle it didn't budge. She wondered what lay on the far side—a store room perhaps. It was of no importance and there would be time enough to find out later. In the meantime she needed to get away from this chamber. She let herself out but, instead of retracing her steps along the way she had originally come, set off in the other direction. It brought her at length to another narrow wooden door. This one was unlocked and yielded quite easily when tried. It led out on to a short flight of steps and thence up to a flat roof area at the top of the tower. Dusk was drawing in. In a little while it would be full dark.

The knowledge did nothing to lighten her mood. Wrapping the cloak closer around her Ashlynn moved to the crenellated wall and peered out between the stone merlons, but there was little to be seen save snow and swirling white mist. She recalled what Iain had said about the weather closing in. Soon they would all be its prisoners. She felt as one standing at the edge of the world in some uncharted waste, a place where different rules obtained and where, just out of view, lurked unspecified dangers. It was very cold out on this exposed place and far from an ideal refuge, but she didn't want to return to her chamber and certainly had no intention of going down to that filthy, cheerless hall where there was a better-than-even chance of meeting her husband.

Now that he had intruded on her thoughts again she found him harder to dismiss than she would have liked. He had told her that he had never forced a woman, but she wasn't naïve enough to think that would hold good for marriage too. It was a husband's right to take his wife whenever it pleased him. She knew full well that it would please him. Involuntarily her mind returned to the great fur-strewn bed. How would it be to lie with him, to yield completely to his will? The memory of the hayloft returned with all its startling intimacy: the warmth of his body against hers, his kisses hot along her throat, the touch of his hands on her naked flesh…

Ashlynn forced the thoughts away even as her mind

reiterated the truth. She was not indifferent to him. That was the worst of it. For men the marriage bed was not about emotion, only a necessity for the getting of heirs. For a woman it was different. Where there was any kind of initial attraction, such intimacy would invariably lead to stronger feelings; in this case, feelings that were not reciprocated. Iain had married her at the king's command, but the human heart could not be commanded. She would be the means by which he sired his heirs, nothing more. Her wishes had counted for nothing in the face of the king's will. She was effectively Glengarron's prisoner but, unlike other prisoners of rank, no ransom would ever buy her freedom. She was tied to this man and to this God-forsaken place for good. In any case, even if she did have her freedom, there was nothing to go back to. Whichever way she looked at it the future seemed every bit as bleak as the landscape around.

Just then the subject of her thoughts was checking on the comfort and condition of his injured men. Iain had made it a rule never to leave an injured man behind to die of cold or wounds, or to fall victim to scum like William's mercenaries. A long and bumpy journey in the back of a wagon was painful and undesirable, but not as bad as the alternative, and all the injured had received good tending at Jedburgh. Iain guessed that if they had survived so far they'd likely live to tell the tale. He stood now looking down at the face of the young man on the pallet before him. For all the waxen pallor of cheeks and brow the Saxon was a good-looking youth and well made too.

'How is he?'

The old woman, who had been examining her patient carefully glanced up for a moment, regarding the laird with cool grey eyes.

'He's lucky to be alive with those wounds and such a bad knock on the head withal. 'Tis small wonder he has a fever.'

'Will he pull through it?'

'He's young, and clearly of a strong constitution or he'd not have lived thus long. God willing, he may yet survive.'

'Tend him well.'

'Depend on it, my lord.'

He nodded. If anyone was going to save the youth it was she. None in Glengarron knew more about healing than Meg. He just had to hope his faith in her would be justified now as it had been so many times before. He continued his round of the injured, stopping here and there to have a quiet word or to put a reassuring hand on a shoulder.

By the time he finished it was dark and the courtyard covered in glittering rime. In a day or two the snow would come in earnest. They had returned to Glengarron just in time. Fitzurse was lost to him for the moment, but there were compensations: a less arduous regime, hot food, roaring fires and a comfortable bed.

That last turned his thoughts in another direction and he sighed. The immediate future was hardly calculated to fill him with unalloyed delight. His new bride was angry and resentful and, behind that brave front she wore, more than a little afraid. He could well understand the reason for it. However, he was her protector now whether she liked it or not. God knew she needed one.

As he recalled the bruises on her face his anger resurfaced. He had no time for the kind of brutality that entailed. No man worthy of the name indulged his strength in such a way against a woman. If nothing else their marriage had put an end to that. No man would ever touch her again, save he.

He had arranged for them to dine alone together in a private chamber prepared for the purpose. It was much warmer than the hall and permitted of greater intimacy. Besides, he knew that his wife wasn't ready to run the public gauntlet just yet and there would be time enough to let the inhabitants of Glengarron see their new lady. Stories would be circulating like wildfire as it was for many of his men had wives and families all too eager for the latest gossip, and the laird's unexpected marriage was the juiciest morsel in years.

For a while he warmed himself by the fire in the hall holding his hands to the blaze. The light shone on the gold thumb ring, giving the metal a reddish lustre: the colour of passion. He grim-aced. A forced match was hardly likely to be the precursor to passion and yet twice, briefly, there had been a spark between them. For a moment the memory of the hayloft returned to tease him. He could not deny the attraction he had felt. Could the spark be rekindled? In a little while he would know the answer.

It had been in Ashlynn's mind to refuse when a manservant came to announce that the evening meal was served. However, a moment's reflection was sufficient to let her see the lack of wisdom in this, for though she had only known him a short time it was long enough to be sure that Iain would fetch her himself if she denied him her presence. Accordingly she followed the servant obediently, expecting that he would lead her to the hall. Instead she found herself in the chamber next to her own. Her husband was waiting for her.

For the space of several heartbeats they faced each other. Ashlynn saw that he had changed his clothes and now wore dark hose and a tunic of crimson wool, belted at the waist and richly embroidered at neck and sleeves, the colour a perfect foil for his dark hair and eyes. Those eyes were now fixed on her, and she was forcibly reminded of the shortcomings of her current attire. However, he seemed to find nothing amiss for he smiled faintly and bowed low over her hand.

'Come and sit down, Ashlynn.'

In fact, Iain had temporarily forgotten that his wife had no other garments besides the borrowed ones she had been wearing. He guessed that Morag had attempted to remedy the matter for the brown woollen gown was clearly a servant's garb. It was also too big and tended to conceal her figure rather than emphasise it. He eyed it with quiet disfavour, realising it was a matter he was going to have to address in due course.

Unable to follow his thought, she felt herself redden, feeling unwontedly self-conscious. The recollection of her bruised cheek and cut lip only intensified the feeling. Rarely had she appeared to such disadvantage and certainly never before a man. Not just any man either. She was more than ever aware of that handsome charismatic presence and it made her feel awkward. He on the other hand seemed quite at ease and led her now to the table.

Although she still had little appetite she was glad of

the business of dining for it kept him at a safe distance. She had no real idea of what she ate that evening but she took her time, dreading the moment when the meal would be over and the atmosphere of cosiness would become intimacy. Covertly she looked around at the appointments of the chamber. It was comfortable enough but practical too, a man's room. She could see a doorway leading off it and guessed with a feeling of mounting dread that beyond it lay his bedchamber. It was then she realised where the locked door in her own room led to.

Iain settled himself back in his chair, his hand toying with his wine goblet. He had taken several of these with the meal but the wine appeared to have touched him not at all. He surveyed her keenly now, the dark eyes shrewd. Ashlynn bridled instantly.

'Must you stare at me like that?' she asked.

'Does it displease you then that a man should look at you?'

To answer yes or no would have been equally ridiculous and she said nothing.

'Besides,' he continued, 'I know it isn't the first time. You told me yourself that you'd had admirers.'

Admirers yes, she thought, but none with the power to unsettle her so thoroughly. Besides, back then she had always been the one in control of the situation.

'I would wager there were many. Yet you never met one who pleased you?'

'No.' She paused and threw him a speaking look. 'I still haven't.'

The dark eyes gleamed. 'That's better. I feared for a moment that you'd lost the fighting spirit.'

'If you did you were much mistaken.'

The challenge was there and unequivocal too. In spite of himself his enjoyment grew. 'I'm glad to hear it, truly. I once thought that a marriage of convenience was like to be dull. Now I am reassured that it will not be.'

Ashlynn listened in disbelief and then returned a faint ironic smile. 'Dull? With you?'

'You flatter me, lass.'

'Not in the least.'

'Of course not,' he conceded. 'I should have known better.'

'Do you want flattery?'

'No, but I doubt you'd deal in it anyway. Your tongue is too sharp for that, and backed up at need with tooth and claw.'

The allusion brought a deeper colour to her cheeks. 'I regret that I can offer you no dowry in mitigation of these faults.'

'I can live with that,' he replied.

'Perhaps you should have chosen a rich wife while you had the chance.'

'I would not have married again, any more than you would have taken a husband.'

For a moment Ashlynn was very still, her eyes fixed on his face. 'This marriage is not your first?'

Iain met and held her gaze. He didn't know why he had said it. It had not been his intention but perhaps it was just as well. Better she should learn it from him than servants' gossip.

'No, it isn't. However, my first wife died some years ago.'

'I'm sorry.' She hesitated but couldn't help herself. 'What was her name?'

His fingers tightened round the cup. 'Eloise.'

'Eloise? That is French is it not?'

'That's right.'

'How came you to meet and wed a Frenchwoman?'

'I spent six years in France completing my military training.'

'I see.' Ashlynn digested this in silence and summoned all her courage to ask the next question. 'Was it a love match?'

'Aye,' he replied, 'it was. But, as I told you, it was long ago.'

Her heart sank. His words might relegate his former wife to the past but he had not been able to disguise the feelings that lay beneath. Clearly the memories were powerful still. The knowledge caused a strange pang. Eloise must have been quite something. *I would not have married again...*

'And now the king has forced you to take me.'

The bleakness in her tone caused the dark gaze to soften a little. 'We neither of us had any choice, lass.' He paused. 'Nor can we change the past.'

For a moment she saw Heslingfield in flames and forced the image back. With an effort she managed to keep her voice level. 'As you say.'

'Your life is here now, Ashlynn. It may not have been the one you would have chosen but I promise you it will be safe.'

She watched him rise from his chair and, with thumping heart, followed suit. He halted a few feet away.

'So what now, my lady?' He glanced over his shoulder

at the door she had noticed earlier. 'Yonder lies my bed-chamber. If it pleases you to join me, I would be most happy and most honoured. If not, over there is the way out.'

Her surprise was total and for a moment or two she could only stare at him, torn between reluctance and something harder to identify. He saw her hesitation and moved in closer. She felt the warmth of his hands on her shoulders. She knew she should pull away now while she could and despised her own weakness for not doing so. His arms slid round her shoulders and waist, drawing her against him. His mouth closed over hers. A familiar flicker of warmth ignited deep within, her pulses racing for that seductive nearness, for the scent and the taste of him. Sensing that reawakening fire, he tightened his hold and the kiss grew more intimate, more knowing, the kiss of a man completely familiar with women and completely confident of his power. Ashlynn tensed. The wife he loved was dead. This meant nothing to him beyond the consummation of a bargain. She could not risk her heart in such an enterprise for her heart was all she had left. That knowledge increased the sense of inner desolation and she shivered.

Iain felt that tremor and drew back a little, looking down into her face. In it he saw reluctance and his eyes narrowed a little. Almost immediately she found herself free.

'You need have no fear that I'll force more on you than my name, Ashlynn,' he said. 'I'll have you willing or not at all.'

'Then you don't mean to…you won't—' She broke off, floundering.

'No, I don't mean to. There's time enough, lass.'

The words, delivered with such quiet assurance, served only to reinforce the truth. He did have time, but underneath that statement was a colder reality. While he had sufficient honour not to force her, the fact that he chose not to prosecute his right was further indication of how deeply he resented this marriage. How could this compare to what had gone before? How far she must fall short in his eyes—an unwilling bride and an unattractive one to boot! Ashlynn lifted her chin and gathered about her what dignity she could muster.

'I think time will make little difference,' she replied, 'since we are together only at the king's command, not personal inclination.'

The barb went deeper than anticipated but his tone remained calm. 'As you say, and yet the situation carries its own inevitability.'

'You may believe that, but it's not a view I share.'

'Maybe not, but if you think about it you'll see that I'm right.'

'I have no wish to think about you at all.'

'None the less, you will abide here from now on and you will see me every day of your life whether you want to or not. In the meantime you may return to your room if you will.'

Ashlynn's jaw tightened as she clamped the lid on anger. 'Gladly, my lord.' She moved towards the outer door and paused a moment. 'I bid you a goodnight.'

Taken by surprise Iain could only watch her retreating figure until the door closed behind her. Then he sighed and turned away toward the hearth, staring down into the flames, his fist clenched above the lintel.

Ashlynn regained the relative sanctuary of her own

room. Now that she was alone, anger quickly cooled leaving her feeling only weary and disconsolate. She should not have let him provoke her but somehow she had been unable to help herself. He was so confoundedly arrogant! Her response had been as much a defensive reflex as anything. Of all the possible beginnings to marriage this surely must rank as one of the most disastrous.

She shivered. In her absence the fire had burned down in the hearth and the room was growing chill for the servants had understandably assumed she would be spending the night elsewhere. Stripping to her chemise she climbed quickly into bed, burrowing under the furs for warmth. Lying there alone in the darkness she could hear the wind against the shutters, a lonely, desolate sound—as desolate as her own heart. In spite of fatigue it was a long time before sleep eventually claimed her.

Chapter Six

When she awoke next day it was to see bars of grey light through the shutters. By their pale illumination the details of the strange room came slowly into focus and with them the recollection of her predicament. She shivered. Raising herself on one elbow she glanced across at the hearth but the fire was reduced to a heap of ash. The room was freezing now.

Ashlynn slipped from the bed and struggled into her clothes as fast as possible. Then she splashed water on her face and dragged a comb through her hair. She had just finished when Morag appeared with a platter of food which she set down on the table. Her glance went to the bed across the room and though she made no comment her expression was curious. However, nothing could have been more courteous than her tone.

'Lord Iain sends his compliments, my lady, and says he will attend you presently.'

Ashlynn felt her heart sink. Now what? She had no desire to see him at all but in truth no way to prevent it.

'Very well. In the meantime, please remake the fire and see that it remains lit. This room is like a tomb. It will take several days to take the chill off the air.'

As Morag bustled about Ashlynn turned her attention to the food, wondering how to comport herself in the forthcoming interview. Though neither of them had sought it they were both trapped in this marriage. Anger and resentment were pointless now. Somehow this must be faced. Besides, she knew from experience that it was worse than useless to get angry with him, and she had need of every ounce of composure she could summon.

However, when Iain appeared a short time later he made no allusion to what had passed before. Nor did he comment on her pallor or the shadows beneath her eyes even though he missed none of it. In truth it touched him more than he expected. He also seemed to recall that his words last evening had scarcely been calculated to win her over. With hindsight they seemed at best to suggest indifference, something he had not intended at all. Ashlynn's wit was quick and sharp and she was becoming adept at finding the chinks in his armour. Even so, he shouldn't have retaliated in that way. Adopting a rather gentler tone he bade her a good morning.

'If you wish it, Ashlynn, I will show you Dark Mount. It is your home now and you should become acquainted with it.'

She forced back the immediate urge to refuse, acknowledging the truth of his words. This was her home now, whether she wanted it or not. It would have been foolish to reject the offer. In any case curiosity overrode apprehension.

She nodded acquiescence. 'As you wish.'

'Come then, lass.'

They spent the next hour on a leisurely tour. Dark Mount was bigger than she had first thought and complete with storehouses, stables, smithy and work-shops. From time to time they stopped so that he could introduce her to some of his people. She made a point too of remembering names and speaking to those whom she encountered, if only briefly. It was too soon to know if she would ever be fully accepted here but clearly it would be as well to get off on the right foot.

She was also conscious of having angered his men by her earlier misguided attempt to escape en route to Jedburgh. It had been foolish in the extreme and she greatly regretted the matter now. No doubt the story had been related round many firesides already. She would not cause his people to hold an even poorer opinion of her behaviour. They were courteous enough and eyed her with frank curiosity, but she knew they were reserving judgement until they should know her better. She could not find it in herself to blame them. Perhaps in their place she'd have done the same. In the meantime she took care to behave to everyone with becoming courtesy and a pleasant word or smile at least. Iain, observing, said nothing, but her manner towards his people pleased him and he saw the guarded approval in their eyes.

Although she was quiet at first Ashlynn began to relax a little as time went on, and, as they walked and explored, he realised he had an attentive companion. She asked intelligent questions and listened to the answers.

She was quick of apprehension and he had but to tell her something once for her to remember it. It reaffirmed his view that the pretty face concealed a sharp mind.

'It is a thriving community,' she said when at length they paused on the threshold of the barn. 'You seem to have everything here you are likely to need.'

'Almost,' he agreed, 'but 'tis as well to be prepared for every eventuality.'

'And are you?'

'Mostly.'

She looked around, her comprehensive gaze taking in the neat stacks of sacks and barrels, the harness and coiled ropes. Then, seeing the items in the far corner, she raised an eyebrow.

'Sledges?'

'Very useful for transporting supplies in the snow.'

'Ah, yes, of course.'

He smiled faintly. 'I try not to be caught napping.'

'I have no doubt of that. Has Dark Mount ever come under attack?'

'Aye, in the past. But no enemy has ever prevailed.'

'Do you have enemies?'

'Few living, and only one of any consequence.'

'Fitzurse,' she replied.

'Aye, he. And one day I'll find him.'

The words had been spoken casually enough but a great deal more lay behind. However, remembering his earlier response Ashlynn didn't dare to question him further. He was not a man to cross lightly. His earlier treatment of her had demonstrated as much, though with hindsight it had also shown considerable restraint. While he was not given to fits of fury she knew instinctively that his anger once roused would be doubly dangerous. Throwing a covert glance at her husband now it was hard to imagine the battle rage on that calm face, and yet she knew it concealed passions that ran deep: a passion for war and a passion for revenge. The ghosts of the past haunted the living. Recalling that snowy field littered with corpses she shivered inwardly.

That evening she ventured down to the hall, knowing that the intimate arrangement of the previous evening would not be repeated. Part of her was glad and another part daunted. From what she had seen of the place, it was clear that dining in the hall was unlikely to be a comfortable experience. Besides, it was a masculine domain and she had not been bidden there. Iain had issued no positive invitation to join him, nor had he said that she should not. Their encounter earlier had been amicable enough but would he welcome her presence in an all-male preserve? If he rejected her how would she deal with the humiliation? For some time she hesitated. Then summoning all her courage she went down.

When she arrived Iain was already there along with many of his men. Ashlynn paused in the doorway surveying the scene, her heart beating a little faster, conscious of being the only woman present. On the other hand was she not the lady of the house now? At that recollection her chin lifted and she crossed the floor to join her husband.

As the men became aware of her presence their conversation died and all eyes followed her progress. Under their keen regard her discomfort increased. Iain looked round and for a moment he seemed surprised to see her there. Her heartbeat accelerated. Was he annoyed? Would he see this as an intrusion and send her away?

However, it seemed that was not his intent. He rose and taking her hand, conducted her to the chair next to his. She sank into it thankfully. Around them the conversation started up again.

'This is an unexpected honour,' he said.

She inclined her head in acknowledgement while he gestured to a servant to fill her cup.

'I thought you might prefer your room.'

'Hardly,' she replied.

Recalling the somewhat austere nature of that chamber he winced inwardly.

'In any case,' she went on, 'is it not fitting that we should dine together?'

'Aye, I suppose it is.'

Ashlynn took a sip of wine, very much alive to that steady regard. What was he thinking when he looked at her? Was he remembering that other marriage, the one he had entered into for love? At least he had not humiliated her before his men and that was something. Iain made no further remark on the matter and then the food arrived, diverting his attention and apparently obviating the need for conversation. Taking her cue from him she addressed herself to the meal.

The other men ignored her for the most part, though she was aware that one or two covert glances came her way. Ashlynn looked ruefully at her humble makeshift attire. It was hardly the dress of a noblewoman. However, by accepting her presence here this evening and seating her beside him, Iain had tacitly established her position. She was not Eloise but she was his lady now and they would accept her as such. It was a small step but a significant one. Her back straightened. She might not look the part but she could at least act it.

It was not until they had finished eating that Iain turned his attention towards her again. She had begun to wonder if he had forgotten about her. Being used to conversation and friendly banter at table she found this silence awkward and a little unnerving. When he picked up the wine flagon and gestured to her cup she nodded, conscious of surprise. He wasn't dismissing her just yet then. Perhaps they might talk a little. Their earlier conversations had whetted her curiosity and so much about this man was still a mystery. Summoning her courage again she put a toe in the water.

'How long have you been Laird of Glengarron?'

'Five years.'

'I thought it longer, coinciding with your return from France.'

'I did not go back to Glengarron then.' He paused. 'I hired out my sword instead.'

'But what of your wife? Was she not with you?'

'Eloise died in France. I returned alone.'

Ashlynn heard the edge in his voice. Most like his wife had died in childbed or from fever. They were common enough occurrences after all. However, she sensed that this was not the time to delve further and dropped the subject, fearing to alienate him. Instead she shifted the focus of the discussion. 'You hired out your sword to the king?'

'Aye. Malcolm was ever one for recruiting able fighters and there was plenty to be done in his service,' he went on. 'It kept me occupied, until my father's last illness. Then there was no choice but to return.'

'You speak as though you were reluctant to do so.'

'I was. My father and I were never close and, after my mother's death, things got much worse. She had always smoothed things over between us but when she was gone…' He made a vague gesture with his hand. 'Dark Mount was not a congenial place to be. I was only too glad to get away in the end.'

Though the words were quietly spoken Ashlynn heard the bitter note beneath. Heard it and identified with it in part.

'Were you reconciled at last?'

'No. He did not favour my support of Malcolm and it deepened the estrangement between us. I was with him at the end but by then he was too ill to speak. Yet I sensed he wanted to.'

'That is something at least. Would that I might say the same.'

He regarded her curiously. 'You quarrelled with your father?'

'Not in that way.'

Iain waited, suddenly wanting to know.

Ashlynn smiled sadly. 'My mother caught a fatal fever shortly after I was born. Her death was a terrible blow to him.'

'I can understand that, but not that he should blame you for it.'

'He tried hard not to, but never quite succeeded in hiding his thoughts. It was always there between us.' She sighed. 'I think it was why he wanted me to marry Ath—' She broke off, conscious of having almost said too much. 'Wanted me to marry,' she amended. 'In that way I'd be out of his sight for good.'

He noted the correction and wondered what she had been going to say. However, he knew better than to push her. A confidence could not be forced. He didn't know why he had spoken to her of his father. It hadn't been his intention, but somehow the words had come out anyway. Perhaps it was no bad thing. Certainly the tension of the previous evening was conspicuous by its absence.

Ashlynn retired a little later leaving the men to drink. Having returned to her room she undressed, laying her garments carefully aside. Once again their ugliness impressed itself on her mind. It was not a problem that would be easily solved since she had no money to buy cloth and thread, even if she knew where these things might be procured locally. The thought of asking Iain for money was anathema. Self-respect forbade it. Clearly he saw nothing amiss with the present arrangement and if he did not, she would not raise the subject. If anyone else found it a matter for remark, that was just too bad. Fine clothes were only a form of vanity when all was said and done, and yet she missed them all the same. They were something else she had taken for granted, like looking attractive. It shouldn't matter, but somehow it did, especially now. Iain's face drifted into her mind. Even if she were appropriately gowned would it make any difference there? Would he ever look at her in the way he had once looked on Eloise? Would she ever be able to influence his thoughts? Somehow she couldn't see it happening any time soon. The knowledge of her powerlessness was oddly lowering. With a sigh she climbed into bed and burrowed under the furs for warmth.

However, sleep would not come and for a long time she lay awake listening to the sound of the wind in the chimney. She shivered, thinking how different it was from her chamber at Heslingfield. Thoughts of home revived the faces of her family and suddenly a lump formed in her throat. The last time she felt like this she had been in a hayloft and Iain had comforted her. The memory of his arms around her then only served to enhance her loneliness now. She tried to check it, to force the lump back again but it resisted every attempt and grew bigger, swelling in size until it threatened to choke her. Turning her face into the pelts she began to sob as though her heart would break.

Iain left his men carousing and made his way up the stairs. Truth to tell he was in no mood to drink for his mind was elsewhere. Ashlynn's appearance at table that evening had served as a sharp reminder that his life had changed. While he had no quarrel with her presence, he had not lied when he had said it was unexpected—unexpected and oddly impressive in its quiet dignity. It could not have been easy for her. Nor could it be easy adjusting to her new life at Dark Mount. Though she never spoke of it he sensed her homesickness. Worse, it was something that he could do nothing to change. Heslingfield was gone for good. Only one small hope remained in that direction.

Having reached his room he took himself off to his bedchamber. He was in the process of undressing when he caught a faint sound from the next room. His brows drew together and he stepped closer to the connecting door, listening intently. The sound of sobbing was unmistakeable, great heart-wrenching sobs that pierced him to the core. For a moment he remained where he was, torn by indecision. His hand went to the handle, hovered briefly, then slowly withdrew. He retreated and, with a sigh, continued undressing.

For a long time after that he lay awake in the darkness, listening to the sounds from the other side of the door. He wanted to go to her and speak what words of comfort he could, but knew he must not. Not yet. This outpouring of grief was long overdue. In its shuddering sobs he heard all the fear and pain and loss that she had kept hidden behind the brave mask she showed to the world. He always knew it must erupt at some time, but he had not anticipated its depth and force. Nor could he ever have guessed how much it would grieve him to hear it.

Ashlynn woke late feeling heavy-headed, her eyelids swollen and pink-rimmed. Reluctantly she slipped from the bed and struggled into her clothes. Then she bathed her eyes in cold water. She had just finished when Morag appeared with a platter of food. She set it down on the table. Her glance went briefly to Ashlynn's face and her expression registered concern.

'Are you quite well, my lady?'

'A slight headache,' Ashlynn replied. 'I slept ill last night.'

'Can I fetch you anything?'

'No, thank you. I shall be recovered soon enough.'

Morag seemed not entirely convinced but did not pursue it. When the servant had gone Ashlynn turned her attention to the food but, after a mouthful, abandoned the attempt. Her appetite had gone and everything tasted like ashes. Pushing it away she went to the hearth and stood for a time, staring down into the flames.

Eventually her attention was drawn by a knock on the door. She took a deep breath, mentally composing herself.

'Come in.'

Iain opened the door and paused on the threshold. For a moment he surveyed her in silence, but if he noticed anything amiss he did not remark on it.

'Good morrow, Ashlynn.'

She returned the greeting and waited, part of her wishing he would go and leave her alone and part curious as to why he was there. Then he stepped into the room.

'I would like you to join me, lass. There is something I would show you.'

'What is it?'

'You'll see.'

It was on the tip of her tongue to refuse and he saw it.

'Please,' he said.

'Is it a mystery then?'

'If you come with me, all will be made clear.'

She hesitated another moment and then rose to join him. To her surprise he led her back to the staircase and down to the next floor. After following the passageway for a little space, he stopped outside one of the chambers. Ashlynn eyed him quizzically and waited, wondering what it meant. He vouchsafed no explanation but merely opened the door and stood back to let her enter.

The room was smaller than hers and even more sparsely furnished, but it was clean and warm with a cheerful fire burning in the hearth. On the far side an old woman was sitting at the edge of a bed. She looked up on hearing the visitors arrive and inclined her head in acknowledgement of their presence. Iain spoke a few words in Gaelic to which the woman responded briefly. However, Ashlynn paid no heed. Her attention had moved on to the bed which was occupied, apparently by one of the injured men who had been brought back to Dark Mount following the battle with the Normans. Then she became aware that her husband was speaking, and in English this time.

'How is the patient today, Meg?'

'A little better, my lord. Conscious anyway, though still very weak.'

Ashlynn looked from one to the other in puzzlement but Iain's hand was under her elbow, drawing her further into the room. When they reached the bedside she looked down at the injured man lying there. He was very pale and his face was stubbled with many days' growth of beard, the same tawny shade as the hair visible beneath the bandage. The eyes regarding her now were deep blue and staring as though they had seen an apparition. For a moment she stood transfixed and the colour drained from her face.

'Ban?'

'Ashlynn?' The voice was weak but familiar for all that. 'Is it really you?'

'Ban!' Then she was beside him, her trembling hands brushing his face, his breast, his hands. All were real and warm. 'I thought you were dead. I thought I'd never see you again in this world.'

'I almost was dead. Fortunately the Normans thought so otherwise they'd have finished me off.'

Her incredulous gaze took in the bandages
swathing his ribs and shoulder and the other round his
head. For a moment she said nothing, and then
suddenly burst into tears. The old woman put a comforting hand on her arm.

'It's been a shock for ye, lass. But the right sort of
shock, I ken.'

Ashlynn was beyond speech and only sobbed the more.

'You're supposed to be glad,' said Ban. 'Now you're
like to drown me and finish what the Normans started.'

It drew a ragged laugh and she tried to dash away the
tears with her hand. With the other she was holding one
of his tightly as though, if she did not, he might vanish
before her eyes. He eyed her critically a moment and
then looked up at the man beside her.

'I think I have you to thank for my life.'

'Others must take the credit for that.'

'May I know who you are and how my sister comes
to be here?'

'I am Iain MacAlpin of Glengarron.' As he spoke the
name he saw instant recognition in the young man's
face. 'I met your sister by chance when she was fleeing
from the Normans. She has since done me the honour
of becoming my wife.'

'Your wife?' Ban stared at him thunderstruck for a
moment before his gaze went swiftly to his sister's face.
For the first time he noticed the fading bruises there and
his eyes narrowed. 'Ashlynn, he hasn't hurt you?'

'No, certainly not!' The words came out more force-
fully than she'd intended but she would not have Ban
under any kind of misapprehension on that point. 'These
came courtesy of a certain Norman lord.'

'But how came you to be married? And to *him* of all men?'

She saw the anxiety in his face and the pain around his eyes. 'It's a long story, Ban, and it will keep for now.'

At this point Meg intervened. 'Aye, it will. You'll have time enough to catch up on all your news. Meantime, the laddie needs rest if he's to recover his strength.'

It was a hint and Ashlynn made to rise but Ban detained her. 'You'll come back?'

'Of course, I'll come back.' She smiled. 'Do you think I'd leave you so soon?'

Only then did he release her hand. Reluctantly and with several backward looks she allowed herself to be led away. However, once the door closed behind them Ashlynn turned to face Iain, her face pale with contained emotion.

'All this time you knew he was alive and yet you said nothing.' Her voice caught on a sob. 'How could you do that?'

'Ashlynn, I…'

'I thought everyone I'd ever loved was dead and you let me go on thinking it when a word from you would have made all the difference.'

'It wasn't like that, I swear it.'

'What kind of man are you, Iain, that you could even consider such a deed?'

'Will you at least let me speak before you judge me?'

Ashlynn bit her lip. He looked at her pale tear-stained face and waited. Then at length she nodded.

'Very well. Say what you want to say.'

'My men and I passed through Heslingfield not long after the Normans had left.' Seeing her expression he

nodded. 'It was on our way north. Fergus and Dougal
found your brother among the injured. He was unconscious but just breathing. We had no idea who he was,
only that he was nigh unto death and certainly not one
of the Normans. We tended him as best we could and
put him in the wagon. I didn't put two and two together
until I heard you speak of your brother. Even then I said
nothing because I thought the lad was going to die, and
you had already lost him once. I didn't want you to
have to go through it again. You had already been
through so much.' He paused. 'If I was wrong, I'm sorry.
Please believe that, if you believe nothing else.'

For a long moment she said nothing, her eyes missing
no detail of his expression. It spoke of remorse and sincerity. He saw her draw in a long shuddering breath.

'I believe you did what you thought was best,' she
said at last, 'but it was a decision you had no right to
make.' The blue eyes filled with tears anew.

'If I've hurt you, lass, I'm truly sorry for it.'

The tone also sounded sincere and she wanted to
believe that it really was but the tears spilled over anyway.
Completely overwrought she had no way to stop them.
Then she felt his arms around her holding her close.

'Shh, lass, don't cry. It's all right.'

Suddenly he felt all the tension go out of her but her
body shook as she wept on his shoulder. For some time
they remained thus while he let her have her cry out.
Eventually the tears subsided a little and she lifted her
head to find him regarding her with deep concern.

'I've been a fool. Forgive me, Ashlynn.'

Even as he spoke he realised that fool was an understatement; he should have listened to his inner doubts

and told her long since. By seeking to spare her pain he had caused her far more. What he had never anticipated was how much her tears would hurt him.

She drew in another shaky breath, searching for the words, but emotion locked her voice in her throat as reaction set in. Her head swam. A strong arm caught her by the waist as she slumped, and another went under her knees, lifting her effortlessly. Then he carried her back upstairs and set her down gently in a chair by the fire. Frowning to see her pallor he put his own cloak around her and then poured some spiced wine, heating it with an iron from the fire, before handing her the cup.

'Drink this.'

Obediently she took it. He watched her sip the hot liquid and with no small relief saw some of the colour return to her cheeks.

'That's better.' Satisfied that she was recovering a little, he poured some wine for himself and pulled up a chair beside her.

Becoming properly aware of her surroundings for the first time Ashlynn realised with a start that they were in his room, the chamber where they had dined together on their first evening at Dark Mount. It aroused some mixed feelings. Iain, watching her closely, guessed at it. Her nerves were raw enough already before this morning's nerve-shattering discovery.

'I'd hoped to cheer you with the news but I see now the shock was too sudden. I should have prepared you for it first,' he said.

'It was a shock,' she agreed, 'but, as Meg said, the right kind at least. It was just a little overwhelming coming so soon after…after everything else.'

Iain's jaw tightened, thinking that the 'everything else' to which she referred had been a fearful load for anyone to bear, let alone a fragile girl.

'I had no wish to be the cause of further tears in you, Ashlynn.'

'I know that now. It was just the discovery that I hadn't lost everyone after all.' She paused. 'Ban and I were always close. He is only a year older than I am.'

'He has the look of you too.'

'The hair and the eyes,' she agreed. 'A family trait.'

'He's a good-looking youth, and a brave one I'm thinking.'

'He was always thus. Nothing would ever stop Ban when he had it in mind to do something, no matter how reckless or how dangerous.'

'And you were right beside him or I miss my guess.'

It drew a faint smile and he saw the blue eyes soften as she looked into the fire. He wondered what she was remembering. There was so much he wanted to know but still he would not try and force her confidence. She was wary of him and with good reason. Accordingly he kept silent and waited.

'We had so many adventures as children, often to our father's grave displeasure. It didn't stop us though. The risk seemed worth the thrashing somehow. We had our share of those for though our father was not a cruel man he was strict. There were limits to what he would tolerate.'

'And you pushed those limits.'

'Often. And many times we got away with it. My father said I was a hoyden and that I needed—' She broke off and her cheeks reddened a little.

'Needed what?'

Ashlynn shook her head.

He wondered what she had been about to say but let it go, being unwilling to stop her in this expansive mood. He poured more wine into her cup.

She drank it down and felt its pleasing warmth spread through her. Once she glanced covertly at the man beside her for she recalled all too well what her father had once said in a fit of exasperation: *'You need breaking to bridle, my girl, and somewhere is the man to do it. You need a husband and one with a firm hand too.'* Would he be amused to know that the prediction had come true, in part at least? Perhaps so, but never would he have dreamed to see her wed to the Laird of Glengarron.

'My father and older brother fought at Hastings,' she went on. 'When the battle was lost they managed to escape and return home. Both my brothers dreamed that one day the Norman tyrant would be overthrown but my father called it a foolish dream. He said they were there to stay. He would not permit Ethelred or Ban to have any part in the rising against de Comyn's men.' She paused. 'Perhaps he should have. At least then Heslingfield would have burned for a reason.'

Iain caught the note of unwonted bitterness in her voice but he could not blame her.

'Innocence or guilt matter not to the Normans,' he replied. 'What happened at Heslingfield is being repeated all across the land 'twixt York and Durham. The Conqueror means to crush Northumbria into the dust.'

'To what end? So that he can be king of a graveyard?'

'To make it absolutely clear that he will suffer no challenge to his power or to his authority.'

'It serves but to make him a more hated tyrant.'

'Hated, aye. But feared more.'

'Must a man be feared in order to govern?'

'Aye, he must, but he has no need of the kind of brutality the Normans rejoice in.'

Ashlynn fell into reflective silence. He saw that she had stopped shaking now and the warmth of the fire and the drink had made her more relaxed. The fur cloak had slid back off her shoulders revealing the mane of tawny hair beneath. In the light of the fire it was shot with red and took on a resinous sheen that served to enhance its beauty. Seeing it, Iain found himself wanting to touch it, to run his fingers through it. He wanted to put his arms around her, to hold her close and kiss away her pain. However, he did none of those things. A fragile bond was being established in this room and he would do nothing to destroy it.

She looked up and surveyed him with curiosity. 'Do your men fear you?'

'They have nothing to fear from me.'

'But they do not cross you.'

'That is why they have nothing to fear.'

It drew a smile from her. 'And those men who do cross you?'

'Only do it once.'

The words were lightly spoken but their import was not and she shivered inwardly. However, it was not totally due to fear. It was a feeling akin to one she had known before, when she and Ban were about to embark on another reckless adventure. It was not totally divorced from apprehension but underlying it was something else, something concerned with excitement and danger and the allure of the forbidden. Regarding him now, it occurred to her that the face she had earlier considered merely arresting was very much more than that, like the dark eyes burning into hers now. The expression there was familiar and disturbing. Shaken by the direction of her thoughts Ashlynn decided it was the wine talking and sought safer ground.

'When can I see Ban again?'

'You will see him tomorrow. As he grows stronger you will be able to visit him for longer periods.'

'How long was he unconscious?'

'Several days. Then he was delirious with fever. For a while even Meg thought he might not live.'

Ashlynn felt only relief and thankfulness. She had been hurt by his failure to tell her but that had been a misjudgement on his part, not done out of malice. She saw that now. In the immediate shock after finding Ban alive she had been overwrought and that, on top of the existing concerns, had caused her to overreact. The knowledge brought a sharp twinge of guilt. The reality was that he had given her back her brother, an unlooked-for gift of inestimable price.

'I did not thank you for saving Ban but I do so now, and unreservedly.'

The tone was gentle and tender, different from any she had used hitherto, and the look that accompanied it likewise. It was also sincere, a realisation that warmed his blood more thoroughly than the wine. With an effort he controlled it.

'You should rather thank Fergus and Dougal. 'Twas they who found him.'

'But I think it was you who made it a rule never to

leave injured men behind,' she replied. 'And you who had him brought here and tended. Were it not so he would never have survived.'

'I'm right glad he has, lass.'

'You have shown him much kindness. More than I could ever have supposed.'

'You find it hard to believe then that simple kindness exists among the Scottish savages?'

She reddened a little. 'The tales about you paint a different picture.'

'Ah, and which particular tales would they be?'

'Tales of murder and kidnap, of rape and theft.'

'It is true I have killed many men but they had just as much chance of survival as I did. Every warrior knows the realities of combat,' he replied. 'I have kidnapped, but 'twas a man as it happened. His father tried to renege on a business agreement and I had to find another means to get what I was owed. I have known different women but never raped one. As to the rest I confess it freely, but I have only ever taken from those who had plenty to give.'

'I'm glad to learn that you live by such a strong moral code.'

'I live by a different code from the one you may be used to, lass, but it is not entirely without honour.'

'No, I think it is not.' She stood on tiptoe and kissed his cheek. 'And I thank you from the bottom of my heart for saving Ban.'

The dark eyes met and held her own. 'No thanks are necessary and I do not want your gratitude, Ashlynn. If you would kiss me let it be for myself.'

Chapter Seven

In the days that followed Ashlynn spent as much time as she could with Ban, though mindful not to tire him. He was still very weak but the terrifying pallor was gone and a healthier colour returned to his cheeks. Moreover, he could take nourishment now and, by the end of a week, was propped up on cushions and looking about him with interest. In the first days of their reunion they had not talked much, being content to know merely that the other was there. Later, as he regained a little strength, they spoke more, of different things, trivial enough in their way, each glad just to hear the other's voice. Sometimes, when he was asleep, she would sit and watch him, willing strength to return and restore him to full health.

She had been sitting thus rapt in thought one afternoon when he awoke. She saw him smile.

'Still here?'

'Where else?'

'I thought I would never see you again.'

'Nor I you.'

For several moments the emotion was too great for words. Ban's sombre gaze was fixed on her face for there was yet a shadow over the joy of reunion. He chose his next words with care. 'There are still many things I would know, Ashlynn.'

'I will tell you whatever you wish.'

'Then tell me what happened after the Normans left. Everything that I have missed.'

'Very well. But I warn you, it's a long story.'

'I'm not going anywhere.'

Taking a deep breath she began to speak, relating the story as she knew it, of her treatment at Fitzurse's hands, of her flight from the barn and her meeting with Iain. How he had saved her from the icy river and brought her along with him, and how she had discovered only later who he was. She spoke of the journey north and of her marriage, leaving out nothing, or almost nothing. His face darkened as he listened and she saw his hand clench on the coverlet.

'He forced you to wed him?'

'He married me at the king's command. For Malcolm it was the obvious solution and the one to cause him least trouble.' She sighed. 'There could be no place at Dunfermline for a penniless, friendless girl and a Saxon to boot.'

'You had me.'

'I did not know that and Iain did not tell me because he did not think you would live. I genuinely believe that now.'

'He has not hurt you?'

'No. On the contrary, he has kept me from hurt, even at the risk of his own life.'

Ban relaxed a little. 'I cannot say I like it, Ashlynn. The man has a reputation of the blackest kind. However, I owe him much.'

'We both do.'

'So it seems.' He paused. 'And if, as you say, he saved your life and has since treated you well then I have no cause to feel animosity towards him.'

'He has treated me well. I have no grounds for complaint on that score.'

Ban shook his head as he tried to assimilate what he had heard. 'It is most strange to hear such welcome and unwelcome things at once. Perhaps his reputation has become exaggerated.'

'I think perhaps it has, but I can only speak as I find.'

'And what do you find?'

'A man of his word, a leader, a fighter, one whom other men follow.' Even as she said it her mind added, *a man unlike any other.* 'He lives by his own rules but he is not dishonourable.'

He shot her a penetrating look. 'Do you love him?'

Ashlynn's cheeks grew pink. What was love exactly? She had heard it described as all encompassing, unchanging in the face of time and adversity, a passion so strong that death could not conquer it. A passion she had only dreamed of. The kind of passion that Iain had felt for Eloise.

'I…I respect him.'

'I see. Well, respect is a good enough basis for marriage. 'Tis said the rest comes with time.'

Ashlynn bit her lip. She would not tell him that respect was as far as it was ever going to go, or could ever go. Unwilling to linger in such dangerous waters she turned the conversation to other things. However, her brother's words stayed with her a long time afterwards. They might have comforted her had she not already known that her husband's abiding passion now was for revenge.

Unbeknown to Ashlynn, Iain paid her brother a visit of his own. He had long meditated it but wanted to give her space and time on her own with Ban, and the young man a chance to recover from his wounds. However, he also knew that the lad did not view the marriage with favour. Ordinarily Iain would not have cared a fig for any man's opinion on the matter but things now were not quite so simple. He could not live in such proximity to his wife's brother and be at odds with him. The nettle must be grasped. Accordingly he chose his moment when he knew Ashlynn was not by and presented himself at the bedside.

While Ban did not greet him with open hostility his expression was carefully neutral. Iain concealed a smile knowing the lad was reserving judgement.

'You are making good progress I see.'

'Yes, I thank you.' The tone was courteous but stiff.

Iain gestured to the stool that Ashlynn had not long since vacated. 'May I?'

'As you wish.'

For a moment they regarded each other in silent mutual appraisal like two combatants weighing each other up.

'I think that there are things you must want to know,' said Iain. 'If you wish it you may ask what you will now and I will answer truthfully.'

For a moment he saw surprise in the blue eyes, then it

was gone and the neutral expression returned. The lad was evidently better at hiding his thoughts than his sister was.

Ban nodded, his gaze never leaving the other man's face. 'It is true that I have questions to ask. Ashlynn has told me much but…'

'But?'

'There are things she did not say.'

Iain was quite sure of it. He waited.

'I cannot pretend that I was overjoyed when I learned of your marriage.'

'I had gathered as much.'

'But she speaks well of you.'

Iain only just managed to hide his surprise. 'Better perhaps than you think I deserve.'

'You do have a certain reputation.'

'True.'

'However that may be, my lord, she has told me how you saved her life and how you took on the role of her protector.' Ban paused. 'For that I must thank you.'

'Believe me, it is an honour.'

Ban searched that handsome face for any sign of mockery but he found none. The tone had been earnest too. Was it mere smooth courtesy or could it be that the man cared rather more than he let on?

'My sister and I are very close. Her well being and her happiness are important to me.'

'To me too. I promise you to look to the first, and that I'll strive by every means for the second.'

Ban unbent a little. 'She tells me that you have treated her well.'

For the second time Iain concealed surprise, feeling strangely pleased. His wife had demonstrated a degree of loyalty he had not expected. Did that stem from mere gratitude or could it be that she had warmed towards him of late? The notion produced an answering heat within, the kind he had not expected to feel again.

'Did she so?'

'Yes.' Ban hesitated. 'I must confess that when I first saw those bruises on her face I thought…'

'That I had put them there?'

The young man reddened. 'Yes. I'm sorry.'

'It was a reasonable suspicion, under the circumstances.'

'She told me what really happened and that you slew most of the bastards responsible.'

'Aye. Now that really was a pleasure.'

The tone was perfectly even but Ban did not miss the glint in the dark eyes. It confirmed him in the opinion that his new brother-in-law was not a man to cross with impunity. Not that he had any intention of doing so. On the contrary, he was beginning to warm to him rather more than he had thought he would. For all the man's dire reputation there was a directness about his manner and speech that Ban liked. Of his prowess in battle there was not the least doubt. However, the Laird of Glengarron had one more surprise in store. Crossing to the door he summoned the servant who had been waiting without. The man entered bearing a sheathed sword which he handed his master before withdrawing once more.

'I believe this is yours.' Iain reversed the weapon, offering it hilt first.

For a moment Ban was speechless. With a trembling hand he reached out and took it. One glance sufficed for the rest. Then blue eyes met brown. It was several more moments before he felt able to control his voice.

'I never thought to see this again. Where did you get it? How did you know it was mine?'

'It was found beside you after the battle. It bears the device of a falcon on its pommel, the crest of the Thanes of Heslingfield, I believe.'

'Yes.' Ban's hand clenched round the hilt. For the first time it occurred to him that he was now the thane, albeit fugitive and dispossessed. The sword suddenly became a most poignant symbol of all that was lost, and his throat tightened.

Seeing the powerful play of emotions on his face Iain made a shrewd guess at the thoughts behind. From the moment he saw it he had recognised the quality and craftsmanship of the weapon but, looking at Ban's expression now, knew it had significance far beyond its own intrinsic beauty.

'It is a fine weapon. I thought you would be loath to lose it.'

With an effort Ban got his voice under control. 'Indeed I would, my lord. It was a gift from my father. I thank you for its return.' He paused. 'It would seem that now I am doubly in your debt, and in truth I know not how I can repay it.'

'If you wish to repay me then you will get well and make your sister much happier.'

Ban found nothing to say for he could not put into words what was in his heart. The dark gaze met his and held it for a moment.

'Get well, Ban.' Iain moved to the door and paused just long enough to bestow one last smile. Then he was gone.

* * *

Ashlynn closed the storeroom door and took a leisurely look around. When Iain had first shown her around Dark Mount it had been one of many chambers they had visited. This was the first time she had been back. Her gaze passed over a stack of empty wicker baskets and a pile of old sacks and moved on, coming to rest on several large chests. Initially they had rated no more than a casual glance but curiosity was roused now and there was time to indulge it.

The chests were heavy and banded with iron, the bolts stiff with disuse, but with perseverance she managed to slide them back and lift the dusty lids. A pleasant scent drifted out to greet her and she realised then that the box was lined with cedar. The reason quickly became apparent. Inside were heavy folds of thick-woven cloth. She ran her hand over the surface, tracing the outline of a colourful embroidered bird. It was beautiful and in spite of herself she gave a gasp of delight. Two other chests revealed similar tapestries, all perfectly preserved by the cedar lining.

Ashlynn's appetite was whetted now. A further search revealed a large and slightly moth-eaten bearskin rug, a mirror of polished metal with an ornate frame, a wooden screen finely carved in the likeness of fruit and leaves and an elegant silver flagon with half-a-dozen matching goblets. Open-mouthed with delight she ran her fingers over the curved handle, marvelling at the workmanship and wondering where they had come from. Such things were made to be enjoyed, not hidden away and forgotten. Her own spartan chamber would benefit greatly by the addition of some attractive furnishings. That would involve asking Iain, of course. She bit her lip and closed the chest lid carefully.

* * *

For two days she had hesitated over the matter before deciding that cowardice was never going to solve the problem. Having made up her mind she went in search of Iain. Knowing he was unlikely to be in his chamber she tried the hall but it was empty of all save servants so she made her way downstairs. She was only halfway down when she heard the din of what sounded like fighting. For one dreadful second her mind was filled with Normans in helmets and chain mail. Then common sense returned. A swift glance out of the lower door revealed the truth: the courtyard was full of men locked in close physical combat or paired off for sword practice. The air rang with the sound of clashing steel and shouts of derision or encouragement. Her startled gaze moved quickly from the wrestlers to the swordsmen, seeking her husband out. Then she saw him and her breath caught in her throat.

Like the rest of the men he had stripped to the waist, apparently unconcerned by the cold air, but the rest were an irrelevance now. Her attention was riveted on Iain. She had not thought before that a man's body could be beautiful, but that had been quite wrong. His arms and torso might have been sculpted so clearly delineated was the heavy musculature beneath his skin. Dark hair tapered from the broad chest and led the eye to a narrow waist and hips and thence to long, muscled legs.

Even though she already knew something of his ability, Ashlynn was still drawn to watch, held by the lithe power of the man and the skill and control with which he fought. He moved tirelessly, testing his opponent's ability, looking for a weakness and when he found it exploiting it ruthlessly. Recalling her lessons with Ban she smiled ruefully. Against such skills, her own were puny. All at once the incident with the robbers returned and she knew without a doubt that she had been lucky. But for the element of surprise she would have been skewered. Given a fair fight she had no doubt Iain could have accounted for his attackers single handed. Even Ban, whose skill she respected, would have been hard pressed to hold his own against him. With that knowledge came the first stirring of pride, as unexpected as it was genuine.

At the end of the bout Iain sheathed the sword and donned his shirt and tunic again. She watched Dougal stroll across to join him. They exchanged a few words and then were joined in turn by one or two others. In a short time the group was engaged in animated discussion. From the accompanying gestures it seemed to be about the finer points of sword play. Once she saw Iain look round, his eyes scanning the spectators. They saw her at once and she felt again the power of that casual regard. Would he disapprove of her presence here? His expression gave no hint of annoyance but then it was often hard to tell what he was thinking. Her pulse quickened. Would he come over now? She hoped he might. His men already had a low opinion of her and, if she went to join him, they might take such an interruption ill.

However, Iain remained where he was, apparently seeing no reason to leave the present company. Around them the exercise continued, drawing his attention that way. He must have made some quip for she saw his companions laugh. The conversation resumed. Ashlynn bit her lip and turned away. The message was clear enough. He was busy and she was unwanted here. She should go.

'The wrestling bouts are fun to watch are they not, my lady?' said a voice beside her.

Ashlynn started and, looking round, recognised Robbie. For a moment she felt awkward for it was he whom she had given the slip when she ran away, but his expression now was genial. If he bore her a grudge it wasn't apparent. From the question she realised that she must have been staring at the wrestlers, though in truth had seen nothing of them.

'Er, yes,' she said. 'Who do you think will win?'

'Fergus,' he replied without hesitation. 'There isn't a man in Glengarron who can match him for strength or skill.'

Looking at the individual in question Ashlynn could see the truth of that remark. Fergus was massively muscled and looked to be roughly the size of a barn door, but for all that he was fast and agile.

She nodded. 'I can well believe it.'

'I'm just thankful he fights on our side.'

Ashlynn took the point as Fergus raised a big and brawny opponent over his head and tossed him into the banked snow at the edge of the courtyard, much to the rowdy enjoyment of the onlookers.

'I think I would not like to meet him on a field of battle.'

'Or in an alley on a dark night,' returned Robbie with a grin.

'Heaven forbid.'

They laughed, each visualising the possibility.

'But then all Glengarron's men are able fighters, are they not?' she continued.

'Aye, my lady, they are. Lord Iain trains them well.'

'So I see.' She eyed him with curiosity. 'Have you ridden with him long?'

'Going on four years now.'

'Four years? A long time.'

'Not so long. There's many have been with him longer.'

'A man to inspire loyalty then.'

'Indeed he is, my lady. He looks after his men and all who depend on him. There's not a braver laird in the whole border country, or one more cunning.'

'I can believe that.'

'You'd be right to, my lady. A man would have to get up very early to catch Iain of Glengarron.'

They lapsed into companionable silence for a while, but the conversation had given Ashlynn plenty to think about. Almost from the first she had recognised in Iain the qualities of strong leadership. It had been evident in the quiet assurance with which he moved among his men and the way in which he spoke to them. He called each one by name. She never heard him raise his voice but his slightest word was obeyed to the letter. Having seen their skill in battle she knew they were a formidable force. If their opinion of their leader was so high then that respect had been earned. Such men did not give their loyalty or their regard easily.

Robbie eyed her curiously. 'I've heard it said you're no so bad with a sword yourself, my lady.'

'Who told you that?'

'Dougal. He said that when you and Black Iain were attacked by robbers you killed six of them single handed.'

She gave a gurgle of incredulous laughter. 'Dougal overrates my skill. It was only two and I took them by surprise.'

Robbie grinned. 'I wish I'd been there to see it all the same.'

Across the courtyard Iain was apparently still engaged in easy conversation. However, he was also keenly aware of the scene opposite. It was too far to catch the words but he heard the pair laugh. His jaw tightened. When she was with him Ashlynn rarely laughed yet somehow, in mere minutes, Robbie had overcome her reserve, God rot him! Iain had always acknowledged his wife to be a pretty woman, but since the bruises had faded from her face it had become obvious that she was more than just pretty. When she appeared in the hall his men followed her with their eyes. Hitherto she had never given the least sign that she was aware of the attention but now she seemed to find pleasure in Robbie's company, apparently hanging on every word. Moreover, the young man was near Ashlynn's age and well favoured withal. Even her clothing blended with his, damn it. In this throng she might, to the casual eye, have passed for a local lass—a local lass or a servant. His brows drew together.

'What does the lady here? This is no fit place for a woman to be.'

The voice had come from the fringes of the group around Iain but the words were clearly meant to be overheard. They recalled him at once and he turned, giving the speaker a long and level stare. Recognising that look the rest fell into awkward silence.

'Well, Archie,' he replied, 'some might say it's not a

woman's place to fight off a gang of armed robbers either, but she did it all the same.'

Beneath the weight of that cool gaze the speaker coloured faintly. 'Beg pardon, my lord. I meant no disrespect.'

'I'm glad to hear it,' said Iain. 'Lady Ashlynn may do as she pleases without reference to you.'

The other lowered his gaze. 'As you say, my lord.'

The words fell into the surrounding silence and rippled outwards. Iain remained quite still, waiting. However, no further comment was forthcoming from any quarter and a few moments later the men turned away and resumed their earlier conversation as though nothing had happened. A remark from Dougal about one of the nearby swordsmen reclaimed Iain's attention and he made some reply, forcing his attention back to what his companion was saying. However, in spite of his best efforts his gaze was repeatedly drawn to the pair on the fringes of the wrestling. Ashlynn's attention was seemingly absorbed by the spectacle and she never looked his way. Then Robbie spoke to her again and she glanced up, smiling. Iain's gaze smouldered.

It was perhaps half an hour later when the combatants stopped to recover their breath and take a mug of ale. The gathering broke up into little groups, all talking and laughing together. Ashlynn excused herself and moved away then. It had been entertaining to watch the proceedings but, even with a cloak on, she was beginning to feel the cold. She was halfway to the door of the tower when a hand on her arm arrested her progress. She looked round quickly and felt her heart miss a beat.

'Iain.'

'I take it you enjoyed the practices,' he said. The words were quietly spoken but carried a nuance of something harder to define.

'Yes, very much, although that was not the reason I came out here.'

'Oh? And what was the reason?'

'I was looking for you.'

'I'm flattered. For a while I thought it might have been someone else.'

His gaze flicked toward Robbie. Ashlynn stared at him in genuine astonishment. Surely he couldn't have thought… For a second she felt a strong urge to laugh, then looked at his expression and decided she had better not. All the same he could not possibly be jealous. That was ridiculous. Before she could say more he took her arm and led her back indoors. Only when they reached the hall did he stop and draw her round to face him.

'What was it you wanted to speak to me about, lass?'

She took a deep breath and seized her chance, explaining about her discoveries in the store room. Listening, Iain was taken aback and, in spite of himself, faintly amused. Whatever else he had been expecting it wasn't that.

'So I wanted to ask…may I put those things to use?'

She waited, wondering if he would be angry. However, his expression did not suggest it and his tone when he spoke was perfectly level.

'You need not ask my permission, Ashlynn. This is your home now. Arrange it as you please.'

Footsteps on the stairs announced the arrival of some of his men and with that he favoured her with a bow and left. For a moment she watched him go, feeling

strangely bereft. Clearly he had no further interest in the
matter or in her either. Turning away, she summoned a
servant and bade him find Morag.

Some hours later Ashlynn surveyed her chamber with
something approaching real pleasure. The cold stone walls
were concealed now by the glorious tapestries, hanging
there in many-coloured splendour. By her bed the bearskin
rug covered a large section of floor. The bed itself and the
chairs were adorned with colourful cushions. In one corner
was the carved screen. The mirror lay on the table with
the flagon and cups. Now that the fire had at last taken the
chill off the air the overall effect was of cheerful cosiness.

'It looks fine, my lady,' said Morag, surveying it
critically.

'Yes, it does,' she agreed. 'Much less like a convent
cell.'

They both laughed. Then Morag turned to go.
Ashlynn saw her check slightly and turned to see Iain
in the doorway. He stepped aside to let the servant pass
and then came in, looking casually around. She experienced a moment of misgiving, wondering what his
reaction might be. However, she needn't have worried.

'You've done a good job, lass.'

'Thank you. I think so too.'

He glanced down at her and smiled faintly. All at
once the room seemed a lot smaller and a lot warmer.
The bed on the other hand seemed to have grown much
larger. Her heartbeat quickened and in the name of self-
preservation Ashlynn took a step away.

'The tapestries are finer even than I expected. Where
did they come from?'

'France,' he replied.

Her heart sank as an unwelcome possibility suddenly dawned. Had these things belonged to Eloise? Suddenly she was mortified. Why hadn't such a possibility occurred to her before now?

'They belonged to my mother,' he continued. 'After she died they were put away. I'd almost forgotten about them, but it seems fitting now that they should return to their rightful place.'

She let out the breath she had been holding, feeling almost weak-kneed with relief.

'Did she die long ago?'

'Aye, when I was four and ten. My father packed away everything connected with her, including me.' He smiled wryly. 'Although I was sent to France rather than the storeroom.'

'That must have been hard.'

'Not really. It was a relief in many ways. As I told you, my father and I were never close. He had a quick temper and frequently exercised it on me, whether it was merited or not.'

Although there was nothing remotely self-pitying about the tone of voice Ashlynn sensed the hurt beneath. Sensed it and identified with it.

'Well, families are strange things, are they not?'

'Aye, lass, they are.'

'Children are vulnerable enough without having to contend with the enmity of a parent.'

The tone was even but he caught the wistful expression in her eyes.

'We play as the dice fall,' he replied, 'and perhaps it makes us stronger.'

'Perhaps.'

'You are strong in spite of your father,' he said. 'Strong and brave.'

There was no hint of mockery in the quiet tone and Ashlynn looked up in surprise. Then she shook her head.

'My father's word was reckless.'

'Then he didn't know you very well, did he?'

Disconcerted by the unforeseen direction of the conversation, Ashlynn changed tack. 'Did you have no brothers or sisters?'

'Three other siblings died in infancy but I have a sister living.'

'A sister? What is her name?'

'Jeannie.'

'Shall I meet her soon?'

'I doubt it,' he replied.

'Oh, she lives some distance away then.'

'Not so far, but in recent years we have become—estranged.'

Ashlynn took a deep breath. 'May I ask why?'

'We quarrelled.'

'I'm sorry to hear that.' She paused. 'Could you not make it up again?'

'No.' He sighed. 'This disagreement admits of no remedy.' Then seeing her puzzled expression he went on, 'It concerns Fitzurse.'

'Fitzurse!' Ashlynn was genuinely astonished. 'How so?'

'Jeannie thinks I should give up my quest to find him.'

'I see.'

'No, you don't. You have no idea.'

The tone was unwontedly harsh. She could hear anger

and, beneath it, something that sounded more like pain. The expression in his eyes was glacial. One part of her mind quailed, telling her to back off and leave it alone. Yet the stronger part knew she could not. This must be faced. She needed to know, to understand. Instinctively she reached out and laid a gentle hand on his arm.

'Then will you not tell me?'

For a moment she thought he was going to snub her as he had before, and tell her it was none of her concern. She saw him draw a deep breath as though to steady himself.

'If anyone has a right to know I suppose it is you,' he replied.

Her heartbeat quickened and she waited, unwilling to do anything that might break the mood now.

'I told you that I was married before and that my wife had died,' he continued. 'Fitzurse was the man responsible for that.'

Ashlynn stared at him, stunned and appalled together.

'My father had sent me to France in order to complete my military training. His sister was… is…married to a French nobleman, the Comte de Vaucourt, a man renowned for skill at arms. It was in their house that I met Eloise. She was…most beautiful. I believe I fell in love with her at first sight.'

As she listened Ashlynn kept her face determinedly neutral, hiding the turmoil of thoughts behind.

'My feelings were reciprocated and, since there were no objections to the match from either of our families, we married. For a while we were very happy. However, I had a jealous rival.'

Ashlynn's gaze met his for a moment. 'Fitzurse.'

'Aye. He had had designs on Eloise himself and took

it much amiss that her hand should be granted to one he saw as a foreign interloper. That it was so clearly a love match piqued his pride even further. So, believing himself slighted, he planned his revenge.'

'What did he do?'

'The Comte de Vaucourt arranged a boar hunt and a large party rode out that day, including Eloise and myself. Somehow, in the course of the chase, she became separated from the rest. Fitzurse's men were waiting and, seeing their chance, carried her off to his castle some few miles distant.'

Ashlynn paled, remembering her own encounter with Fitzurse and knowing too well what the man was capable of. Iain took a deep breath.

'He raped her repeatedly and then, when he had done, gave her to his men. When they had had their sport they released her. We eventually found her in the fields not far from Vaucourt. Somehow she must have made her way back there. She was in such a state that only the greatest effort of will could have kept her going. Above all else she wanted to see Fitzurse punished, to be avenged. Having gained that holy assurance she seized the dagger from my belt and ended her life.'

'Dear God.'

'The shame was not hers but she could not live with it.'

'What did you do?'

'I sought redress through the law. Like a fool I thought that having right on my side must result in justice. However, when the matter was brought before Duke Richard, Fitzurse swore that Eloise had gone with him of her own volition, that it had been only the two of them involved. He had powerful friends who bore false witness to that effect. And since those same men had provided the gold to fund his wars, the Duke inclined to their part. I would have killed Fitzurse anyway and to hell with the consequences but, knowing that, my uncle had me forcibly returned to Scotland for my own safety.'

'How did he do that?'

'He drugged the wine one evening. I woke up on board a merchant ship bound for the Firth of Forth. I cursed my uncle's name at first but, with the wisdom of hindsight, I saw that he was right. I'd live to fight another day. In the years that followed he sent me regular intelligence from France. In that way I learned Fitzurse had taken service with Duke William and was bound for England. Then I knew my turn was coming.' He paused. 'My one fear was that my enemy might have perished at Hastings along with all those others. Happily he did not.'

'And you have sought him ever since.'

'Aye, and one day we will meet.'

There could be no mistaking the cold purpose in his tone and Ashlynn shivered.

'That day may be far distant,' she replied.

'One year or ten, it makes no difference. I shall keep my vow.'

As the ramifications became clear, Ashlynn knew a moment of deep sadness. Would the evils of the past never be exorcised? If they were ever to build a life together its foundations could not be those of hatred and revenge. And if they did build a future could he ever feel for her what he felt for Eloise?

Mistaking the cause of her silence he eyed her

ruefully. 'It's not a pretty story. Perhaps I should not have told you.'

'No, it isn't pretty,' she replied, 'but I'm glad you did all the same. It makes so many things clear.'

'Does it?'

'Yes, among them why your sister should have asked you to give up your quest.'

He frowned. 'Jeannie doesn't know what she asks.'

'I think she does. She wants you to move on.'

'That is not possible.'

'Isn't it?'

'Not until I have rid this earth of Fitzurse.'

'I know as well as anyone why you hate this man, but we cannot alter what is past, Iain.' She squeezed his arm. 'Let it go. Look to the future instead.'

Her touch, though gentle, was warm. He could feel it beneath his sleeve. The effect was both soothing and sensual. He forced himself to ignore it along with the haunting expression in her eyes. 'There can be no future until this is settled. My vow was made in blood and it will be met in blood. I will not be forsworn.'

'Will you sacrifice everything to that end?'

'If needs be.'

'Does that include me?'

'This has nothing to do with you, Ashlynn.'

'How can you say so? How can you even think it?' she replied. 'I too have cause to hate Fitzurse, but if I let hatred govern my life he will have won. Don't you see?'

Iain's jaw tightened. He could not doubt the sincerity of the words or mistake the plea in her tone, but nor could he cede the point. 'You will deal with him in your way and I in mine.'

With that he turned and left her. She knew then beyond doubt that she was one of the things that would be sacrificed to this cause. Iain had married her only because he must. He wouldn't let that get in the way of his ambition. Nor, she reflected sadly, could she hope to win his heart. Quite clearly, Eloise had it still.

Chapter Eight

In the meantime, Ban was recovering well from his wounds and Ashlynn observed his physical progress with satisfaction. Of more concern was his state of mind. He never spoke of Heslingfield or what had occurred there but the events had inevitably cast their shadow over him. Although he had not entirely lost his former cheerful demeanour he was subject now to long periods of silent introspection. She had no need to ask what he was thinking about; the expression in his eyes was more eloquent.

Typically, he wanted to get back on his feet and left his sick bed at the first opportunity. Ashlynn went to visit him one morning to find him up and dressed.

'Ban, what on earth are you about? You're not strong enough yet.'

'I cannot lie there any longer, Ash. It has been weeks.'

'Three weeks. If you're not careful you'll tear those wounds open.'

''Tis but the shoulder I need to favour for a while. The rest are almost healed.'

'I'd say the one to your head has addled your brain.'

'Not so, sister mine. You fuss over nothing.'

'True enough, I suppose. A blow there could never do serious damage.'

Ban grinned. 'If I were not wearing this sling I'd make you pay for that impertinence.'

'I'm trembling at the narrowness of my escape.'

Suddenly she became aware that he was looking past her towards the doorway, and turned to see Iain there. To judge from his amused expression he had overheard much of their exchange. Ashlynn appealed to him now.

'My lord, tell him he should not be abroad so soon.'

'Alas, I fear my words would fall on deaf ears for I detect a strong streak of stubbornness in your family.' He came into the room and surveyed Ban keenly. 'Besides, I think lying abed has but a finite charm.'

'You speak truth, my lord.' Ban regarded his sister in triumph.

'This is a conspiracy,' she replied.

Iain smiled. 'Not at all, though I fear you are outvoted on this occasion.'

'All right. I know when I'm beaten.' Ashlynn fixed Ban with a speaking look. 'Just don't do anything foolish for a while, I beg.'

'You know me.'

'Yes, quite.'

In fact Ban showed remarkably good sense for several days, taking things slowly at first and contenting himself with gentle exercise within doors. However, he, like Ashlynn, loved to be outside, and before too long proposed a turn about the courtyard for some fresh air. It was with some misgivings that she agreed to accompany him, but she knew that even if she refused he would go anyway.

When Iain had said her brother was stubborn it had been no more than the truth.

In fact, her worries were unfounded. Ban showed no signs of a relapse and, as the days passed, the fresh air restored his colour and his appetite. Gradually he increased the time he spent out there and when the men were practising with swords he would linger to watch and gradually, through her husband's agency, was drawn into their conversation. Finding him interested and knowledgeable the men accepted his presence among them and Ashlynn, observing from the sidelines, was grateful for it. He needed their company and with it a chance to think about something other than the past.

'Your brother looks much better,' Iain observed, coming to join her one morning.

'Yes, he does.'

'He seems much more animated of late.'

'Male companionship is proving beneficial. He has been shut up for too long with mine.'

'I think no man would object too strenuously to that,' he replied.

The words were casually spoken but the look that accompanied them was not. For many reasons it was disturbing, not least for its lingering warmth. Moreover, she could detect no sign of tension in his manner now; their former conversation might not have happened.

'All the same fresh conversation is always welcome,' she replied. 'It is not good to be too long alone with sombre thoughts.'

'No, it isn't.' He paused. 'Perhaps you too might find new company stimulating.'

'New company?'

'Yule is almost upon us. It is the custom here to hold a feast.'

'Yule,' she murmured. 'I had forgotten.'

Ordinarily she would have looked forward to it. This year she had been dreading it but since the destruction of Heslingfield it had become an irrelevance and she hadn't given it a thought. It was as though her mind had deliberately blotted it out. Guessing at some of her thoughts Iain laid a gentle hand on her shoulder.

'I'm thinking it will not be an easy time for you, lass, or for your brother either. Do you wish me to abandon the feast this year?'

She regarded him with real surprise and for a moment found it hard to speak, not least for the warmth of his touch and his look. Then she shook her head. 'Thank you, but no. It will not be easy, as you say, but it must be faced. Besides, I would not put a damper on other people's enjoyment and neither would Ban.'

'Neither would I…what?' inquired a voice behind them.

Ashlynn turned to see her brother. 'Iain was asking whether we wished the Yuletide feast to be abandoned this year on account of what happened to Heslingfield.'

Ban met his sister's gaze and held it. Then he turned to look at Iain. 'No, my lord, not for the world would I have you do so. Rather, let the occasion be held as it always was at Heslingfield. In that way all the right memories may be kept alive.'

He reached for his sister's hand and squeezed it. Ashlynn managed to return his smile. The sight of it pierced Iain to the heart.

The following day the fine weather broke and the grey sky grew leaden, threatening snow. The wind was bitter. One brief exposure to that icy blast on the roof terrace sent Ashlynn hurrying back to the warmth of her room. She had not been there very long before someone knocked on the door. Feeling sure it would be Ban she bade the caller enter. However, it was a very different figure that appeared on the threshold.

'Good morning, Ashlynn.' Iain surveyed her in silence for a moment and then smiled faintly. 'May I come in?'

Gathering her wits she answered in the affirmative and watched him step into the room. Then he turned and beckoned to someone without. To her astonishment four women entered, all total strangers and all of them carrying a variety of large bags and bundles. They smiled as they made their duty to her. In bemusement Ashlynn looked from them to him.

'Madame and her assistants have just arrived from Dunfermline. They'll be staying with us for a few days.'

'Will they?'

For the first time she realised he carried under his arm several bolts of cloth which he laid on the bed. His companions bore several more. Soon the fur coverlet was transformed into a riot of colour.

'What's this?' she asked.

'Your new wardrobe, my lady,' he said, 'or the basis for it, at least.'

'New wardrobe?'

'Aye, and not before time.' He eyed her homespun gown with disfavour. 'Since the day I first saw it I've wanted to get that ghastly dress off you. I'd have done it a lot sooner but the ladies here had commitments at the royal court and could not be spared.'

'They've come from the royal court?'

'That's right.'

Incredulous and speechless Ashlynn watched him cross to the door again. He paused on the threshold.

'I'll leave you to it then.'

With that he was gone. Ashlynn tried to gather her scattered wits and turned to look at the rolls of cloth on the bed. The elder seamstress hastened to fetch the azure silk. Drawing out a length she held it against Ashlynn.

'The colour looks well on you, my lady.'

'It's beautiful,' she replied, running her fingers over the surface of the material. 'I never saw anything so fine.' It was no more than the truth. Never would she have dreamed of owning such a gown.

However, before she had finished admiring the blue, Madame gestured to an assistant to fetch a bolt of red velvet, considering it intently, letting her gaze rest on Ashlynn's face and hair a moment and thence to the slender form below, taking in the whole picture.

'This will also look well,' she said. Seeing Ashlynn remain silent, the seamstress regarded her keenly. 'Does the cloth displease you, my lady?'

'No, it's beautiful. It's just that I find it hard to choose between the two.'

'No need, my lady,' replied the other, 'since we are to make half-a-dozen new gowns.'

For a moment Ashlynn was rooted to the spot. Half-

a-dozen new gowns! Never in her life had she been permitted more than one new dress at a time and, even
then, not in fabrics like these. Madame smiled.

'So we keep the red I think.'

'I, er…yes.'

The red bolt joined the blue.

Half an hour later those two had been joined by four
others in gold, cerise, forest green and mauve. Then
she found herself being measured by the giggling assistants. From time to time Madame spoke to them in the
French tongue, apparently giving detailed instructions.
Ashlynn looked on in awed silence. She dreaded to
think what all this must be costing. Never could she have
envisaged so generous a gift. These cloths were sumptuous, fit for the royal court indeed. Apart from the dress
material there were also lighter, finer fabrics of the type
suitable for chemises and stockings. These too came
under close scrutiny as Madame picked out the shades
that would complement the rest. Then, when she had
taken her client's measurements, the dress patterns
emerged from a leather bag. Ashlynn regarded them
with concern.

'Aren't they a little revealing?'

'These are the latest styles, my lady. Let me show
you.' She gestured for the younger woman to come
closer. 'Notice the wider sleeves. They allow the colour
of the chemise to show to advantage. The bodice fits
close to the body.' She let her gaze rest on her client a
moment. 'A figure like yours should also be shown off
to best advantage, my lady.'

Ashlynn wondered what on earth Iain was going to

say about that. The proposed style was so far removed from the modest drape of a Saxon gown that it was vaguely shocking, but the woman in her found it hard to resist. The thought occurred that such a fashion might also be pleasing to a man, if for rather different reasons. Would it please Iain? Would he truly *see* her then? With almost uncanny prescience Madame interjected.

'My lord was most insistent on this point.'

'He was?'

'Oh, yes, my lady. Gowns in the French style. Those were his instructions.'

Ashlynn made no more demur. There was little time to dwell on the matter because the seamstress's assistants wanted to measure her feet. Having done so, they traced out the size on soft leather prior to cutting out shoes which would later be sewn to fit her.

'It will take a few days to complete the work,' said Madame, 'but I hope it will meet with my lady's approval.'

Ashlynn was quite sure of that. She could hardly wait to see the results. Iain's face imposed itself on her mind. Would her choice meet with *his* approval? She hoped so. He had made her a most generous gift and one she had certainly not been expecting. It behoved her to thank him at least.

When the session ended she sought him out and found him in the hall.

Iain heard her in silence and then replied, 'As the wife of a laird it is fitting that you should dress as one. Do not feel obliged to thank me.'

'I did not thank you from a sense of obligation, my lord, but because I meant it.'

There followed another short silence before he inclined his head in acknowledgement. 'Then I accept your thanks in the spirit they were meant.'

After he had left Ashlynn took herself off to the roof terrace needing space to try and order the riot of her thoughts. She was tempted to pinch herself to find out if she woke or slept. It would not have surprised her in the least to discover the last couple of hours had been a dream. Never in a thousand years would she have expected him to think of this, but she was woman enough to appreciate it and to look forward to seeing the finished gowns. It would be good to wear truly flattering feminine garments again. Would he find her attractive then? She glanced down at the homespun dress and sighed. He obviously considered her a perfect fright at present. Almost at once she was ashamed of the notion; she ought to be beyond this sort of foolishness. They would have company over Yuletide and he wished her to look the part she played, that was all. Had he not made it clear enough? She could have no hopes of him.

Quite deliberately she turned her mind away from Iain to the matter of Yule. If they were to have a feast then arrangements needed to be made for that and for the guests. Rooms must be cleaned and beds prepared. Then there was the hall. The very thought of it was enough to bring a grimace to the face. After years of neglect and solely masculine influence it was more like a temple to barbarism than the heart of the house. However, that was about to change. Ashlynn lifted her chin. Like it or not, she was mistress here now. Had she not been told to arrange matters as she pleased? Having made up her mind she returned within doors and summoned Morag.

'Gather all the household servants in the hall. I want to talk to them.'

Some time later a disgruntled steward waylaid Iain below stairs with a string of queries. Did his lordship really mean for the hall trestles to be taken down and scrubbed? Was the straw to be changed when it had barely been down six months, and the floor swept at that time too? Since when had dust and cobwebs ever hurt anyone? Had his lordship really intended that the majority of the servants should be taken from their regular duties to carry out such work, or that two of them should go out for a whole morning to collect greenery and leave him, Davy Kerr, shorthanded as a result?

Iain listened with concealed surprise but said nothing at first, waiting till the man ran out of breath.

'Who ordered this?' he asked then.

'Lady Ashlynn, my lord.'

'Did she so?'

Davy Kerr's pigeon breast swelled with virtuous indignation. 'Aye, my lord.'

Iain eyed him steadily. 'Then you'd best get to it, man.'

For a moment the steward could only stare at him in disbelief. 'Beg pardon, my lord?'

'You heard me. Get to it.'

'Very well, my lord.' Kerr threw him a fierce stare and then bowed stiffly before turning to go.

'Oh, and Kerr…'

'My lord?'

'Don't ever question Lady Ashlynn's orders again.'

The tone was soft but the look in the laird's eyes was not. Kerr swallowed hard and nodded, then scuttled away as fast as he could.

Iain continued on up the stairs and came to the hall. He stopped in his tracks on the threshold. The room was a hive of frenetic activity with servants bustling about in every direction, armed with brooms and pails and scrubbing brushes. Ashlynn's slender regal figure stood in their midst directing operations. Homespun gown or not she had an air of natural authority about her and no one questioned the instructions she delivered with such cool and firm assurance. The men looked slightly bemused but the women's expressions approximated more to triumph. For a while Iain stood and watched in silent amusement and considerable enjoyment. If he'd ever entertained any doubts about her ability to run his household they had just been removed. He'd seen military commanders with less skill.

'What the devil's going on?' asked a voice beside him.

Iain glanced over his shoulder to see Ban. 'I believe your sister is readying the hall for the Yuletide celebrations.'

'Ah.'

'I take it you've seen this before.'

'Oh, yes.'

'She looks to be very thorough.'

'You have no idea.'

Iain grinned. 'So what would you advise?'

The younger man surveyed the scene for a few moments longer. 'That we make ourselves scarce.'

'My thought exactly. How about a jug of ale and a game of chess?'

'A most excellent suggestion, my lord.'

* * *

It took most of the day and a small army of servants to clean the hall to Ashlynn's exacting standards. By then the men she had sent out earlier returned with a cart full of fragrant greenery to decorate it. When it was carried indoors it filled the air with sweet fresh scent. Ashlynn drafted all available hands to help and by the time they had done she surveyed the result with real satisfaction. Beside her Morag nodded approval.

'The place looks like it used to in the old days, when Lady Alice was alive.'

'Lady Alice?'

'Lord Iain's mother, God rest her soul.' Morag shook her head. 'She always had the hall decked thus for the feast. After she died things were never the same. But then men have no sense of these things.'

'Some might say they have so sense at all,' replied Ashlynn.

Morag chuckled. 'You're not wrong there, my lady.'

Ashlynn gathered all the servants together. 'You've done a magnificent job. Now go and get something to eat and drink. You've earned it.' Having dismissed them she went to sit down by the fire feeling weary now herself.

Ban and Iain found her there a little later. Both men stood looking round the room in open-mouthed amazement.

'God's bones,' murmured Ban, 'it looks like a different place.'

Iain mentally agreed. It did. Apart from the obvious cleanliness it smelled wonderful, a mingling of green foliage and fresh straw and scrubbed wood. The old tallow lights had been replaced with fine beeswax candles which threw a sweet soft-scented glow over the whole room. In an instant he was transported back to his childhood when his mother had been alive, and he felt his throat tighten. Then he became aware that Ashlynn was watching him.

'Do you like it?' she asked.

'I think it's perfect, lass. Just perfect.' He took her hand and carried it to his lips. 'Thank you.'

He had never used quite that tone before. It was gentle and tender and it took her unawares, like the warm touch of his fingers on hers and the imprint of his kiss on her skin. She made no attempt to withdraw her hand from his and he seemed in no hurry to relinquish it. Only when a servant appeared with a query for Ashlynn about the serving of the evening meal did he reluctantly let her go.

The atmosphere in the hall was different that evening, for once the men had recovered from their initial astonishment their mood lifted to match the cheerfulness of the surroundings. There was more laughter and good-humoured banter. Ashlynn too relaxed in the lighter atmosphere, and she was gladdened to see Ban smile. However, as time wore on the exertions of the day began to take their toll and eventually she excused herself from the gathering. This time Iain rose with her and escorted her as far as the door. For a moment the dark gaze surveyed her in concern.

'You look tired, lass.'

'I am,' she admitted.

''Tis not to be wondered at.' He paused. 'Thank you for your efforts today. It has been a long time since Dark Mount looked like a home.'

There could be no mistaking the sincerity of the words or the expression in his eyes as he raised her hand to his lips. Not knowing quite what to say she remained silent, every fibre of her being alive to him. Would he take her in arms now? If he did, what then? Recalling the power of his kiss and how it had set her aflame it took but a second to know the answer to that. He surveyed her just a moment longer and relinquished her hand.

'Goodnight. Sleep well, lass.'

In silent confusion she acknowledged that what she felt was not relief but something akin to disappointment. She bade him goodnight and turned away. He watched her until she was out of sight.

Two days later the weather changed and it snowed again overnight. By morning all the landscape was transformed. Ashlynn surveyed it for a while from the roof terrace before making her way down to the hall. Finding no sign of Iain or her brother she went outside.

The courtyard had been cleared and the snow banked high against the walls. It was bitterly cold but the wind had dropped and the ice crystals courted the sunlight like flung diamonds. Ashlynn smiled and breathed deeply, enjoying the moment. She would take a turn or two before starting work. In spite of what had gone before there was plenty to be done. Her mind moved ahead, thinking of food for the feast. She would consult the cook about that in due course…

Her thoughts were rudely interrupted by a large ball of snow which caught her squarely in the chest. Looking up indignantly she saw her brother some yards off regarding her with a speculative smile. In that moment he was so much the old Ban again that her heart swelled. The feeling was short-lived as another snowball caught her shoulder. Ashlynn's eyes narrowed.

'Just you wait!' With a speed born of expertise she fashioned a missile and lobbed it back. Ban ducked and it skimmed his cloak but, when he turned round again, the next one hit him in the face. Spluttering, he heard her laugh.

'My aim is still good, brother.'

'Too good, you minx.'

Several more men had emerged from the hall and other bystanders watched with interest, among them Iain who had just emerged from the smithy hard by. Ban fired off several more shots with varying success for he was still using his left hand to avoid straining the recovering shoulder. However, he kept up the pressure. Ashlynn found herself trying to dodge Ban's missiles while throwing her own, and her usually accurate aim became less so. A large snowball, intended for Ban's chest, flew past and hit Iain instead. She heard several sharp intakes of breath from the on-lookers and then muffled snorts of laughter. Ban guffawed. For a moment Ashlynn was still, but remorse was short-lived and mischief reasserted itself in a wide grin.

Seeing it, Iain lifted an eyebrow and strolled casually towards her. Undeceived by this apparent nonchalance, Ashlynn turned to flee. He caught her in six strides and lifted her off her feet with no more difficulty than he would have lifted a wisp of straw. Her shriek of protest went unheeded. Then he glanced down at his struggling burden with a glint in his eye that boded no good at all.

'Throw snowballs at me, would you, lass?'

'You don't understand…'

'Oh, I think I do.'

He carried her to the edge of the courtyard where the cleared snow was banked in great heaps. As she saw him grin an unwelcome suspicion dawned.

'Iain, no!'

'No?'

Ashlynn struggled harder. 'Don't you dare!'

'You know better than that, lass.'

'You wouldn't…'

The sentence ended on a shriek of outrage as he dropped her into the huge white drift. Roars of laughter erupted from the spectators. Then, almost as though at a signal, other missiles began to fly amid yells and curses and laughter and soon the air was thick with them. For a moment Iain surveyed the scene, grinning. Then he glanced down at Ashlynn who, almost completely engulfed, was trying unsuccessfully to extricate herself.

'Help me out, you villain!'

'Villain is it now?' He shook his head. 'Not content with an unprovoked attack you insult me into the bargain.'

Torn between laughter and frustration she moderated her tone. 'I beg your pardon, my lord. Won't you please help me up?'

His grin widened and he surveyed her a moment longer. Then, reaching down a hand, he caught hers and hauled her out of the white mound. Covered from head to foot she was grinning herself now. He shook out her cloak and then began to brush some of the snow from her hair. As he did so a stray missile caught him round the ear. Unable to help herself Ashlynn laughed out loud. His expression was eloquent but far from stopping her amusement served only to fuel it.

'It seems to me, wife, that you do not demonstrate the proper respect due to your lord and master. I am minded to show you the error of your ways.' He crooked a finger. 'Come here.'

Ashlynn backed away. 'I shall not.'

'Is that right?' He advanced slowly. 'And I thought I'd cured you of disobedience.'

The tone was decidedly ambiguous. Withal there was an expression in his eyes that she hadn't seen before but it was definitely not to be trusted.

'Iain?'

She backed up a few more steps but still he came on. Then, without warning, his hand shot out and grabbed her wrist. Ashlynn gasped and tried to resist but in a matter of seconds was thrown over a broad shoulder. Ignoring the accompanying yells of protest he carried her across the courtyard and back to the tower. When eventually he set her down again they were in the great hall.

For a moment they faced each other, she half-laughing and half-panting as she tried to draw her breath, he drinking in every detail of her. Much dishevelled now, with snow still clinging to her cloak and melted drops in her hair, she seemed to glow for the cold had brought the colour to her cheeks and her eyes sparkled with mischief yet. There was withal a most provocative smile on her lips. He drew her closer, looking down into her face with an expression that was both alarming and exciting together. Then his mouth was on hers and excitement superseded alarm and banished it as Ashlynn swayed against him, surrendering to the moment, knowing this was what she had wanted him to do. Her mouth opened beneath his and the kiss grew deeper and more intimate. Involuntarily her arms stole around his neck, her hand stroking the warm curve at the nape of his neck beneath the dark mane of hair.

The touch sent a thrill to the core of his being re-awakening the hunger he had felt before, a hunger he once thought he could not know again. His hold tightened about her, lifting her off her feet, crushing her closer. He felt her mouth respond to his and tasted again its sweetness on his tongue, breathing the fresh clean scent of snow on her hair and clothes and beneath it the subtle erotic scent of the woman. He wanted her, here, now, wanted to lose himself in her completely...

A discreet cough alerted them to other presences and they surfaced, looking round to see Fergus and Dougal. Ashlynn's cheeks turned a much deeper shade of pink. With a wry smile Iain relinquished his hold on his wife and watched her turn away toward the hearth. As the men approached Ashlynn drew in a deep breath to try and compose herself, to still the dangerous thumping of her heart. A covert glance at Iain revealed nothing of his inner thought and certainly none of the powerful emotion that gripped her now. His voice when he spoke to his men was calm, unforced. It recalled her to reality. What had occurred had begun as a bit of harmless fun and somehow gone further than either of them had intended. She smiled ruefully. It was certainly no more than that to him. Yet she had seen a side of him today that she had never dreamed existed, a side that was mischievous and playful and, she admitted, doubly attractive. When he laughed it lit his whole face and brought a warm gleam to his eyes. She realised then it was the first time she had ever seen him laugh like that.

'If it pleases you, my lady, the new gowns are ready for your inspection.'

Ashlynn looked round to see Morag. 'I beg your pardon?'

'Your gowns, my lady?'

'Of course, I'll come directly.'

Throwing a swift glance at the men she left them to talk, and moved quietly to the stairs. She never saw the dark gaze that followed her every step of the way.

The finished gowns exceeded her expectations in every way. They had been beautifully made and she looked at them with delight. Morag was open-mouthed to see the array of garments: chemises, bliauts, shoes, even a cloak made of good wool cloth and lined with marten fur. It was far warmer than the old one and Ashlynn knew she would be glad of it as the winter tightened its grip. She spent the next hour trying each of the garments in turn under the critical eyes of the seamstress and her assistants. Ashlynn had no fault to find. Madame's instinct for colour and style had been unerring. The gowns fitted her figure to perfection and she could see from the women's expressions that they became her well. Would Iain approve? She hoped he would for in truth it had been a most generous gift—generous and unexpected. The timing couldn't have been better either. Now she would have no cause to feel ashamed before the Yuletide guests.

In the meantime she gave orders for one of the big cedar-lined chests to be brought to her chambers. It would be ideal for the safe storage of the new gowns. Having organised that, she helped Morag lay the dresses within. The servant eyed her quizzically.

'Will you not change your gown now, my lady?'

'Not now. Tomorrow.'

'Ah, for the feast.'

'Just so.'

'I think you'll break hearts, my lady.'

Ashlynn smiled wistfully knowing there was one heart at least that would remain for ever out of reach.

Chapter Nine

The Yuletide feast saw the arrival of many guests. Ashlynn had dressed with care for the occasion, donning the forest green bliaut. It was simple and elegant, set off by the soft cream chemise beneath, the combination enhancing the tawny sheen of her hair. With Morag's help this was now neatly braided down her back with matching green ribbons. A girdle embroidered with brown and gold flowers rode her waist.

Ban, calling in a little later, surveyed her critically. Ashlynn smiled and gave him a twirl. 'Do you like it?'

'It's stunning,' he replied. Then, glancing over his shoulder, 'What say you, my lord?'

Iain, who had just appeared in the doorway, stopped in his tracks. For a long moment he surveyed his wife in silence, his gaze missing no detail. In fact he found it hard to tear his eyes away. Ban had not overstated the case; she really was stunning. The new gowns might have cost a small fortune but, looking at the result, it had been worth every penny.

'I think the assessment quite correct,' he replied.

There could be no mistaking the expression of warm approval in his eyes or the way they lingered on her figure. For the first time since she had left Heslingfield Ashlynn felt as though some lost part of her had just been restored and it lifted her spirits in an instant. She laughed and swept a low curtsy.

'I thank you, my lords.'

Ban grinned. 'Are you ready, Ash? The guests are approaching.'

'Yes, I just need my cloak.'

She retrieved it from the chair nearby but Iain stepped forward and relieved her of it.

'Allow me.'

He settled the garment on her shoulders and then fastened the brooch at the front. His hand brushed the neck of her gown, a casual and lightly caressing touch that set her flesh tingling in response. Then he held out his hand.

'Shall we?'

They descended the stairs and reached the bottom in time to see the riders clatter into the courtyard. Now that they were closer Ashlynn scanned the faces with interest. Counting the servants there were a dozen all told, ranging in age from four to forty. It took her by surprise to see the children among them but it was a pleasant discovery. How long it must have been since Dark Mount had heard children's voices.

Before she could pursue the thought she became aware that Iain's attention was not on them but rather on the accompanying adults, and suddenly there was tension in every line of his body. Following his gaze she saw it was fixed on a pretty dark-haired woman. The woman returned his stare for a moment or two and then allowed her male companion to help her from the saddle. Ashlynn had an impression of a burly bearded individual clad in a great fur cloak. For a moment he and Iain faced each other in silence. All around them the others were silent too, as though waiting for something. The tension was almost palpable. Then the newcomer held out his right hand. Iain stepped forward and took it in a firm clasp.

'It has been a long time, Duncan.'

At this the others relaxed visibly. Ashlynn's curiosity mounted. She exchanged glances with Ban and saw him raise an eyebrow. Evidently he too was at a loss. Then she turned her attention back to the little scene before them.

'Aye, it has,' Duncan replied. 'Too long, I'm thinking.' He glanced down at the woman beside him. For a moment she didn't move, her eyes fixed on Iain's face. In it Ashlynn saw both wariness and longing. Iain returned her gaze and held it.

'This is an unexpected pleasure,' he said.

'Unexpected I have no doubt,' she replied. 'As to the last, I wonder.'

'Then be in no doubt. You are welcome here, Jeannie.'

Ashlynn's heart missed a beat. This had to be the mysterious sister he had mentioned before.

'It is good of you to make the journey in such weather,' Iain continued.

Duncan snorted. 'It wouldn't have mattered if the drifts were five feet deep. Jeannie was determined to come.'

'I'm flattered.'

'Aye, you are, you rogue,' retorted the lady.

Undisturbed by this mode of address, Iain regarded her keenly. 'Can it be that you have missed me, sweet sister?'

She ignored the gibe. 'I wanted to know for myself if the rumour I've been hearing is true.'

'Oh, and what particular rumour would that be?' he replied.

'The one about you carrying off a beautiful woman and then marrying her. Duncan wouldn't have it, and I must admit I thought it ridiculous at first, but when I had the story from more than one source I became curious.' She fixed him with a sharp eye. 'What have you been up to, brother?'

Iain's lips twitched. 'I carried off a beautiful woman and then married her.'

Her jaw dropped for a moment but she recovered quickly. 'If you are trifling with me, Iain MacAlpin, I warn you now…'

'I wouldn't dream of it.' He turned toward the two figures behind him and smiled. 'Come. Allow me to present my wife, Lady Ashlynn, and her brother, Lord Ban. Ashlynn, this is my sister, Jeannie, and her husband, Duncan McCrae of Ardnashiel.'

For a second there was a pregnant silence. Duncan's blue eyes sparkled and he laughed softly in utter disbelief.

'Well, in the name of all that's wonderful.' As he ran his eye over Ashlynn his smile grew. 'I am truly delighted, my lady, although where this ugly brute found anything so beautiful I'll never know.'

Ashlynn curtseyed and returned the smile. 'The pleasure is mine, my lord.'

Duncan turned then to Ban and held out his hand. 'I'm

glad to make your acquaintance, sir. Did he carry you off too by any chance?'

Ban grinned. 'Aye, my lord, he did—in a manner of speaking.'

'Is that so? Well, by heaven, there's a good story here or I miss my guess, and I would fain hear it.'

'I also,' replied his wife.

The two women faced each other and Ashlynn found herself looking into an arresting face framed with curling dark hair. Jeannie was perhaps five or six years her senior. She was taller too and her figure fuller, but it was the eyes that one remembered for they were dark and piercing like her brother's. They missed no detail in their frank appraisal.

'I once thought that nothing my brother could do would ever surprise me again, but I see I was wrong.' She softened the words with a smile. 'For once it feels good to be wrong.'

With relief Ashlynn saw the smile reach the dark eyes and with it came the first glimmer of hope that she might now find a woman friend. Jeannie indicated the three children who stood nearby.

'My sons, Jamie and Andrew, and my daughter, Fiona.'

As the children made their duty to her Iain surveyed them with frank astonishment. 'Good God, but they've grown. I hardly recognise them.'

'How should you?' replied Jeanne. 'You haven't set eyes on them in nigh on three years.'

The tension was back and Ban interjected quickly. 'Children always grow fast, do they not?'

'So it would seem,' replied Iain.

His young relatives looked up at him with wide-eyed

apprehension for the tallest of them came no higher than his belt. The little girl's lip trembled. Ashlynn smiled.

'You are all welcome here,' she said. 'Now you are come I see that we shall have great fun this Yuletide.'

The gentleness of her tone seemed to offer reassurance and they began to look a little less anxious.

'We shall have feasting and music and, if you wish, we shall play some games. Would you like that?' she asked.

They nodded solemnly.

'Good. In a little while we shall go in together and you shall tell me what games you like best.' She held out her hand and after a moment's hesitation the little girl took it.

Iain watched the scene in fascination. He would never have suspected that she might like children or have such an easy way with them. They seemed to like her too and pressed round her now, clearly sensing safety. Him they continued to regard warily. He supposed it was scarcely to be wondered at. They must have forgotten his existence. Almost three years! The realisation caused an unexpected twinge of guilt. To cover it he introduced his wife and brother-in-law to the various cousins who made up the remainder of the party. When at length that duty was performed he gestured to the door.

'Shall we go in then?'

Jeannie smiled at Ashlynn. 'Aye, let's do that. Then we'll find a quiet corner somewhere and you can tell me how you had the misfortune to be married to my brother.'

Iain threw his sister a speaking glance which she ignored. Ashlynn began to like her more and more. She caught Ban's eye and saw him grin. Then they all went in together. After their guests had taken refreshment and been shown to their various quarters, Ashlynn went to inquire if Jeannie had everything she needed.

'I shall do very well. In truth I had not expected to find such comfort here,' she replied, looking round. 'You have made your mark already.'

In fact Ashlynn had raided all the upper storerooms for rugs and hangings and with the aid of Morag and the other servants had put them to use. She had also commanded that fires be lit in the guest chambers some days before, in order to take the damp chill off the air. In consequence the rooms looked and felt much more cheerful. It was pleasing to discover that her efforts were appreciated.

Her sister-in-law gestured to the chair opposite. 'Will you not sit awhile? Then you can tell me your story for I long to hear it.'

Ashlynn related the main events, leaving out only what was too personal to be shared. As she listened, Jeannie's face registered horror and sympathy but when it came to the part about the wedding her dark eyes narrowed.

'Did my brother force you to wed him?'

'He could not do other than marry me, my lady, since the king commanded it.'

'Malcolm disposes as he sees fit and always to suit himself,' replied Jeannie. She eyed Ashlynn closely for a moment. 'Has my brother treated you well since?'

'Yes, very well. He has been most generous.'

'Has he indeed? I'm relieved to hear it.'

'I have no cause for complaint.'

'You must be the first person ever to say so.' Jeannie smiled. 'But that's enough of him for the moment. Tell me about *your* brother.'

Ashlynn explained how she and Ban had been reunited. When she finished there were tears in her listener's eyes.

'It is a strange fate indeed that brought you here, but I am so glad it did.' She paused. 'Iain and I have been at odds for some time, and I began to fear that our estrangement might never end. It is in part due to you that it has a chance of doing so.'

'Then I am glad of it. Families should be united.'

'Aye, they should.' Jeannie eyes her quizzically. 'Did my brother tell you the nature of our quarrel?'

'He said that it concerned Fitzurse.'

'It is true. What Fitzurse did was cruel beyond believing.' The older woman sighed. 'Yet I could not bear to see Iain so consumed by rage and hatred.'

'I can understand that.'

'He and I were very close at one time. He was the person I looked up to most. Our childhood was not an easy one and he stood up for me many a time against our father.'

Ashlynn remained silent, listening avidly. She wanted so much to know more about the man she had married.

'He took some beatings on account of it,' Jeannie went on, 'but I never saw him cry. It was as though it had become a point of pride with him not to. When our mother died the situation got much worse. Iain said it was our father's unkindness that caused her death. Perhaps in part he was right.'

'I'm sorry to hear it.'

'He and Father had a terrible row and came to blows as a result. A short time later Iain was sent to France.'

'But what of you?'

'I was rescued by an aunt, one of my mother's sisters. She was ever a kindly soul and her house seemed like heaven to me. The three years I spent with her were among the happiest of my life. It was there I met Duncan. He came courting after that and when I turned sixteen we married.'

'Did you ever hear from Iain?'

'He would send word from time to time. It was clear that France agreed with him.'

'He married there, did he not?'

'That's right.' Jeannie paused. 'Did he tell you what happened to his wife?'

'Yes.'

'It almost destroyed him. I never saw a person so changed. For a while I thought he might run mad. However, he channelled his energies into fighting instead.'

'That was when he joined Malcolm.'

'Aye, and began to carve out a reputation for himself into the bargain. He always was a good swordsman and he honed his skill. Those who saw him in battle said he was fearless. As time went on he became involved in a lot of other wild exploits and his reputation grew.'

'I had heard of it long before I met him,' replied Ashlynn.

Jeannie nodded. 'He had learned the value of being feared.'

'But you did not fear him?'

'No, I feared *for* him. I dreaded what hatred and rage might turn him into and begged him to give up the quest for Fitzurse, but he would not and so we quarrelled.' She sighed. 'Heaven knows how often I have regretted it.'

'You did what you thought you had to do.'

'Yet it got me nowhere and earned his enmity into the bargain.'

'But surely that is at an end now,' said Ashlynn.

'I hope so, for this quarrel has resulted only in tears and bitterness and we have seen enough of that.' Jeannie regarded her keenly. 'Perhaps now that he has you my brother will put aside the thought of revenge.'

Ashlynn smiled sadly, knowing she possessed no such influence. Iain was set on a course that could only end in bloodshed and death—for him or for Fitzurse, or both. Nothing she could say would ever change his mind.

Further friends and relations appeared later that day, braving the weather to make the ride to Glengarron. All were warmly welcomed and, Iain having performed the necessary introductions, all received the news of the laird's marriage with frank astonishment. Suddenly Ashlynn found herself the centre of attention.

'She's a bonny lass and no mistake,' said Duncan who was standing next to Iain by the fireplace, watching as Ashlynn and her brother talked with Jeannie and some cousins across the room. 'You've done well for yourself there.'

'I know it,' replied Iain.

'I like the brother too. He's a brave lad if what you say is true.'

'That he is.'

'They've had a bad time, the pair of them.'

'Aye, they have.'

'The rumours are true then. William really is laying waste to Northumbria.'

'It's true all right. Heslingfield was only one of many manors to fall victim to his revenge.'

Duncan shook his head in disgust. 'It's indefensible to punish the innocent. The man's a monster.' He darted a glance across the room to Ban. 'What is the lad going to do once he's fully fit again?'

'I don't know. We've not discussed the matter as yet.'

'Well, there's time enough.'

'So there is.' Iain held out his cup to be refilled by a servant. 'No doubt he'll tell me his mind when he's ready.'

His gaze returned to the group across the room, though in truth the only one he saw was Ashlynn. He was glad to see her developing friendship with his sister and gladder still to see her smile and laugh. Today she looked every inch the lady she was. As his eyes lingered on the curves of her slender figure now so enticingly revealed by the new gown, his mind dwelt tantalisingly on what lay beneath. He knew he wasn't alone in his admiration; he had seen the way the eyes of other men were continually drawn back to her. It did not displease him. Let them look. None would dare to touch: she was his. The knowledge did nothing to diminish his pride.

The feast that evening was a splendid and sumptuous affair and the hall was filled with conversation and laughter. Iain, watching the succession of dishes appearing from the kitchen could not but be impressed. Once again Ashlynn's ability to plan and organise surprised him. It was a facet of her personality he had not suspected. Watching her smiling and talking to their guests she looked every inch the lady of the manor. There was no trace now of the boyish imp or the wildcat and yet he knew both were still there. This unpredictability was, he reflected, part of her considerable charm. He never knew what facet might be revealed next and it both intrigued and fascinated him, arousing his curiosity and making him want to discover more.

Keenly aware of that apparently casual regard Ashlynn turned to meet his gaze and saw him smile.

'An excellent feast,' he said. 'You have surpassed yourself.'

His words brought a glow of pleasure and she returned the smile. 'You must thank the cook for it, not I.'

'Had it not been for you I doubt we'd have seen anything like this. His imagination seemed not to run much beyond a haunch of venison or a side of mutton before this.'

'I added a few ideas of my own.'

'So I see, and I'm glad of it. This board would not disgrace a king.' He paused. 'Where did you learn all this?'

'Even Sassenach girls are brought up to know about the managing of a household, my lord.'

'Who'd have thought it?'

She shook her head. 'It's no use. I shall not allow myself to be provoked.'

'What a pity.'

'I think you enjoy provoking people.'

'Only where there's such a strong element of unpredictability.'

Ashlynn laughed. 'I hardly think that applies in this case for you know full well that I have a temper and one too easily roused.'

'Not so. You were ever unpredictable, lass, but as to the rest, you never lost your temper without good cause.'

The quiet tone held no trace of levity and it caught her off balance for, while she felt perfectly capable of holding her own with him in any amount of verbal sparring, it was harder to know how to deal with this.

In the event she was saved the trouble because the musicians struck up and heralded the start of the dancing. Iain rose and held out his hand.

'Will you honour me, my lady?'

Once again she was caught unawares. However, after a moment she gave him her hand and allowed him to lead her out. Soon the other couples formed around them. Dancing was not an activity she would have associated with him, but it soon became apparent that, for so tall a man, he moved with considerable grace.

'Where did you learn to dance?' she asked as the figure brought them together.

'In France. In my aunt's house it was *de rigueur*, just as it was for every page and squire to learn how to comport himself in company.' He grinned. 'Six months under her tutelage was enough to knock off the rough edges.'

'I thought you went there for military training.'

'So I did, but the two things went hand in hand. Sometimes it was hard to tell the difference.'

Ashlynn laughed. Then the dance separated them again but his words had given her much to think about. The wider reputation of the man they dubbed Black Iain concealed a personality far more complex, and it intrigued her.

When the measure ended her hand was claimed by other partners and he as host invited other ladies on to the floor. She noted that, without exception, they never took their eyes off him, looking up into his face and smiling, clearly hanging on his every word. It was borne upon her yet again that her husband was a very attractive man.

Later, when the musicians took a break, the company demanded the appointment of a Lord of Misrule to lead the future festivities. After some lively banter a youth called Hamish was duly elected. Ashlynn recalled that he was one of Iain's many cousins. Lord of Misrule was a role he stepped into with ease. His first act was to call for a game of blind man's buff, a suggestion received with much favour, especially by the younger members of the gathering. Accordingly a blindfold was produced. Then Hamish turned to Ashlynn.

'As Lord of Misrule I decree that you shall wear the blindfold first, my lady.'

Taken totally by surprise Ashlynn held up her hands in protest but the company would have none of it and in the end she yielded, laughing. The guests cheered. As Hamish fastened the blindfold over her eyes, Iain handed his cup to Duncan.

'It has been a while since I've played this. Let's see if I remember how.'

To his brother-in-law's amused surprise he joined the others in the centre of the hall to the general approbation. Ashlynn heard the increased laughter but knew not the cause. Then Hamish spun her round and let go. Swaying a little she regained her balance, edging forward with outstretched hands. She heard rustlings in the straw underfoot as people skipped out of the way, and heard giggling and laughter all about her. For a while she stumbled around and then, unexpectedly, her hands met the woollen fabric of a tunic. Exploring further they discovered a man's arms and then a pair of broad shoulders. The laughter grew. Suddenly the arms closed round her waist and shoulders and crushed her against a lean hard body. Then a man's mouth was over hers in a kiss that had nothing of gentleness in it but something quite other.

Taken by surprise Ashlynn had no time to struggle and the hands that had moved instinctively to push him away suddenly lacked the will or power to do so for deep within a treacherous spark awakened and then flamed, spreading like fire through her veins. It was a kiss so blatantly passionate that it drew shocked gasps from the delighted spectators. When eventually he released her there was a moment of complete silence. Then roars of approval shook the rafters of the hall. Breathless and astonished Ashlynn removed the blindfold and stared into her husband's face. His eyes were alight with amusement. He was also very clearly enjoying her evident confusion. Speechless, Ashlynn relinquished the blindfold to Hamish and, since there was no help for it, allowed Iain to lead her aside. When they were a safe distance from the others she confronted him.

'You did that on purpose, didn't you?'

'That's right. It's the point of the game you see.'

The words took her straight back to their wedding day. He had kissed her then for the benefit of others. She hadn't been able to help her response then either. *'By God, lass, you play the game well.'* Was this part and parcel of the same thing? Indignation was replaced by hurt and uncertainty.

'This is all a game to you, isn't it?'

Amusement faded. 'A game? What are we talking about here, Ashlynn?'

'You know full well.'

'I don't think I do. Explain it to me.'

'This…this whole situation.'

'You're angry because I kissed you in public?'

'No.'

'Then why?'

Even as she sought the words to tell him, Duncan appeared beside them.

'Forgive me, but I need to borrow your husband, my lady.' He grinned and jerked his head towards the far side of the room. 'There's an argument over yonder that would be settled.'

Her heart sank but there was only one possible answer. 'By all means.'

Iain gritted his teeth knowing there was nothing for it save graceful compliance. However, before he left he fixed Ashlynn with a penetrating look.

'I'll be back, my lady, and this discussion will be resumed.'

Sick at heart she watched him walk away. Just when everything seemed to be going well she had alienated him. What had possessed her to say it? Of course it was a game! Why couldn't she have left it at that? She knew perfectly well where his feelings lay.

When Iain left her he fully intended to return as promised and have the matter out. However, that was easier said than done. By the time he had settled the argument amongst Duncan's circle the dancing had started again and Ashlynn's hand was claimed for every measure. He noticed too that she made no attempt to seek him out or even look in his direction. What had happened to anger her so much? Surely a kiss could not be the cause, no matter how public.

From his vantage point Iain watched his wife laughing and talking with the other guests. To anyone else she would have seemed quite at ease. Iain, looking more closely, was undeceived. He could sense the tension in her. It occurred to him then that what had happened earlier might be due to reasons other than he had initially supposed. She must be missing her home and her family. With her emotions in this fragile state it would not take much to upset her. What was it? How he wished she would tell him. He was so preoccupied with the thought that at first he failed to notice the woman who had come to stand beside him.

'She's very beautiful, Iain.'

He looked round and saw Jeannie. 'Aye, she is.'

'And charming too,' his sister went on. 'She has but to smile to have men eating out of her hand. Women as well it seems.'

'She has charm and to spare.'

'I had not realised your taste was so good.'

'I'll take that as a compliment.'

'I can quite see why you wanted her to wife.' She paused. 'What is much less clear is why she agreed.'

'Don't flatter me, Jeannie, whatever you do.'

'You forced her to wed you, did you not?'

'When the king commands it is unwise to do anything other than comply. I had no more choice in the matter than Ashlynn. Malcolm solved the problem with as little inconvenience to himself as possible.'

'And yet you have not done so badly by the bargain.' She shook her head. 'In truth it is Ashlynn I feel for. A woman has no chance when pitted against the will of powerful men.'

'She has an honourable position here. The alternative would have been a lot worse.'

'So you were the lesser of two evils then?'

'If you choose to put it like that.'

'Oh, I do. As I said, I know you well, brother. All the same, I'm fascinated to see you in the role of protector to a lovely woman.'

'I can assure you it is a role I take most seriously.'

'I'm glad to hear it. The lass has had a bad time of it by all accounts.'

'Aye, she has, but that is over now at least. Nothing shall hurt her again if I have the power to prevent it.'

The words were quietly spoken but Jeannie heard the resolution that underlay them and looked up in surprise, yet there was no mistaking the ingenuous tone. Recalling the cold and bitter man he had been before, she realised that something fundamental had changed and her heart knew a glimmer of hope.

Iain tossed off the remainder of his wine and cast another look across the room. Seeing his wife surrounded by a crowd of admirers all vying for her attention, he experienced a re-awakening of the feeling he'd had when he saw her with Robbie that day in the courtyard. Annoyance turned in on itself. He had no grounds for jealousy. Ashlynn was beautiful and men admired her, wanted her. Yet for all her banter and smiles she knew how to hold them at arm's length. That of course just had the effect of making them try harder. He should know. He too was fully alive to his wife's physical charms. At night he lay awake knowing there was but a door between them and that he had the key, knowing how easy it would be to use force. However, he wanted more than mere bodily submission. She must come to him or it meant nothing. And so he waited…and waited. Just when he thought he was making progress he found himself back where he'd started.

Watching her now he saw her excuse herself from the group and move to speak to her brother who was standing nearby. She put an arm about him, a casual and loving gesture that meant nothing and everything. His jaw tightened as jealousy resurfaced for the second time. What on earth was the matter with him that he should lose his customary sense of perspective over something so trivial? Ban was her brother and she loved him. Why should she not? The lad was handsome and brave and good company withal. In his presence she opened like a flower in the sun. With him her smile was unforced, her laughter from the heart. Ban too played his part well. It was a testament to their spirit that they would not inflict their sorrows on others even though the wounds were still raw.

His admiration grew, along with his frustration for, while he knew that Ashlynn wasn't totally indifferent to him, she never looked at him as she looked at Ban, never smiled in quite that way. He had once told Ashlynn that she would see him every day of her life whether she wanted to or not. How ironic then that it was he who now suffered the torment of seeing her every day, of speaking to her, of being close enough to touch her and yet knowing himself as far away as ever. Be that as it might, he would know the cause of her displeasure before this evening was over.

* * *

Ashlynn felt only relief when the female members of the company started to drift away. Soon she too could escape and seek the sanctuary of her chamber. Out of the corner of her eye she could see Iain talking to Duncan and Jeannie. She saw him take his sister's hand and smiled to herself, glad to see that some degree of amity had been restored. The two of them strolled towards the door to be joined by several other ladies. There they paused while he bade them all a courteous goodnight. When they had disappeared from view he turned back to the room at large, his gaze searching. It found Ashlynn at once and held her. If she had been expecting him to return and mingle she was mistaken; he remained exactly where he was, waiting. The message was plain. To leave the hall she must pass him first and he wasn't about to let that happen.

Knowing there was no point in delaying the inevitable Ashlynn excused herself from the company. Iain watched her come. For a moment they surveyed each other in silence. Then he took hold of her arm. The grip didn't hurt but it would not be resisted either. He drew her with him into the corridor. Ashlynn glanced up, expecting him to stop but he didn't. Instead, and much to her consternation, she was conducted up two flights of stairs and along the corridor to his room. He pulled her in with him and closed the door behind them. Then he leaned upon it, surveying her keenly.

'Now that we are quite private, you and I going to talk, lass.'

'There is nothing to say.'

She took a step towards the door but he did not move.

'I think there is, and you're not leaving until this matter is resolved.' He paused. 'Now, tell me what it was so offended you that you must avoid me all the rest of the evening. I cannot believe it was just a kiss.'

Ashlynn shook her head sadly. Just a kiss. That really was all it meant to him. 'It doesn't matter.'

'It does matter. If my memory serves me aright, you spoke of playing games. It carries an imputation I don't much care for.'

'Did it strike a nerve, Iain?'

His eyes narrowed a little. 'You think that my kissing you was some kind of game?'

'Wasn't it?' she replied. 'Wasn't it just a charade for the benefit of your guests? You did it very well too I may say. I think they were convinced.'

He gave a hollow laugh. 'Is that what you think?'

'What else is there to think?'

'That I might have kissed you because I really wanted to, that the passion wasn't feigned, that you're so beautiful I don't know how to keep my hands off you.'

'Because you want me in your bed you mean.'

'Aye, I do, in case it's not already clear. What's wrong with that?'

She swallowed hard. 'Everything, when you love someone else.'

'What!' His brows drew together. 'Who is it that you think I love, Ashlynn?'

'Eloise!' She flung the name at him. 'You told me as much yourself. She's the reason you never remarried, would never have remarried until the king commanded it. I believe you only agreed because you needed heirs to continue your line.'

For a moment he was quite still, regarding her intently, his face white. Then, when he was sure he could keep his voice under control, 'Do you so?'

'It's the truth.'

'I think you and I need to get a few things straight.' He took a deep breath. 'Since you've raised the subject we'll start with Eloise.'

'I don't want to hear it.'

'You're going to hear it,' he replied. 'You'll not make such statements without giving me the right of reply.' He fixed her with a gimlet stare. 'You accuse me of loving Eloise still and so I do, but not in the way you seem to think. What I cherish is not a hopeless, pointless passion but the memory of a brief happiness; happiness I never thought to have until I met her and which, for a long time after her death, I believed was lost for ever. Then you came into my life.' He made a vague gesture with his hands. 'I'll not pretend I fell in love with you at first sight; it wasn't until the first time I kissed you that I realised there was an attraction. Even then I tried to deny it, but the longer I was with you the more difficult it became.'

'Very difficult,' she agreed. 'So much so, that it was the king who ordered our marriage.'

'Malcolm had his own reasons. Whatever they were he was several moves ahead of me at that point. But, when he compelled us to marry, it made me think about what I really wanted.'

'Oh, and what did you decide?'

'That I want to build a future with you. That I want a family, children who will grow up knowing a father's care. If all I wanted was to sire heirs I'd have done it long since. The reason I haven't is that I never met the woman I wanted to share that with. After what I had with Eloise I could never settle for anything less. I thought I could never have that again, until I met you.'

Ashlynn's gaze searched his face, her heart thumping painfully hard. The words had sounded sincere. 'Is that the truth?'

'On everything I hold sacred.'

Ashlynn turned away, trying to make sense of her chaotic thoughts. They both wanted the same things— almost. He had not spoken of his desire for revenge but the word hung there between them. She knew it hadn't gone away; that it was still an issue; that they needed to confront it. But if she spoke its name the spell would be broken, the moment lost. She had alienated him once tonight already through ill-considered words. Now he was trying to put things right. How could she destroy what had been so hard won?

Iain didn't move, made no attempt to touch her, but his voice was calmer now, steadier. 'I know as well as anyone can what you've been through, lass, and no one could have faced it with greater courage. When you took my name I swore to protect you, and if I had the ordering of the world nothing should ever harm you more.' He paused. 'With you I have found what I never thought to have again with any woman. I hoped that you had begun to care a little for me. Was I wrong?'

She shook her head. 'No, you weren't wrong. It's just…'

'Just…?'

'That I was afraid.'

'Of me?'

She turned to face him again. 'Of being hurt.'

'I would never deliberately do anything to hurt you.'

In spite of all attempts to blink them back the tears welled in her eyes and spilled over. Very gently he drew her against his breast and let her rest there, safe in the circle of his arms, and for the first time all the tension went out of her and she knew only the rightness of being there.

He dropped a kiss on her hair and then, as she looked up, another on her mouth. Ashlynn returned it, a slow and lingering embrace that turned his blood to fire. For a moment the dark gaze burned into hers and saw there what he had hardly dared to hope for.

'I want to kiss you again, lass, but I'm afraid if I do it'll not stop there.'

'Who said I wanted it to?'

His heart performed a sudden and dangerous manoeuvre and for a moment or two he didn't move, being entirely unsure he had just heard her aright. Then she reached up and drew his face down towards hers. This time it was she who kissed him, a passionate affirmation of the feelings she could no longer conceal.

He lifted her in his arms and carried her into his bedchamber and undressed her there, laying aside her garments before removing his own. Ashlynn caught her breath, taking in all the lithe and sculptured beauty of the hard-muscled body. Then he was beside her, drawing the furs over them, his mouth on hers, his hands exploring the curves of her flesh, subtle, arousing. And the world became a fusion of sense impressions, the coarse linen sheet and the soft wolf pelts, flickering light from the fire, the faint smell of wood smoke and the warmth of his flesh against hers, the erotic scent of musk on his skin, the taste of wine on his lips. His mouth moved lower, caressing neck and throat and breasts, sending a delicious shiver the length of her body. Ashlynn yielded herself up to it, wanting this, wanting him, no longer able to deny what she felt. Now there was no fear or doubt, only the sweetness of belonging, as though something long sought had been found.

He took his time, restraining desire, controlling passion, fighting the predatory urge that would make possession an act of violation. She would be his, finally and absolutely. He knew now he had wanted this from the first, a knowledge he had tried to deny, just as she had. And so he relearned the beauty of her body whose perfection his eyes had ascertained long before, his hands moving across waist and hip and thigh, and thence to the secret place between, gently stroking, teasing, rousing, feeling the answering rush of hot warmth, feeling the first shudder in her body's core. A body made for this. His knee parted her thighs and he entered her, gently, encountering resistance, moving past it and then deeper into her, moving in slow rhythm, holding back, feeding the fire and bringing her with him.

Ashlynn gasped, feeling him thrust deeper into her, moving with him now, her body arching into his, each rhythmic stroke sending pleasure coursing through every fibre of her being. The cry caught in her throat. And then restraint was gone and there was a final fierce possession before release and the hot sweet rush of a mutual shuddering climax.

For a little while he remained inside her, breathing hard, looking into her face, seeing there an echo of his own wonder. He had expected to enjoy this; what he had not anticipated was the sheer soul-filling delight of it. Gently he withdrew and collapsed beside her, deliciously sated. He had given her pleasure in order to leave her wanting more; he had not realised that the effect might rebound on him with such force.

Beside him Ashlynn drowsed, exhausted. He smiled and drew the pelts over her again, dropping a kiss on her shoulder. Then he curled his body round hers and held her close, listening to her soft breathing until he too fell asleep.

Chapter Ten

Ashlynn stirred and then stretched luxuriously, her body filled with a sense of well being. Opening her eyes slowly to the new day she became aware of a strange room and for a moment or two couldn't remember how she had got there. Then memory began to wake and she smiled to herself. Turning her head she let her gaze drink in the details of the sleeping face beside her. While the realities of the marriage bed had come as no surprise, she could never have imagined they would be anything like what had happened last night. The recollection sent a flood of warmth through her loins. The only cloud on her horizon was that he had not actually said he loved her. Not in so many words anyway. *Cared for* was not quite the same thing. Perhaps he found the words too hard to say.

In the meantime, she was aware of the advancing hour and that they had a house full of guests. Casting a furtive glance upon the sleeping figure she turned away, looking around for her clothes and finally spied them across the room. She began to ease herself from the bed. An arm closed about her waist, pulling her backwards. A moment later she was looking up at Iain's face. He smiled.

'Where did you think you were going, wife?'

'We have social obligations, my lord.'

'Let them wait.'

'But it's broad day. Too late to be lying abed.'

He grinned widened. 'I assure you, 'tis early yet, my sweet, and in truth last night did but whet my appetite.'

'You are quite shameless.'

'You're not the first person to say so.'

'I can believe it. Whoever dubbed you Black Iain knew you well.'

The dark eyes gleamed appreciatively. 'Well then, perhaps I should live up to my name.'

As the implication dawned Ashlynn's inner demon woke. It might have been entirely seduced last night but that didn't mean it was tamed. Without warning she twisted, trying to escape the restraining arm but it held her with consummate ease. Iain laughed softly. The sound caused her to redouble her efforts. She twisted again but instead of pulling away threw herself forward, landing across his chest, hands forcing his shoulders back against the bed. She smiled triumphantly. A moment later triumph turned to a gasp of dismay as he rolled, pinning her beneath his weight and cutting off all protest with a kiss. Pleasurable warmth spread the length of her body. Moreover, it was clear her efforts had done nothing to diminish his desire either. Ashlynn writhed, testing his hold. It yielded not an inch.

'Let me go, villain.'

'Not a chance, lass.'

* * *

The sun was considerably higher before they emerged to face the world. However, no one seemed to find it amiss and their arrival in the hall was greeted with amused smiles. As they broke their fast Ashlynn kept her attention on the food, feigning nonchalance and trying not to dwell on recent events in the bedchamber. Even now her flesh seemed to burn with the recollection. When at length she had finished her meal she glanced up to meet Iain's eye and saw him smile.

'What shall we do today?' he asked.

'Since the snow is here we might as well make the most of it.'

At these words the children who had been playing nearby fell silent, their eyes on her face. Seeing all those hopeful expressions Iain was intrigued.

'What exactly did you have in mind?'

'Well, there are some sledges in the barn,' she replied. 'Perhaps we could take them out on to the hill.'

A babble of excited chatter erupted and was promptly shushed by the older ones. All eyes turned to Iain and they waited, hanging on his reply with painful longing. He let the silence drag out for a few seconds more and then grinned.

'Why not?' he said.

A cheer rent the air. He beckoned them closer. They obeyed, though still keeping to a respectful distance.

'The older boys can fetch the sledges from the barn.'

At the word sledges other ears pricked up.

'We'll go with them, my lord,' said Hamish, throwing an eloquent look at Donald.

'Absolutely,' his friend replied. 'Just to be sure they come to no harm, my lord.'

Ban got to his feet. 'I think I'd better go along too. There are lots of children to take care of after all.'

'Indeed there are,' Iain replied. Then he looked at Ashlynn. 'I think some responsible adults should go accompany them, don't you?'

She laughed. 'You just read my mind.'

'Can I come too, Aunt Ashlynn?' said a timid voice beside her.

She glanced down and saw Fiona. 'Of course you can come.' Smiling she took the child's hand in hers. 'You shall walk with me.'

Iain grinned. 'It looks like we have a full complement then.'

Five minutes later they went to join the excited little crowd in the courtyard. When the boys re-appeared with the sledges they all set off. The older children soon drew ahead, some of the lads engaged in a running snowball fight on the way. Ashlynn's pace was of necessity slower to accommodate Fiona's shorter strides. Iain paused to let them catch up. He could hear Ashlynn speaking to the child, her tone gentle and patient, drawing her companion out and making her laugh. Clearly she had a way with children.

'I never thought of you in this role,' he said when they had rejoined him. 'It suits you.'

'Does it?'

'Very much so.'

The words were quietly spoken but they contained a nuance she had not heard before. It turned her thoughts in another direction entirely and sent a flush of warmth through her entire being.

They walked on for a while but, as they drew nearer their goal the snow became deeper. Fiona stumbled over the skirt of her gown. Ashlynn's hand prevented her from falling but it was clear that progress was going to be slow.

'You go on ahead,' she told Iain.

'I have a better idea.' He bent and lifted the child up on to his shoulders. 'Hold on tight now.'

Fiona was quick to obey, torn between anxiety at being so far from the ground and the thrill of having so exalted a position. However, as they walked on she began to relax and enjoy herself, exchanging occasional shy smiles with Ashlynn. In fact Ashlynn was amused and oddly touched. She had never imagined Iain unbending this far and yet he did it so lightly and withal so naturally. He would make a good father. The ramifications to that sent another flush of warmth through her. She shot him a sidelong glance and saw him smile.

By the time they reached the slope the older members of the party were already organising themselves. Iain lifted Fiona down and gave her into the safe keeping of two older girl cousins and then watched as Hamish and Donald embarked on their first run. However, their balance was awry and the sled went hurtling off course towards the burn. With yells of dismay they tried to take evasive action, only to lurch sideways into a hidden boulder just below the surface of the snow. The collision pitched them headfirst down the hill, to the huge enjoyment of the onlookers. Undeterred the other participants climbed aboard their own sledges and went speeding away. The air rang with shrieks and laughter.

Having seen the others underway Iain turned to his wife. 'Will you adventure with me, Ashlynn?'

The tone was casual enough but there was a mischievous expression in his eye that gave her pause. Seeing her hesitation Iain seized the advantage and went straight in for the kill.

'What's the matter, lass? Are you afraid?'

He saw her chin come up and grinned, knowing his faith hadn't been misplaced. Taking her hand he led her away from the main group to a much steeper part of the hill. Ashlynn looked at it with trepidation. The lower slope had produced speeds that were hair-raising enough. This was something else again. At the base of the slope the ground curved out and then ended abruptly in a sharp drop to the burn, dark and deep and swift-flowing at this season.

'Are you sure about this, Iain?'

'Of course. Jeannie and I came here often as children. It's an exhilarating run I promise you.'

Unwilling to back down from the unspoken challenge she seated herself gingerly on the sledge and he climbed on behind, locking his arms around her.

'Can you swim by the way?' he asked.

'Swim!'

'Aye, for when we end up in the burn, ye ken.'

Before she could reply he pushed off and heard her shriek as the sled gathered speed, hurtling down the hillside at a dizzying rate. Ashlynn gasped as the wind stung her face and brought the water to her eyes, seeing through blurred vision the burn approaching with horrifying rapidity. Uttering a wail of dismay she closed her eyes. However, what she hadn't known was that the view from above was foreshortened and where the land flattened out at the bottom of the slope there was in fact a considerable distance to the stream, easily enough space for the sled to come to a safe stop well short of the water. Speechless she sat for some moments in stunned disbelief, her heart in her throat. Iain too was unusually quiet. When she looked round it was to see him shaking with silent laughter. Ashlynn glared at him.

'You horror! You frightened the life out of me.'

Rather than expressing any kind of remorse Iain's merriment seemed to increase. Incredulous she could only stare at him, her body still trembling with reaction. Then, as the initial shock subsided, the humour of it struck her and somewhat ruefully she began to laugh too.

'Truly you are well named!' she said.

'Admit that you enjoyed it.'

'If terror can be said to be enjoyable then, yes, I admit it.'

'Is it not such moments of terror that make us feel most alive?'

'Don't try to philosophise, villain. What you enjoyed was scaring the daylights out of me.'

'I canna deny it.'

Ashlynn grabbed a handful of snow and pushed it in his face. 'Take that!'

The words were succeeded by a gasp as, without warning, he tipped her backwards into the snow and then followed her down, pinning her beneath him. Worse, there was a gleam in those dark eyes that she recognised all too well.

'Have you not learned that there are fearful penalties attached to that kind of thing?'

Then his hands were round her, tickling her ribs unmercifully. Ashlynn shrieked, trying in vain to escape.

'Now then, beg for mercy, wife.'

'I will not.'

'Say you so?'

His efforts intensified. Helpless with laughter she had at last to cry quarter. 'Enough, Iain, I yield.'

'Then I claim the right as victor to name the terms of surrender.'

'Which are?'

For answer he took a leisurely kiss. Powerless to prevent it she had perforce to submit. However, the experience was enjoyable to a most disquieting degree. Furthermore the expression in his eyes did nothing to detract from that. For a long moment they remained thus, until other voices broke the spell. They looked round to see Hamish and Donald approaching along the path at the top of the crest followed closely by Ban with James and Andrew.

'Such perfect timing,' murmured Iain between gritted teeth. 'I swear Hamish does it on purpose.'

Ashlynn laughed and he threw her a speaking glance. Then she felt his weight shift as he got to his feet. A moment later he reached down and took her hand, pulling her up after, and together they toiled their way back up the hill.

As the oncoming quintet drew nigh Ashlynn saw her brother's speculative grin as he took in her dishevelled appearance. However, before he could comment Hamish spoke up.

'We're following your example, my lord. This looks like much more fun.'

'Indeed it is,' replied Iain. Then in an aside to his wife, 'The slope's quite exciting too.'

Ashlynn gave a snort of laughter and then hurriedly turned it into a cough. Donald regarded her with hopeful eyes.

'Will you come with me, my lady?' he asked.

'Thank you no. Once was enough.'

In evident disappointment he joined Hamish on the sled. Beside them Ban followed suit with James and Andrew. Then all five set off down the hill again.

For a moment Iain followed their progress and smiled. However, when he turned to his wife his expression was quite serious.

'Was once really enough or will you adventure with me again, Ashlynn?'

His eyes met and held her own and she recognised in his face the invitation that was both challenge and promise. Her spirit leapt, remembering the heart-thumping excitement of the first dizzy rush down the icy slope. She knew now that she had never been in danger, that he would not have let anything happen to her. It had been exhilarating and not just because of the purported risk. Being with him was the real exhilaration. She saw him smile and hold out his hand to her. For the briefest moment she hesitated, then smiled in return.

'Yes, I will.'

Iain's fingers closed around hers. 'Come then, my sweet.'

This time there was the thrill with none of the terror and they reached the bottom of the hill in gales of laughter.

* * *

At the end of that afternoon when they walked back through the snow to Dark Mount, Ashlynn's cloak was soaked along with the hem of her gown and her shoes, and her fingers tingled inside her gloves, but there was a glow inside her that rendered such details irrelevant. In truth she had not thought two months ago ever to feel so alive again. For the first time she began to glimpse a future that was not filled with fear, a possibility that she might, after all, find happiness here in this remote and wild land.

Ashlynn returned to her chamber and changed out of her wet garments. The task had not long been completed when there was a knock at the door. Her heart leapt as she bade the caller enter. As the door opened she saw her brother on the threshold.

'Oh, Ban.'

He smiled faintly. 'Were you expecting someone else?'

'I thought it might have been Morag.'

'Ah.' He glanced round, taking in the pile of discarded garments. 'Am I interrupting?'

'No, of course not. Come in.'

'I need to talk to you, Ash.'

Seeing that he looked unusually preoccupied she gestured to a chair. 'Well then, won't you sit down?'

However, he ignored her invitation and moved closer to the hearth, looking down into the fire. Ashlynn waited, puzzled, feeling the first stirring of unease.

'I have been thinking,' he said at last.

'About what?'

'The future.' He turned to face her, regarding her with a steady gaze. 'Your husband has been a most generous host, but I cannot stay here indefinitely. I must make my way in the world. Since the best chance of doing that is to go to Dunfermline and seek military service, that is what I mean to do.'

'But your shoulder is not completely healed yet.'

'No, but it grows stronger with every day. In the New Year I shall get back into training and by the spring I shall be fit again.'

Ashlynn bit her lip, fighting the rising sense of dread. 'I don't want you to go, Ban.'

'I know but I must. Surely you see that?'

'Yes, but…'

'But what?'

'You are all I have left of family. I will miss you dreadfully.'

'And I you,' he replied, 'but we will see each other as time and occasion permit. Besides, you will be too busy to miss me for long.'

Ashlynn turned away to hide the tears that threatened. Frowning, Ban took her by the shoulders.

'No need to be despondent. I'm not leaving yet. There's plenty of time for you to get used to the idea.'

'I think I will never get used to the idea.'

'You must, Ash. Our ways lie along different paths now.'

'Does Iain know about this?'

'Not yet, but I shall speak to him soon.'

She turned and regarded him with imploring eyes. 'Must you really go?'

He gave her a gentle smile. 'You have found your place, Ash. Now I must seek mine.'

He left shortly after this and Ashlynn paced the floor

in mounting distress. In a matter of weeks Ban would be gone. He was an able swordsman and she had no doubt of his finding the situation he desired. And after Dunfermline what then? He had spoken of their meeting again from time to time but she was realist enough to know it could not be often. What if something were to happen to him? Life was precarious; doubly so for one who earned a living by the sword. He was the last remaining tie with everything she had held dear. If she lost him… Suddenly, all her former fears rose like a tide and she sank trembling on to a chair.

That evening she was quieter than usual and despite the music and laughter all around the feeling of heaviness persisted. Involuntarily her thoughts turned from the present to the last Yuletide celebrations at Heslingfield, to the hall and the great log burning in the hearth and all the walls festooned with winter greenery. She could see her family and hear again their laughter and merry banter as they moved among their guests. Almost she could hear music and song and smell the rich fare issuing from the kitchen for Lord Cyneric was renowned for keeping a fine table. Not only was he a good host, no one was ever turned away from his door no matter how humble. Remembering it, she felt the tears start. Yule would never be celebrated more in Heslingfield. A great Saxon house was gone, along with all its tradition of hospitality and good fellowship.

'Ashlynn?'

Jeannie's voice recalled her and she looked up with a start to find both her sister-in-law and husband regarding her closely. 'Forgive me.'

'Are you all right?'

'Yes, perfectly.'

With an effort she dragged her attention back to the room and the company.

'Duncan and I want to invite you to Ardnashiel in the spring,' said Jeannie. 'You will come, won't you? I would not lose you so soon.'

'I would be delighted.' Ashlynn looked up at Iain. 'That is, if…'

He smiled and then turned to his sister. 'I will bring her, I promise.'

'I shall hold you to it.'

'I wouldn't dare disobey,' he confided to his wife. 'My sister has a fearsome tongue on her.'

Ashlynn smiled. 'Then I'll look forward to the spring weather.'

'It will come soon enough.' Jeannie threw her brother a shrewd glance. 'And you will be off adventuring again no doubt.'

'That depends on the adventure,' he replied.

Neither of them had spoken the word revenge but it was tacitly understood and Ashlynn felt a sudden sense of foreboding. When all the festivities were over and the guests were gone would his thoughts turn that way? Would the thaw see him gone too? He was a man of action, a man driven by a blood oath. Once the fine weather came he would be drawn from Dark Mount to ride with his men once more, and her brother too would leave for Dunfermline to sell his skills. This magic winter world that held them was only a dream, an illusion that would vanish with the snow. She knew it now and a strange feeling of dread entered her heart.

The two people she loved most would be gone and she would be alone again. She also knew that what she felt for Iain was much more than physical attraction. Somehow she had come to care for him more deeply than she would ever have thought possible. It was a very different emotion from the one she felt for Ban, and it could not be denied.

Iain, alive to every nuance, sensed that something was wrong and determined to know the reason for it. However, the demands of the guests were many and the laws of hospitality required that their needs came first.

It was therefore much later when they had retired that he found his moment. Ashlynn had gone ahead of him and when he entered the room he was surprised to see her still up. She was sitting by the fire and had evidently been deep in thought for she started on hearing him enter. He saw her smile and crossed the intervening space to take her in his arms. Then he sat down and drew her on to his knee.

'Something is amiss, Ashlynn, and has been all evening. What is it?'

'How did you know?'

'Your face speaks before you do, my sweet. It always has.' He smiled. 'So tell me.'

'It's what Jeannie said earlier.'

'About what?'

'About you leaving in the spring.'

He surveyed her in surprise. 'When the warmer weather comes I'll ride again with my men. But do you really think I would stay away from you for very long?' He kissed her lightly on the brow. 'It couldn't be done.'

'But you will still seek out Fitzurse.'

'You know I must.'

'Yes, and if you find him he may kill you and if he does what shall I do then?'

'Hush, lass. There's no need for you to be afraid of that.'

'How can I not be?'

'Fitzurse likes to win by treachery. In a fair fight he has little chance and he knows it.'

'Can there ever be such a thing as a fair fight with such a man?'

'Aye, there can, and one day he'll have to meet me.'

Ashlynn sighed and looked away. Very gently he turned her face to his.

'The ghosts of the past must be exorcised, Ashlynn, or haunt us ever more.' He paused, surveying her closely. 'But this is not just about Fitzurse, is it?'

She shook her head. 'Ban is going to leave.'

'Ah.'

'He plans to go to Dunfermline and seek service there.'

'I'd say he'd every chance of success.'

For a long moment she was silent and the blue eyes were veiled beneath sooty lashes. Then he saw a glistening tear slide down her cheek.

'Ach, lass, don't cry.'

Unfortunately this had the opposite effect to the one he had intended and more tears followed. He regarded her in concern. Ashlynn took a deep breath and tried to recover herself.

'Forgive me. I know that you must go and Ban too, but I cannot bear the thought of anything happening to either of you, of losing you.'

His arms tightened about her. 'You'll never lose me, lass, no matter how hard you try, or Ban either if

I know aught about him. Not at odds of less than twenty to one anyway.'

It drew a reluctant laugh. 'I never used to be insecure—until the Normans came.'

'You need never feel insecure. Nothing shall hurt you if I can prevent it.'

He took her face in his hands then, brushing her tears away, kissed her very gently on the mouth.

'You mean a great deal to me, lass, and I would never wish to be the cause of tears in you.' He smiled. 'As for that brother of yours I will speak with him as occasion permits. If his mind is set on going to Dunfermline, then I might be able to help him; I have certain acquaintance there who could be useful.'

'Thank you.'

'Now, my dove, the hour grows late and you should be abed.' He got to his feet bringing her with him. 'I mean to see to it that you are—right soon.'

In a very short time he had unfastened and removed her gown, tossing it over the chair. Then he led her to the bed and watched her climb in, burrowing down beneath the pelts. Without taking his eyes off her he removed his own clothing and came to join her. Then he made gentle and tender love to her, afterwards holding her close until she slept.

The following day dawned with leaden skies and rain. Mist shrouded the hills and the air was bitter. It was no weather to tempt the guests out of doors so the men amused themselves with chess and dice while the women talked. Hamish took the younger members of the company aside and devised pastimes for their amusement.

At his suggestion that chill afternoon they gathered for a game of foxes and hounds. Hamish carefully established the physical parameters within which it could be played.

'The foxes may hide anywhere in the tower, but not beyond. The hounds will give them the count of one hundred to get away. Then they'll come looking. Whoever is found last wins the game.' He paused. 'However, first found must pay a forfeit.'

The youngsters clapped delightedly. Hamish looked around to where his host was standing with several older members of the gathering.

'Will any of you ladies and gentlemen join in? Can I prevail upon you?'

They laughed and shook their heads. Hamish shrugged and looked at Ashlynn.

'How about you, my lady?'

She laughed. 'Why not?' She glanced at her brother. 'Ban?'

He returned the grin and nodded. 'Why not indeed?'

A cheer went up as they crossed the room to join the children. Hamish turned to Iain.

'And you, my lord?'

Iain grinned. 'How could I refuse?'

His words were greeted first with looks of surprise and then an even louder cheer. Ashlynn watched as he quit the group of adults and came over.

Hamish called the group to order. 'Very well. Lady Ashlynn, Lord Ban, you are the foxes in this first round. You have till the count of a hundred to find somewhere to hide. One…two…'

They exchanged startled looks and departed for the stairs with alacrity. Once out in the corridor they paused.

'We need to split up,' he said. 'I'm making for the storerooms. You?'

'Upstairs,' she replied.

'Good luck.'

With that he took off, heading swiftly down the staircase. Ashlynn grinned and then fled for her own chosen sanctuary.

Back in the hall Iain waited through the count. When at last it was complete he left with the others, watching as the children scattered. It was in his mind that none but he should find his wife. He moved into the passageway and up the first flight of stairs, feigning to look in different places on the way, but ever heading away from the rest, moving towards the top of the tower for he knew with near certainty where she would be.

Ashlynn smiled to herself, well satisfied with her hiding place. Although the roof terrace itself offered no hiding place the recess in the adjoining wall of the tower served the purpose. Located behind the door it was out of the line of vision and anyone taking a cursory glance at the terrace would easily miss it. She wrapped her cloak more closely about her though in truth she was not cold for the marten fur was snug and the chill air against her face was invigorating. Luckily it had stopped raining for the time though the clouds held promise of more.

Suddenly she caught the sound of voices in the near distance and she drew in a sharp breath, shrinking back against the stonework. A few moments later she heard someone open the door that gave on the roof. Then she heard Donald's voice.

'No, there's no one here. Let us try below.'

Another male replied in the affirmative and the door closed. Ashlynn grinned. The chances were good now that she would not be caught at all. That was something of a relief for Hamish would certainly think of some dastardly forfeit. At times that young man's imagination took a distinctly wicked turn. She was recalling some of the more recent examples when she heard the door open again. This time there were no voices, only the sound of footsteps, unhurried and deliberate and heading in her direction. Her heart leapt, knowing before she saw him who it would be. A moment later she was face to face with her husband.

'My lady.'

He smiled then, a mischievous expression that told more clearly than words his discovery of her had been no mere chance. Ashlynn returned the smile, eyeing him speculatively.

'You knew from the first where to find me, didn't you?'

'Let's just say I had a pretty good idea.'

'I had not thought to be so transparent.'

'It's usually a mistake,' he agreed. 'It gives your opponent the advantage.'

The expression in those dark eyes was enough to stir deep misgivings and she stayed where she was. He surveyed her with amusement.

'You cannot escape, Ashlynn. Besides, it's very unsporting to try.'

She grinned. 'It's very unsporting to cheat, villain.'

'No cheating; just a thorough knowledge of the ground and the quarry.' He nodded towards the recess. 'Ordinarily that's a very good hiding place. I have used it myself before now.'

The easy conversational tone didn't deceive her for a minute. However, she was powerless to escape her fate and mentally resigned herself.

'Come, my lady.'

Iain took hold of her wrist in a grip that, though it caused no discomfort, was as inflexible as steel. Then he drew her back inside and shut the door.

'Did you and Hamish collude over this?' she demanded.

'Hamish is completely innocent.'

'That's unusual for him. Even so I dread to think what forfeit he will dream up.'

'Hamish is not exacting this forfeit. I am.'

For a moment she could only stare at him. 'You?'

'That's right.'

As the implications dawned Ashlynn glanced around. The passageway was quite deserted and, in spite of the torches, dimly lit for the afternoon light was fading. Her heart began to beat a little faster.

'You can't do that.'

His expression was suggestive of polite interest. She tried another tack.

'It's against the rules.'

'I don't play to the rules, lass. You should know that.' Without relinquishing his hold he retraced his steps along the passage as far as his chamber and drew her inside. She heard the key turn in the lock. In no doubt now as to what he intended Ashlynn felt her heartbeat accelerate dangerously. She saw him smile and advance. Undeceived by the smile she backed away.

'There's no escape, Ashlynn.'

'Is that so, villain?'

'Aye, it is.'

Ashlynn hid a smile of her own, remembering the interconnecting door that led to her own room. If he thought he'd trap her so easily he was mistaken. Enjoying the thought of his forthcoming chagrin she turned and fled, darting through the open doorway into his bedchamber, heading for the exit. Iain watched her go and his grin widened. Then he strolled after her towards his room arriving in time to see Ashlynn reach the connecting door. Her hand closed on the handle and tugged hard. It yielded not at all. Automatically her gaze went to the lock and found it empty.

'Is this what you're looking for?' he asked.

She whirled round and saw him on the further threshold. In his hand was a large iron key. Speechless she watched as he closed the bedroom door behind him and locked that in turn, the full extent of his plan now apparent. She was exactly where he had intended her to be.

'You devious rogue.' Her voice was low and the tone indicative of grudging admiration as she watched him advance. 'You had it all worked out, didn't you?'

'In any campaign one must have a plan.'

Then his hands were on her shoulders and suddenly his face was much closer, the dark eyes burning into hers.

'Kiss me, Ashlynn.'

Annoyed with herself for falling so neatly into the trap and even more annoyed for enjoying it, she made a token attempt to resist. His hold tightened. He took the kiss at leisure, a knowing and insistent embrace that ignored resistance until resistance was abandoned. Then he carried her to the bed.

* * *

Later as they lay together beneath the furs Ashlynn glanced up at his face and seeing him smile returned it.

'That was quite a forfeit, my lord.'

'No,' he replied. 'The forfeit was only a kiss.'

'A kiss!' She pushed herself up on one elbow. 'Why you utter…' Words failed her in the face of that blatantly unrepentant grin. Then she launched herself at him. Iain guffawed. There followed a short unequal struggle before he grabbed her wrists and pinned them to the bed.

'All's fair in love and war, lass.' He was still holding her lightly enough, but still leaving no possibility of escape for the blue eyes held a militant light. 'And now I have you captive I'm not about to let you go.'

Reluctantly she laughed. 'We can't stay here, Iain. What about the game?'

He bent and kissed her again. 'Do you know, lass, I have a feeling you're going to be the undisputed winner.'

Chapter Eleven

After two days of rain the sky cleared and, as the snow had melted away from the lower lying areas of ground, Hamish suggested that the men might go out for a ride. It was an idea that met with instant favour. Ashlynn looked at her brother.

'Will you join them?'

He shook his head. 'I'd love to, but I'm not sure if my shoulder would stand the pace just yet. I need to put the matter to the test—on my terms.'

'Let's go out by ourselves then, and we can set the pace to suit.'

'I'm game if you are,' he said, 'and it has been a while after all. If I don't get back on a horse soon I'll forget how.'

She laughed. 'Very well, but I think we should not go too far at first. You are like to be sore else.'

Iain, who had followed the exchange, surveyed them with a smile. 'I'll have a groom go with you since you're not familiar with the country hereabouts.'

They went down to the courtyard together and mounted up. For a little way their paths lay together and Iain rode beside them to the fork in the trail where he and his men were to leave them. He bade farewell to Ban and then leaned down to drop a kiss on his wife's cheek.

'Until later, Ashlynn.'

He smiled and turned his horse's head. For a moment or two her gaze followed the dark-clad figure on the grey stallion. She was regretting his absence already. Telling herself not to be so foolish she brought her mount alongside her brother's.

They kept the pace steady but Ashlynn could see that Ban was enjoying the excursion and it pleased her to see him smile in the old way. Their guide led them through the length of Glengarron, intending to ride a wide loop round the valley. While it was good to get some fresh air again, the damp cold was penetrating and Ashlynn wasn't at all sorry that they'd opted for a shorter excursion this time around.

They had reached the end of the valley when the groom reined in, staring at the distant hillside. Ban frowned.

'What is it, Callum?'

'I'm no sure, my lord. I thought I saw movement up yonder.'

All three remained still, their eyes straining to see, but the hillside seemed deserted.

'It might have been a deer,' said Ban.

'Perhaps,' Callum replied. The tone suggested he was unconvinced.

'What else? Surely no one would ride into Glengarron uninvited?'

'They'd be wiser not to, my lord.'

Ashlynn's gaze searched the scattered rocks and clumps of rain-darkened heather but could detect no sign of movement. She decided it must have been an animal of some kind which, startled by their approach, had made off through the undergrowth. All the same the stillness felt suddenly eerie.

'I think we should go back now,' she said.

Callum nodded. 'A good idea, my lady.'

Ban eyed them both thoughtfully and then glanced once more at the silent hillside. 'Just as you wish.'

They turned the horses' heads and began to ride for home, picking up the pace a little. Once Ashlynn glanced over her shoulder, but there was nothing to be seen save the hill and the shrouding mist above.

The others returned some time later, all mud spattered and all in high good humour after the fresh air and the exercise. Iain rejoined his wife by the hearth and sliding an arm about her waist, kissed her soundly. Ashlynn smiled.

'I take it you enjoyed your ride, my lord.'

'Indeed I did, though I missed your company.'

'Liar. You were far too busy talking about horses and hunting if I know anything about it.'

He grinned. 'Not so busy as to put all thoughts of you out of my head.'

'What thoughts?'

He bent and whispered in her ear. Ashlynn blushed scarlet.

'You are incorrigible.'

'So I've been told.' He paused. 'All the same, your guess about hunting wasn't so far wrong. The next

suitable day we get, we'll take the hounds for an outing.
Will you come?'

Her eyes brightened. 'Can you doubt it?'

He looked at Ban. 'How did your excursion go today?'

'Well enough, my lord,' he replied. 'The shoulder
is mending apace. It won't be long before I'm fully
fit again.'

He made no mention of what had passed earlier and
Ashlynn decided he was right. What was there to say
after all? It was suspicion only. They had seen nothing.

'I'm glad to hear it,' Iain went on. 'The rain will
clear soon enough. Then we'll see some action. In the
meantime a little sword practice wouldn't come amiss.
What say you to a short bout?'

'I'd be honoured.'

Ashlynn darted a glance at her brother. 'Are you sure
about this?'

'Why not?' he replied. 'I won't overdo it, but I need
to start some time.'

She looked from one to the other in disbelief. 'In
this weather?'

Iain grinned. 'I'm not such a martyr to the art. We'll
use the barn.' Then, seeing his wife's anxious expression, he continued, 'Have no fear, my lady, I will return
him safe and sound.'

She sighed and watched them go. In a few weeks Ban
would indeed be fit again. After that he would leave. It
was time to face the unpleasant truth. Her brother had
his own life to lead and she had no right to expect him
to remain at Dark Mount if it was his inclination to go.
Their destinies lay along different paths for a while at
least but perhaps, if the fates were kind, they might

overlap from time to time. Besides, she too had duties and responsibilities now and must face up to them.

Out in the barn the two men moved through the warm-up routine and Ban was cautiously optimistic. As he had said, some of the strength was returning to his shoulder. Daily exercise would re-educate the muscles and help him build up the stamina he had lost erewhile. From time to time he glanced at his brother-in-law but if Iain noticed he gave no sign, his concentration entirely on what he was doing. It was habitual with him. Whatever he undertook he did with commitment and attention to detail. It occurred to Ban then that he could learn a great deal from a man like that. When he remembered his initial doubts he felt foolish. Iain MacAlpin might have his faults but he was also a man to respect. Would he find another such among the lords at Dunfermline? He hoped it might be so. All the same he knew he was going to miss Dark Mount for in the few weeks he had been there it had become like a home to him, a home he had never thought to have again. Leaving Ashlynn would be hardest of all, like losing her anew. It was comforting to know at least that she would always be safe, safe and loved.

Ban was startled out of his thoughts by Iain's voice.

'Shall we try a little practice now?'

'Why not?'

The blades engaged and they moved through the regular drills. Ban, tense at first, began to settle into the familiar rhythms. Though he had already seen Iain fight he was once again awed by the lithe power of the man, of the tireless repetitions and the grace of the movements in which the blade became an extension of his arm. Ban was a capable swordsman but all at once he knew he was seeing the standard to aim at. However, it soon became evident that it was going to take a while to achieve his goal for after a short spell of more vigorous use his shoulder began to ache and the weight of the weapon to increase dramatically. Seeing it shake in the young man's grasp Iain lowered his own blade.

'That's enough for today, I think.'

Ban smiled apologetically. 'I fear it is.'

'Even so that shoulder has made remarkable progress.' Iain sheathed his sword. 'It will not be long before it's as good as it ever was.'

'I pray you are right for I hope to make my living thus.' Ban brushed beads of moisture from his forehead, noting as he did so that his brother-in-law hadn't even broken into a sweat as yet. With a rueful smile he sheathed his own blade. 'I imagine my sister has told you as much.'

'Aye, she did.' Iain bent to retrieve his tunic. 'She said you were thinking of going to Dunfermline.'

'That's right.'

'Well, if you still wish to do so then I'll gladly furnish you with an introduction.'

'That is most generous, my lord. Particularly when I consider how much I already owe you.'

'You owe me nothing.'

'I think you understate the matter.'

'Not so.' Iain shrugged himself into the tunic and belted it. 'Family must stick together.'

Hearing those words Ban felt a surge of pride and pleasure for in that one brief and casual comment he was brought into the fold, given a place and a sense of belonging.

'You speak true, lord.'

'That being the case I have a proposition to put to you.'

Ban stopped in the act of reaching for his own tunic. 'A proposition?'

'Aye. Stay here at Dark Mount. I can always use a good man.'

For a moment there was silence. Iain smiled faintly.

'You don't have to make up your mind now. Take your time. Think it over.'

The younger man reddened but recovered himself quickly. 'You mistake, my lord. My silence was not due to hesitation but surprise. Do you really mean it?'

The dark eyes met and held his. 'I should not have said it else. Besides, I would be loath to see you go.'

'I would be loath to go, my lord.'

'That's settled then.' The easy smile appeared again. 'Now I need to speak to Dougal. In the meantime perhaps you should go and tell your sister.'

Ban found Ashlynn in the hall by the hearth. She looked up and smiled as he entered.

'How was the practice?'

'Well enough, but there's a long way to go yet.' He flexed the shoulder and winced a little. 'It still lacks much of its original power.'

'It is like to take some weeks, but there's no hurry. You can't leave anyway until the warmer weather comes.'

'I'm not leaving at all.'

'I don't understand.'

'Iain has asked me to stay. To join him.'

'What…what did you say?'

'I said yes of course.'

For a moment she was speechless for the feeling of joy and relief was so intense that her throat was too tight for words. Then she was out of her chair and hugging him tightly.

'I'm so glad.'

'To tell you the truth I'm glad too.'

'Are you really?' She held him at arm's length for a moment and her blue gaze met his. 'You're not just saying that? It's not just because of me?'

'No. When Iain made the offer to ride with him I was more than happy to accept. He's a man I respect, a man I could follow.'

Ashlynn nodded. She had seen his growing admiration for his brother-in-law and had been glad to see the friendship between the two. However, she knew that Iain had not just made the offer because he saw potential in her brother. It had been done to please her. The knowledge warmed her to the core of her being. With that simple gesture he had made her happier than he could ever know.

Even as she was thinking about him he arrived with Dougal, and the two of them came over to the hearth where she and Ban were standing. Dougal beamed to see them and held out his hand to her brother.

'Lord Iain's just told me the good news. I'm delighted.'

Ban reddened a little as he took the proffered hand. 'It is an honour, believe me, sir.'

'Let us drink to it.'

Iain called for wine and presently proposed a toast. 'To friendship and brotherhood.'

Ban raised his cup solemnly as he repeated the words, a brief and informal version of the oath of fealty he would swear later before his lord and in the sight of his men. Once he looked at Ashlynn and saw her answering smile. When the toast was done the conversation fell into more general topics and she let the men talk, allowing the words to wash over her, having eyes only for Iain. He had done this for her. With a full heart she met her husband's glance and saw him smile, the familiar easy smile that made her heart leap.

Seeing Dougal and Ban deep in conversation he came to join Ashlynn. She looked up at him with shining eyes.

'How can I thank you?'

'No thanks are necessary. It was a logical step to take. Ban needs to make his way in the world and I need good men. Two birds with one stone, you see.'

'Three,' she replied, 'for you have also made me very happy.'

'If you are happy then I am content.'

'I am happy, Iain, more than I ever dreamed of being again. After Heslingfield was destroyed I could see no future. You made me look beyond that.'

His throat tightened for he had never thought to hear such words from her. Yet they were heartfelt, of that there could be no doubt.

'We will build a good future, you and I,' he replied.

'Will we?'

'Can you doubt it?'

'I want so much to believe, Iain, to let go of the past but it lours over us yet.' Her eyes met his and he saw the quiet anguish there.

'What is it, lass?'

'Fitzurse.'

For a moment or two the name hung between them. Ashlynn laid a hand on his arm.

'If you really want to build a future let go of your hatred, Iain.' She paused. 'Such ancient grudges cast a long shadow and they are corrosive. I do not want our life together to be tainted with the evils of the past.'

His expression grew sombre. 'You do not know what you ask, Ashlynn.'

'Yes, I do know—more than anyone.'

'I made a sacred promise. Would you have me break it?'

'I demand nothing. I ask only that you think about it.'

'This is not fair, Ashlynn.'

'It was not fair that Fitzurse destroyed Heslingfield and murdered my kin,' she replied, 'and I have thought often of revenge. But it will not restore my home or make my family live again. They are gone and nothing will change it.' She paused. 'The only way now is forward, to make the most of what we have.'

'With you I have found what I never thought to have again, but I cannot know true peace until Fitzurse is dead.'

'Will you allow him to taint the future as well as the past, Iain? If so, then he really will have won.'

She turned sadly away, leaving him alone. He sighed, watching her go, torn between wanting and frustration. Did she expect him to break his oath? To be forsworn? Time might have made his memories easier to bear but it did not change the instinct for revenge. His hand tightened around his cup. What Ashlynn asked was impossible. How could he have the kind of future he wanted and know all the time that somewhere his enemy lived and prospered?

* * *

Ashlynn did not return to her room but instead left the tower and took a turn about the courtyard, needing the air and the space to clear her mind. At least it had stopped raining now though everything smelled of damp. She glanced up, watching rags of cloud scudding across the sky above the water-darkened stones of the tower, and shivered, drawing her cloak closer. It wasn't the weather to be out of doors and yet she had no wish to return to the hall just yet. Seeing the stable door just a few yards away she made for it. It was dry within and warmer too, the air sweet and pungent with hay and horses. Letting her eyes adjust to the dimmer light she walked along the stalls until she came to the one that housed Steorra.

The mare heard her step and turned, whickering softly. Ashlynn smiled, and slipped into the stall, rubbing the horse's nose affectionately. When the bad weather let up it would be good to get out for a ride. Iain had mentioned a hunt. The prospect was alluring.

The thought of Iain brought their recent conversation to the fore again and she sighed. She had hoped her arguments might prevail with him but in retrospect wondered if she had done right to raise the topic again. A blood oath could never lightly be forsworn and he had every right to want revenge. Considered dispassionately it was understandable, and yet how hard it was to be dispassionate when considering the possible price of such revenge. Would it take him from her? Was this new-found happiness to be so soon destroyed? She understood then that her request had been in part about her own insecurities. The knowledge did not make her feel any better.

A footstep behind her made her turn, expecting to see one of the grooms. However, it was a very different figure that stood there. For the space of a dozen heartbeats they faced each other in silence.

'I thought I might find you here,' he said.

Ashlynn gave Steorra a final pat and came to join him at the entrance to the stall. 'Iain, what I said before…I'm sorry. I had no right to ask it.'

For a moment the dark eyes registered surprise. Then he sighed. 'You had the right, lass.'

'No, an oath like that is sacred. I see it now and I apologise.'

'Ach, lass, you've nothing to apologise for. Besides, there was much truth in what you said.'

Now it was her turn to feel surprise but before she could say anything he went on. 'I have carried the desire for revenge in my heart for so long it has become part of me. Not one of the better parts, I fear. Even now, I'm not sure I can let it go.'

'Iain, I—'

'No, hear me out, I beg.' He took a deep breath. 'If ever our paths cross, I will slay Fitzurse, but I'll not deliberately seek him out any longer.'

Her heart began to beat a little faster. 'Do you mean it?'

'I would not have said it otherwise, lass.' He eyed her keenly. 'Will that content you?'

It was so much more than she had ever expected that for a moment it was hard to speak. Then she nodded. 'Yes.'

Iain knew that a week ago, a day even, he could not have made that promise, but for the first time he had glimpsed something he wanted more than revenge. At some deep level he understood that a fundamental change had taken place and that it was due to his feelings for Ashlynn. He should have felt angry or resentful but he didn't. The feeling was liberating, as though a burden had been lifted.

'Then let the matter rest there,' he said.

'Thank you. In truth I did not expect so much.'

'I want that future we spoke of.'

'And I also. I want your children, Iain, and I want them to grow up knowing their father, not hearing about him at second hand.'

He smiled wryly. 'They'll come to know me well enough. More perhaps than they'll like.'

'I doubt that. It's my belief you'll make an excellent father.'

'Is it so? And what put that thought in your head?'

'Watching you with your little niece. You have a talent there.'

'Well, I've been practising, ye ken, for the real thing.'

'God willing, you'll have the real thing soon enough.'

She stepped closer and reaching up drew his face down to hers for a lingering kiss. When at length they came up for air he saw her gaze move beyond him towards the far end of the building. Instinctively his own turned to follow it and came to rest at the rear on the ladder that led up to the hayloft. Then he gave her a quizzical look.

'When first I came here you took me on a tour of Dark Mount,' she said.

'So I did, lass.'

'But you never did show me what lies up there, my lord.'

Iain felt his heart miss a beat. Then he grinned. 'That can soon be rectified.'

They made the ascent and he drew the ladder up after them, before leading her deeper into the loft space. There he spread his cloak on the hay under the eaves. For a moment they faced each other. Then he knelt, drawing her down with him, closing his arms around her. He felt her mouth open to his letting him taste the sweetness beyond while her body moulded itself to his. He withdrew just long enough to unfasten his belt and tunic and discard them. Then he rejoined her, his lips grazing her cheek, moving thence to her neck and throat while his hands raised the skirts of her gown. Ashlynn moved to accommodate him and felt him lift the fabric clear and then the warmth of his hands on her skin. Her flesh tingled in response. She slid her arms around him, running her tongue along his throat, tasting its salt warmth, breathing in the erotic musky scent of the man, letting her hands explore and caress the hard muscled flesh of his back beneath the shirt. The kiss grew deeper. Her hands slid to the fastenings of his breeches and loosened them, stroking the flesh beneath, feeling the hardening response. She heard him draw in a sharp breath, then pushed him back on the cloak and sat astride him, feeling him slide into her, taking the full length of him.

Iain had fantasised about making love to her in different ways and places but the reality far exceeded the dream. Moreover, there was an expression in her eyes that he had not seen before. It was both teasing and mischievous and it sent a wave of heat through his loins. He wanted her, reached for her hips, drawing her down on him, arching into her, thrusting deeper, desperate to answer that mounting fire. Ashlynn smiled, refusing to be hurried, making him wait.

'Ashlynn, I beg you…'

'All in good time, my lord.'

Bending forward she brought her mouth down on his, taking the kiss at leisure before resuming where she'd left off before, moving against him with deliberate and teasing slowness, fanning the flames. Iain's breath caught in his throat as another wave of pleasure hit him.

'Have mercy, lass.'

She heard him groan and smiled again, a very wicked and provocative smile that did not go unnoticed. Iain gritted his teeth.

'I warn you, my sweet, I intend to have my own back for this.'

'Revenge again, my lord?'

'Don't be in any doubt about it.'

He moved deeper into her and this time she made no reply save for a long and shuddering intake of breath. Then she was moving with him, building the tempo until it ended a little later in a mutual protracted climax.

Afterwards, they lay together beneath her cloak, sharing their warmth. Ashlynn snuggled close drowsing, her head against his shoulder. He bent to kiss her forehead and tightened his arms about her, still finding it hard to believe what had passed or the extent of the pleasure he had experienced. In truth he had not thought to find this again with any woman; had not thought to feel this way again about any woman. Yet somehow it had happened and he could no longer deny it. Nor could he deny the fascination she held for him. Each time he thought he was nearer to knowing her she surprised him anew. If this was a foretaste of what was to come… It led his mind along new and delightful paths and he felt his groin grow warm again.

Ashlynn was roused from her doze a short time later by a kiss, gentle and lingering at first but becoming deeper as she roused to consciousness. His hands drew her skirt and shift upwards. Ashlynn opened her eyes, regarding him quizzically.

'My lord?'

The dark eyes gleamed and he smiled, a deeply disturbing smile that sent a thrill of excitement the length of her body.

'I did warn you, lass.'

'About what?'

'That I intended to get my own back.'

By the time they returned to the tower it was dark and the smells from the kitchen indicated that the evening meal was about to be served.

'Now that was good timing,' he observed with a grin.

'Is food all you men think of?' she replied.

'Not all.' He drew her hard against him for another kiss.

'No more, my lord. I must go and change. Anyone seeing me now would think I'd been for a tryst in a hayloft.'

He shook his head. 'Shocking how people always think the worst. Heaven knows where they get such scandalous ideas.'

She smiled. 'I cannot imagine.'

They made their way up the stairs and, by sheer good fortune, reached the top floor unnoticed. There she left him and went to her own chamber to bathe and change her attire. Her body still burned with his love-making and every limb ached from that delicious and protracted revenge. Recalling the details she smiled to herself. Then, having hastily stripped off her clothing, she washed and donned a fresh shift and gown. With Morag's help she combed and braided her hair with matching gold ribbons. By the time she had finished no vestige remained of the tousled wanton and in her place was the elegant and gracious hostess.

Iain noted the change and grinned as she took her place beside him at table. For a moment or two he let his gaze linger on the curvy figure beneath the golden gown, letting his memory dwell on what lay beneath. It also recalled what had passed that afternoon. When in the early days of their marriage he had dreamed of her surrender he could never have guessed that her passion would equal his own, or that she would have the power to arouse him so far.

Aware of that penetrating gaze Ashlynn kept her attention first on the food and then on her guests lest with one glance she revealed the thoughts going through her mind. However, much of the talk that evening was about hunting and, since it had actually stopped raining outside, the tone was optimistic.

'If the cloud breaks up we might get a day yet,' said Duncan.

'Aye, we might.' Iain looked at Ashlynn. 'Do you still wish to come?'

'I wouldn't miss it,' she replied. 'Besides, I think some fresh venison would be most welcome among our guests.'

He turned to his brother-in-law. 'What say you to some hunting, Ban?'

'I'd like nothing better, my lord.'

'That's settled then.' Iain smiled. 'We're due for some sport.'

'A hart of ten?'

'With any luck. If the weather holds up we'll send Sim out early with his lymer and see what it can find for us. There's not a dog with a keener nose for miles around.'

Knowing the risk now of an endless male discussion about the minutiae of hunting, Ashlynn caught Jeannie's eye and saw an answering sympathy.

'I am sure we all look forward to some good sport tomorrow, brother. However, for now shall we have some music?'

Ashlynn recognised her cue. 'What an excellent idea.'

At her speaking look the suggestion was picked up and endorsed by several other ladies.

Iain smiled and submitted graciously. 'Very well. What would you have?'

Some called for music and others a song. Much to her surprise Ashlynn saw a servant hand her husband a lute and she watched him move to a stool nearby. Then he began to tune the instrument. She had not known he possessed any musical skill. Others evidently did for his acquiescence drew applause. Then he turned to Duncan.

'Will you favour us with a song, brother?'

Another chorus of approval greeted this, intensifying as Duncan got to his feet. It seemed the audience had a song in mind for they called out their choice most emphatically. With a laugh he inclined his head in consent. Listening attentively Ashlynn discovered that he had a good voice and he sang well to general acclaim. Then Jeannie was called upon for a rendition. Her protests availed her naught and at last she capitulated. The song was a ballad as near as Ashlynn could tell for the words were in Gaelic. The voice was strangely beautiful and arresting with an elusive quality that tugged at the heart for it seemed to her to be filled with heartache and loss. Unbidden and unheeded tears sprang to her eyes. The tune held her to the end and she joined in the thunderous applause. Glancing at Ban she could see that he too had been moved.

She had been expecting Jeannie to sit down after this but Iain said something to her and, having gained her agreement, he began to play again. However, when she sang this time he joined with her. His voice was fine and strong, a perfect complement to hers and again in the sweet Gaelic tongue. Ashlynn listened in complete amazement wondering how many more unknown facets there might be to this man she had married. When they finished the applause was tumultuous. This time Jeannie did sit down and presently her brother began another tune.

On the opening bars the conversation faded and the listeners fell silent. Iain fixed his gaze on Ashlynn and began to sing, a soft and beautiful melody that was unmistakably a love song. It wasn't necessary to understand the words to know it. In stunned surprise she listened, held by the expression in those dark eyes that spoke more than the words. She could not have looked away even if she had wanted to. With the swift thumping of her heart came the knowledge that this was much more than a song: it was a public declaration. That understanding was followed by a moment of exquisite pain in which everything around them vanished until the room contained only the two of them and the only sounds were the lute and the voice fused in that haunting expression of love and longing. Her heart acknowledged it and in that instant understood what it had tried so hard to deny.

When eventually the song ended the silence stretched out for several heartbeats before the room erupted. With one part of her consciousness Ashlynn heard the applause wash around them, but her eyes never left his. Then she saw him smile and her breath caught in her throat. Iain handed the lute to Hamish and returned to reclaim his place beside her.

'That was beautiful,' she said. It was the truth, like the emotion overpowering her now. 'I did not know you could sing.'

'Another example of my good aunt's training,' he replied. 'She was ever fond of music and encouraged the pursuit in others.'

'Did she teach you that song?'

'No, I knew it long before I went to France. It was one of my mother's favourites.'

'I see.'

He took her hand and pressed it to his lips. 'Indeed I hope you do, lass.'

Across the room Hamish strummed a few opening chords and launched into a rollicking tune whose chorus demanded loud audience participation, and the ensuing noise precluded further conversation.

It was much later before the singing ended and some of the guests began to take their leave.

Ashlynn expected Iain to linger as was his wont but to her surprise he accompanied her up the stairs. They strolled together along the passageway until they reached his chamber. Drawing her gently inside, he shut the door. Then he turned to face her, for a moment or two regarding her in silence.

'There is something I would give you, Ashlynn. I've been waiting for the right moment.' He reached into a pocket and drew out a small square of folded cloth. 'This is long overdue but I hope you'll think the wait worthwhile.'

He took her hand and placed the little package in her palm. She returned him a swift glance but his face revealed nothing. Curious now, she unwrapped the gift carefully, and then drew in a sharp breath. Inside was a ring. It was made of gold and exquisitely fashioned in an intricate pattern of love knots. For a moment she stared at it in silent wonder and then looked up at him.

'Where ever did you get this?'

'I had the smith make it. He does subtle work from time to time, in between his regular tasks.'

'He is highly skilled.'

'I'm sorry it's taken so long. I'd meant you to have it long since but Ewan will not be hurried.'

'Quite rightly,' she replied. 'He's a true craftsman.'

'You like it then?'

'It's beautiful, Iain.' She extended her hand. 'Will you do the honours?'

He took the ring and slid it on to her finger. Then he smiled faintly. 'It fits a lot better than the last one.'

'It's perfect. Thank you.'

He led her to the adjoining chamber and undressed her there, before removing his own clothing. Then he followed her to bed. Mindful of the demands he had made earlier he made none now, being content just to hold her close. She felt his body curl protectively around hers and smiled, sharing his warmth until they both slept.

Chapter Twelve

The following morning the chief huntsman went out at dawn. He returned from the quest with the intelligence that the lymer had found red deer in the wooded depths of a neighbouring glen. Among them was the coveted prize of a hart with a ten-tined rack of antlers.

Thus it was that a large party of riders, male and female, met in the courtyard. Spirits were high and the air filled with laughter and good-humoured banter. Ashlynn, mounted on Steorra, went to join her brother. Together they cast a critical gaze over the hunting dogs, part mastiff, part alaunt, huge lean beasts with wicked fangs.

'They look to have the strength and tenacity of the one breed and the reckless courage of the other,' he observed. 'If anything is going to bring a wild animal to bay, I think they will.'

'You're right,' said Iain who had reined his horse in alongside. 'Once they get the scent they don't give up.'

Soon the company set off, riding at a steady pace, reserving the stamina of the horses and dogs until they would be required. Ashlynn could feel Steorra's excitement. The mare longed to be off and made no secret of the fact with prancing steps and pricked ears. Like her the bigger animals were champing at the bit too. Stormwind essayed a half-rear and received a sharp word of warning from his rider in return. The big horse dropped his head and snorted in disgust. Ashlynn shot a sidelong glance at Iain and saw him slap the dappled neck good-humouredly.

'Behave yourself, you great lummox!' he told the horse. 'You'll get your chance soon enough.'

She laughed. 'He is impatient, my lord.'

'Aye, you'd think he'd never heard a hunting horn or seen dogs before.'

'All horses love the chase.'

'That they do.'

'They are not alone in that.'

His smile faded and for a moment his face grew serious. 'Stay with the other women, Ashlynn. This is wild country, and you're a stranger to it just now. It would be easy to get lost.'

'I'll do as you advise, my lord.'

He nodded. 'The border lands can be dangerous. This is not a good place to be alone.'

Recalling their encounters on the way north she could see the reason for his caution. 'Do you suppose there may be any danger?'

'Not for a party this size,' he replied.

'That's good to know.' She threw him a mischievous grin. 'I have no sword to hand this day.'

He returned the smile. 'That's as well for any robbers hereabouts. Not that I think there will be many of those. Your reputation will have frightened them off for sure.'

Ashlynn laughed. 'Not *my* reputation, I think.'

Iain turned to Ban. 'Did you know that your coaching had been so successful?'

'How so, my lord?'

'Did your sister not tell you that she single-handedly accounted for some very desperate villains?'

His brows drew together. 'Ashlynn never mentioned anything of the sort.'

'No? Well, she's very modest, ye ken.'

'So it would appear,' said Ban. 'Will you not bring me up to date on the subject, my lord?'

'I'd be delighted.'

Ashlynn threw her husband an eloquent look which he noted with enjoyment and promptly ignored. Then he favoured his brother-in-law with a colourful account of what had happened on the way to Jedburgh. Ban listened with mounting shock and incredulity but underneath it all was pride.

'You're a dark horse, Ash,' he said when the account was done at last.

Iain nodded solemnly. 'That's just what I said.'

'I was lucky,' she replied.

'Even so.' Ban grinned. 'Remind me not to make you angry.'

'She's a terror when her dander's up,' Iain informed him.

'You don't have to tell me, my lord. I grew up with her.'

'So you did. Was she always like it then?'

'You wouldn't believe the half of it.'

'Really. You must fill me in on some of the detail I've missed.'

'This is outrageous!' Ashlynn stared at them in disbelief. 'A conspiracy in fact.'

Iain's enjoyment mounted. 'Aye, lass, that's right.'

'In truth I don't know which of you is worse. I think I shan't stay to find out.'

With that she turned Steorra and rode back a way to join Jeannie, leaving the two men to their conversation.

It took about an hour to reach the glen where the lymer had found the deer. There the hunters deployed relays of hounds along the known tracks of the quarry. Ashlynn studied the wild and rugged terrain and understood why Iain had counselled caution. It would indeed be easy to lose oneself in this countryside. However, she had no intention of doing anything so foolish.

The lymer had done its work well and the other hounds picked up the scent very quickly and streamed away in full cry. Hearing the huntsman's horn the riders followed as fast as the terrain would permit. The men on their bigger, more powerful mounts soon drew ahead. Knowing that the chase could be lengthy Ashlynn made no attempt to push the mare too hard at this stage. Her stamina might be needed later when they came to more open ground. With care they would both have strength enough to last the day. Mindful also of what Iain had said, Ashlynn kept close to the other women riders. Most of them would have ridden here before and some like Jeannie probably knew the ground well. It was only common sense to be guided by their knowledge and experience.

The trail led along the glen for some way, threading through heath and rock before turning off up the wooded hillside. For a while the pace was reasonably swift for the trees were big and widely spaced. However, as the quarry made for the denser thickets the pursuit became more challenging because the rider's concentration was on the avoidance of low branches and slashing twigs. The pace slowed somewhat of necessity and Ashlynn took a swift look around. Just then the horn sounded some way off to the left and all the riders turned in that direction.

The hounds flushed the deer from the covert and made for open country. Here the relays would come into their own since, over distance, the hounds lacked the hart's stamina. With fresh reinforcements however, the chances of catching up with the quarry were greatly increased.

The ride was exhilarating as Ashlynn had known it would be and she gave the horse a little more rein, revelling in the speed and the clean cold air on her face. Up ahead she could see Iain's grey with the other leading horses and once she caught sight of Ban before his mount was swallowed up among the bays and chestnuts around him. She smiled to herself. Her brother was certainly fitter. The hunt would do him good in other ways too. Her thoughts were interrupted a few moments later as the foremost huntsmen disappeared into the cover of some trees.

It was at that point when, out of the corner of her eye, she became aware of other riders. A cursory glance revealed a group of about a dozen horsemen, approaching fast at an oblique angle. Curious, she took another, closer look. It seemed likely they were more of Iain's men and certainly there was nothing to tell them apart, being clad in the same leather hunting costumes. However, something about them gave her pause. She frowned, knowing something wasn't right but being unsure what. As the horsemen came on she realised it wasn't their appearance that was amiss but their course, for it became increasingly clear that they weren't following the main hunt; they were heading for the group in the rear. Now the leading body of huntsmen were in the trees the women riders were caught in the open and ripe to be cut off from the rest. Ashlynn felt the skin prickle on the back of her neck. A glance at her sister-in-law revealed she'd seen the horsemen too.

'Who are they, Jeannie?'

'I don't know,' she called back, 'but I don't like the look of them.'

'Nor I.'

Some of the other ladies had noticed the oncoming riders now and were looking distinctly nervous. Jeannie shouted across to them, 'Spread out and ride for the trees! Go!'

They needed no second bidding. Ashlynn bent low over Steorra's neck and gave the mare her head. The chestnut leapt forward in response. Now more than ever she was glad she hadn't pushed the horse before. Nearer and nearer came the thundering sound of pursuit. Another horrified glance revealed how much closer they were; she could see the riders' faces set in lines of grim determination. In that second Ashlynn knew she wasn't going to reach the shelter of the trees. It was too far. Their mounts were bigger and more powerful and, at each stride, closing the gap between. In desperation she shouted to Steorra, urging her on, but the little mare was already running flat out.

In helpless anger Ashlynn could only watch as a horseman swept alongside and seized her reins. She heard shouts and then both horses were pulled to a plunging halt. Moments later she was surrounded. Only then did she realise what it was that been eluding her: the costumes might have disguised their identity from a distance but the cropped hair marked them immediately as Normans. Wild-eyed she looked around and saw with rising horror that Jeannie had been taken too. The other women were unmolested and fast disappearing into the distance. Then a man's voice broke into her consciousness and her stomach lurched as she recognised the speaker. De Vardes! For a second he favoured her with a gloating smile before turning his attention to her companion.

'Tell McAlpin that if he wants his wife back he must win her in single combat.'

Jeannie's face was pale but her dark eyes flashed fury. 'Against whom?'

'He'll know.'

'Where?'

'The circle of standing stones beyond Glengarron. Tomorrow at dawn. He's to come alone.'

'No! Don't do it!' Ashlynn broke in. 'Tell him to stay away!'

'You'd better pray he doesn't, my lady,' replied De Vardes. 'Otherwise we'll return you to him a piece at a time.' He looked back at Jeannie. 'Just deliver the message.'

'I'll deliver it,' she replied. 'I'll tell you something too:

if you harm Lady Ashlynn there won't be a corner of hell for you to hide in after.'

'The lady will not be harmed, so long as McAlpin does as he's told. However, any attempt to follow us now will result in me cutting her throat the moment we sight pursuit.'

With that he jerked his head at the man holding the reins of her palfrey. He relinquished his hold. Jeannie threw Ashlynn an eloquent anguished look and then reluctantly turned her horse and rode away towards the wood. For a moment De Vardes watched her go. Then he brought his mount alongside Ashlynn's. Without a word he pulled the reins from her grasp and drew them over Steorra's head. Then, he led her away.

Iain heard his sister in expressionless silence, his eyes like iced flint in the pallor of his face. Beside him Ban turned white. All around them the others fell silent too as they listened to the message, every countenance registering anger and disbelief.

'He said you'd know your opponent,' Jeannie went on. 'What did he mean? Who is it, Iain?'

'Fitzurse.'

'Dear God, not he.'

'The same.'

Ban shot him a piercing look. 'Fitzurse! Was not he the man responsible for the destruction of Heslingfield?'

'Aye, he was.'

'You know him by more than repute, I think.'

'Aye, I do, and but for circumstances I'd have slain him long since. But he'll not escape again. This time I'll rid this earth of him once and for all.'

'What are you going to do?' asked Dougal.

'Meet him. What else?'

With that he turned his horse for home. For a moment they watched him go, then gathered their wits and set off in his wake, silent and grim-faced.

Iain rode mechanically, his mind elsewhere and his gut knotted with cold rage. Eight years rolled away, to another day and another hunt. Two women he had loved; two women taken from him by the same man. This time however, there was going to be a different outcome. He had once thought that he could never love again, a mistaken belief if ever there was one. It was a love hard earned but all he could see now was Ashlynn's face. Eloise had been the glorious passion of his youth, a wonderful romantic dream whose beauty would remain with him always. This was different again, a love found in maturity, slower to grow but engendering a deep and lasting need, an emotion that engaged mind, body and spirit. His love for Ashlynn had made him whole again. With her image came the knowledge that this wasn't just about settling an old score now, it was about his reason for living and his hopes of a future.

The swift pace brought them back to Glengarron an hour later. Within a very short time of their return everyone at Dark Mount knew what had happened and the atmosphere so cheerful before became brooding and angry. The insult to the laird was an insult to them all. However, it was Ban whom Jeanne watched now, not her brother. The young man's face was so white it looked bloodless. Guessing only too well at the thoughts behind, she laid a gentle hand on his arm.

'Have no fear,' she said, 'we'll get her back.'

'Aye, but alive or dead, my lady?' he replied.

'Fitzurse will not harm her,' said Iain. 'She's too valuable to him alive. He means to use her to get to me.'

'You canna believe he'll meet you in single combat?' said Dougal. 'It's a trap for sure.'

'Of course it is, and yet I mean to make the bastard face me.'

'How? You ride in alone and you're dead.'

Iain shot him a piercing look. 'Who said anything about going in alone?'

His lieutenant returned the look and held it. 'You've got a plan.'

'Aye. Have all the men come here to the hall. I need to talk to them.'

As Dougal hastened to obey, Ban stepped in. 'I mean to do my part in this, my lord, whatever you decide upon.'

Iain nodded grimly. 'You shall, good brother. I swear it.'

Ashlynn had no idea how long they travelled or of where they went, her mind being too full of dread for Iain. Recalling the day she and Ban had ridden out with Callum she guessed that it had been no deer on the hillside. Glengarron had been watched. Moreover, for the enemy to get so close argued that they had help, somewhere local to use as a base. A man like Iain had enemies. Had the Norman been able to exploit that? The more she thought about it the likelier it seemed.

Her captors rode until they came to a lonely grange. It was an imposing building and clearly the property of a man of some substance, but the grey stone walls

and high arrow slit windows gave it a dour and for-
bidding aspect. The cavalcade clattered through an
arched gateway and into the courtyard beyond. There
Ashlynn was pulled off the horse and taken into the
building. Thence she was led up a spiral stone staircase to the topmost floor and thrust into a small turret
room. Then the door was slammed shut behind her and
locked. Footsteps retreated down the stairs.

Trembling she massaged her bruised wrist and
looked around. The room was cold and gloomy, the
only light filtering in through one small window set
high in the wall, and was devoid of all furnishing save
for a thin straw pallet and, in one corner, a slop bucket.
The narrow door was iron bound oak and had no handle
on her side. There was to be no escape from her prison.
For some time she paced the floor in helpless rage but
eventually gave it up to sink disconsolately on to the
straw pallet.

Some time later she heard more footsteps on the
stairs and then the sound of a key in the lock. Ashlynn
sprang to her feet and moved away toward the far wall.
The door opened and then a man stepped into the room.
Her heart leapt towards her throat. Fitzurse!

He surveyed her for a moment and then smiled
faintly. 'We meet again, my lady.'

He advanced a step or two and a second man
followed him in. He was younger than Fitzurse by about
ten years or so and shorter by a head. She had an impression of a stocky and slightly corpulent frame clad
in a stained tunic. Lank and greasy brown hair hung
about a stubbled face whose pale blue gaze was now

fixed on their prisoner. Then he smiled, revealing stained teeth.

'So this is McAlpin's woman.'

Fitzurse shot him a sideways glance. 'That's right.'

'I'd heard tell she was fair but the tales didna do her justice.'

Ashlynn swallowed, clutching the edges of her cloak, and her gaze returned to Fitzurse.

'Allow me to introduce our host, Sir Robert Fraser. He's been looking forward to meeting you.'

'That I have,' replied the other.

Fighting down a sense of foreboding she forced herself to remain calm.

'Why have you brought me here? What do you want?'

'I want Iain McAlpin,' Fitzurse replied. 'With your help I'm going to have him too.'

'You have no right to pursue him here. This land is not under your king's jurisdiction.'

'A minor point, and one that need not trouble us.'

'Where is this place?'

'Dungavan,' replied Fraser. 'Does the name mean anything to you, my lady?'

'No, should it?'

'Perhaps not,' he returned, 'though you'll be hearing a lot more of it in due course.'

'You speak in riddles.'

'Like my lord Fitzurse, I have a bone to pick with your husband too.' He gave her another nasty smile. 'It's concerned with kidnapping and extortion.'

Warning bells went off in her mind as the words revived a memory, but before she could identify it precisely he went on.

'I've waited a long time to even the score but, as the saying goes, everything comes to him who waits.'

'What do you mean to do?'

'Tomorrow my enemy will die, but before he does he'll know I take his wife.'

Ashlynn's stomach knotted and only with a supreme effort of will did she force herself to meet his gaze.

'You will never take his wife.'

He laughed softly, a sound that chilled her to the core. 'Your loyalty does you credit, my lady, but after a night in my bed you might change your mind.'

'I doubt that.'

The pale eyes hardened. 'You are haughty, but that will soon change, I promise you—if my lord Fitzurse doesn't humble your pride first.'

Ashlynn's heart hammered in her breast and she darted a swift look at the Norman. He saw it and nodded.

'Ah, yes. We have unfinished business you and I.'

'We have no business of any kind.'

'You're wrong. We were interrupted as I recall, but I always finish what I start.'

'Finish it now if you like,' said Fraser. 'It makes no odds to me. I'll have her later after all.'

The icy knot in her stomach grew larger as the walls of the room began to close in. There was only one door and they were between it and her.

'No,' replied Fitzurse. 'I'll finish it tomorrow when I take her in front of McAlpin. He can watch—before I cut his throat.'

'I think it will be you who dies tomorrow,' said Ashlynn. 'You are no match for him in single combat.'

'Single combat? How naïve. Say rather a ring of steel.'

'I might have guessed you'd resort to treachery,' she replied. 'But Iain won't fall easily into a trap.'

He moved towards the door, pausing on the threshold. 'He will.'

'You seem very sure of that.'

'I am sure. After all, you are the bait.'

They left her then, locking the door behind them. Ashlynn leaned back against the wall, trembling in every limb. The tears she had controlled before welled behind her eyelids. Iain would ride to meet his old enemy tomorrow but he would not ride away. This time he would die. She knew then that if he did she would die too and by her own hand. Rather a swift death with him than a lifetime without him, or dishonour at the hands of his enemies. In that moment she understood why Eloise had ended her life. The knowledge gave her courage. If it came to the choice she knew she would do no less.

No one else came to her prison after that and she was offered neither food nor water, though in truth she could not have eaten anything. Gradually the light faded and the cold intensified. Ashlynn wrapped her cloak closer about her and curled up on the straw pallet. As evening turned to night she began to doze intermittently but every time she closed her eyes she saw Iain's face and the feeling of sick dread increased. Miserable and shivering she waited for the dawn.

Having gone over the plan in detail Iain dismissed his men and repaired to the roof terrace, needing some time alone. He stood by the stone parapet, looking out over the darkening glen but in truth it was not the hills that he saw. Somewhere out there was Ashlynn. The thought of her fear and despair tormented him, but it wasn't that alone. For all his calm words to Ban and the rest his heart was riven by doubt. Had they hurt her? Had Fitzurse sought to finish what he had begun before? Would he do to Ashlynn what he had done to Eloise? Iain's fists clenched and he drew in a deep breath of cold air to combat the nausea that knotted his stomach. The Norman was ruthless and cruel and he knew there was no surer way to hurt his foe than this.

'Dear God, let her be unharmed,' he murmured. 'It took so long for me to find her. Let me not lose her now. Let me not lose the hope she brings.'

With a bitter sense of irony he remembered his promise to forswear all thought of revenge. *'Unless our paths cross.'* And now their paths had crossed. Was Fitzurse always to be his evil nemesis? Was it part of some divine plan? Well then, he would not seek to circumvent it. Tomorrow he would ride to meet his enemy, and his destiny.

Chapter Thirteen

⧸⧹

The circle of stones stood on the hill beyond Glengarron. Higher than a man and twice as wide, the silent monoliths remained unchanged by the vagaries of time or weather though the race that built them had long since vanished. Their brooding presence commanded the hill top. All around in every direction open moor land stretched away beneath a louring sky, the sere heath dark and sombre beneath a chill wind. The only other sounds were of creaking saddle leather and muffled hoof falls on peaty soil. As they drew nigh the place, Ashlynn saw with sick despair that Fitzurse and Fraser had chosen well. Here their enemy would be completely alone, isolated from any form of help. They, on the other hand, had with them a dozen armed men, murderous odds by any standard. The party reined in and came to a halt some yards outside the ring of stone.

Fraser looked around at the empty heath. 'He's not here.'

'Then we wait,' replied Fitzurse.

'He will not come. It would be madness and he knows it.'

The Norman glanced at Ashlynn. 'He'll come.'

She forced herself to meet his eye, regarding him with cold contempt. 'He will not be so easy to kill.'

'On the contrary, I expect it will be very easy, in the end.' Seeing Ashlynn's cheeks turn a shade paler, Fitzurse smiled appreciatively. His cold gaze stripped her, bringing back other memories. 'I'll say one thing for McAlpin. He always had good taste in women. It's the one thing we share.'

Fraser returned the smile. 'The one thing we're all going to share.'

Sickened with disgust she turned away, refusing to dignify the gibe with a reply. As she did so her gaze fell on the lone horseman approaching out of the east. Her heart began to thump painfully hard. Even from a distance there could be no mistaking the dark-clad figure on the dapple grey stallion.

'Iain,' she murmured.

In that second she knew that she loved him, unconditionally and beyond all reason. He was her lord. There could be no other as long as she lived. In that moment of awful clarity she knew the sublime terror, the awful vulnerability of loving and all its aching need.

Following her gaze Fitzurse saw the advancing figure and his smile widened as he glanced at Fraser.

'There we are. I told you he'd come.'

He turned then to his men and ordered them to dismount. Two of them dragged Ashlynn off her horse and hands like iron closed round her arms as they flanked her, dragging her forward to stand in clear view, while the rest ranged themselves in a semi-circle behind their leader who alone remained mounted. All eyes watched the oncoming rider.

Fitzurse spoke quietly, never turning his head. 'Let him get closer before you shoot. There must be no mistakes. I want him alive.'

De Vardes nodded. 'There will be no mistake, my lord.'

For the first time Ashlynn noticed the crossbow he held at his side and her throat dried as she realised the intent. When the quarry was close enough for a clear shot De Vardes would use it to cripple and bring him down. Once Iain was injured and unable to defend himself, they would take him prisoner. Then they would exact their final revenge. Panic stricken she tried to break free but the restraining grip on her arms only tightened in response, holding her still. Seeing it, Fraser laughed.

'It's no use, my lady. Nothing can save Glengarron now. Two hours hence his head will adorn my gates.'

Sick at heart she could only wait and watch as the man she loved rode towards his death.

Iain approached at a leisurely pace, his gaze taking in every detail of the scene ahead, undeceived by the apparently quiet demeanour of the waiting men. He mentally numbered fourteen, including Fitzurse. Three stood off to the side, holding the horses, the rest were arrayed in a semi-circle, watching him come. All their attention was focused on him. It was what he had counted on.

As he drew nearer his gaze never left the waiting Normans. He knew full well Fitzurse had no intention of meeting him in single combat; most likely the plan

would be to bring him down and capture him alive.
Everything depended on what happened in the next
couple of minutes. Even as the thought formed itself he
saw with silent satisfaction the several dark-clad figures
that rose like wraiths from the heather behind the
Norman force. Seconds later the three men who had
been holding the horses fell silently with their throats
cut, never knowing what hit them. Iain smiled grimly.
Unaware of what was taking place behind, Fitzurse kept
his eye fixed on the approaching horseman.

'Get ready, De Vardes.'

The Norman raised the crossbow and took careful
aim. Ashlynn screamed a warning. The bolt flew and
seconds later the horseman lurched in the saddle and
then slipped sideways. Fighting deadly faintness she
could only stare at the spot and the riderless grey stallion
now standing with trailing reins.

'Got him.' De Vardes was quietly exultant.

'Excellent,' said Fitzurse. 'Now bring him in.'

'Aye, my lord.'

De Vardes cast aside the bow and drew his sword.
'You three men, come with me.'

Ashlynn watched in helpless horror. In a short time
now Iain would be their prisoner and they would kill
him, but not quickly, dear God not quickly.

In torment she saw De Vardes and his companions
advance, but they had taken no more than half-a-dozen
paces before they checked, frozen in mid-stride. Then
they dropped like stones. Only then did she see the
crossbow quarrels embedded between their shoulder
blades. Before her brain could take it in she heard a
warning cry. More thuds followed and the hold on her

arms slackened as the two men on either side of her fell away with cries of pain, bolts sunk deep in their ribs. Seconds later the heath all around erupted with living forms, dark clad, their faces stained with peat as though the womb of earth had just delivered them. Taken totally by surprise the Normans had not even time to draw their weapons before the Scots were upon them with sword and dirk. What followed was brief, bloody and brutal. Ashlynn gasped, looking around in shocked bewilderment. Before her frightened eyes a savage figure seized Fraser by the hair and yanked his head back. He had time for one strangled cry before the naked dagger slit his throat from ear to ear.

Hard by Fitzurse fought to control his plunging horse, realising too late how he had been tricked, even as his furious gaze took in the scale of the disaster. Then, seeing the day was lost, he turned and spurred away. Off to the left of the fleeing figure Ban lifted his bow and took aim. The quarrel flew. A moment later the horse screamed and fell, crashing on to its side in the heather and pinning its rider to the ground.

'Good shot,' said Dougal. 'For a Sassenach, that is.'

Ban returned him a cool smile, never taking his eyes off the struggling figure on the ground. His hand went to the hilt of the blade at his side. 'Say the word and I'll finish him.'

'No.' The Scot turned to the men beside them. 'Bring him here—alive!'

Trembling with reaction, Ashlynn looked around in stunned disbelief, her mind unable to accept what her eyes were telling her. Somehow, in a matter of minutes, the Norman force had been annihilated. Her gaze came to rest again on the riderless stallion standing some hundred yards off, and her cheeks paled.

'Iain!'

Then she was running, her heart sick with dread, knowing what she must find. But before she got halfway there another dark-clad figure rose out of the concealing heather and caught hold of her. Ashlynn shrieked, kicking and struggling, fighting furiously. It took several moments before she recognised the voice speaking her name. Then she froze and looked up, seeing his face for the first time.

'Iain?'

Half-fainting with relief she felt him draw her close, crushing her close to his breast as though he could never let her go, and for a moment neither of them spoke. Then he looked down into her face.

'I thought I'd lost you. I thought…' He took a deep breath, summoning the courage to ask the question uppermost in his mind. 'Are you all right, lass? Did he hurt you? Did he…?'

'No.' She shook her head. 'I'm not hurt.'

He experienced the sensation of heartfelt relief. 'Thank God. Every moment since he took you from me I've lived in dread of what he might do.'

'He was saving his revenge for today. He and Fraser both.'

'Fraser! So that's who was helping them.'

'He spoke of a long-standing grudge.'

'I'm sure he did. 'Twas he I kidnapped once when his father reneged on an agreement.'

'But what of you, my lord? Are you not hurt?' She

held him at arm's length, her anxious gaze searching for signs of injury. 'De Vardes shot you.'

'I let them think he had.'

He smiled down at her and then his mouth was on hers in a passionate and lingering kiss. When he eventually drew away it was to see tears on her face.

'They meant to kill you, Iain. They meant to make me watch…' Her voice caught on a sob.

'Ach, lass, I'm sorry.' He drew her to his breast until her sobs quieted a little. 'You should not have had to suffer for my fault.'

'It doesn't matter now. His plan failed. It's over.'

Iain glanced towards the waiting men. 'No, lass. Not yet.'

She looked up quickly. 'What do you mean?'

'There's one more thing I have to do.'

Her heart beat a little faster and with a sense of dread she followed his gaze to where his men stood. Then she recognised their prisoner.

'Iain, you promised…'

'I promised not to seek him out and I have kept my word. He has sought me.'

'That is true, but even so I beg you…'

'This must be settled, Ashlynn, and I mean to see that it is,' he replied.

The tone was implacable and she knew that no words of hers would change his mind. They walked back to where Dougal and the others waited. In their midst stood Fitzurse, his hands bound. Seeing his sister, Ban hastened to greet her with a glad smile, folding her in his arms. Then, as he glanced down and saw her tear-stained face, his joy faded a little.

'Dear God, are you all right, Ash? Did this scum hurt you?'

'No, he did nothing, beyond holding me prisoner.'

'I thank heaven for it.' Ban threw a cold glance at the captive. 'But this vermin will pay for his crimes in due course.'

'Aye, he will,' replied Iain.

'It is your right, my lord,' said Ban, 'for yours is the prior claim. I acknowledge it and yield in obedience to the duty I owe you. But let his payment take into account the destruction of Heslingfield and the slaying of our kin.'

'It will, good brother, I swear it.' Iain looked at Fitzurse and then at Dougal, nodding toward the ring of stones. 'Take him in there.'

His men moved into the ancient monument and formed up in a large inner circle leaving Fitzurse at its centre. Then each one drew his sword. The Norman darted swift looks around him but could find no way out. Moreover, the faces that met him there were cold and hard, entirely without pity or remorse. He licked dry lips. The Scottish laird strolled into the circle, a naked sword in his hand. He halted a few yards away.

'Cut his bonds.'

When Dougal had obliged, Iain thrust the sword into the earth and left it quivering there. Then he drew his own blade and looked at Fitzurse.

'Defend yourself.'

The tone was soft but there could be no mistaking the intention behind. Fitzurse edged forward, his gaze darting between the sword and his waiting opponent, half-expecting some trick. It never came; the other man made no move towards him. Then his hand closed on the hilt and the weapon was his.

The two men circled each other and Ashlynn caught her breath as Fitzurse rushed forward. Iain side-stepped, parrying the thrust easily. The blades engaged again as the Norman attacked with a rain of fierce blows. Each time his sword was met and turned aside. Then, without warning, Iain lunged. Too fast for the eye to see, his blade caught his opponent across the upper arm. The only sign of its passing was the sudden red stain that bloomed through the rent sleeve of the leather tunic. Fitzurse glared at it and then retaliated with another series of savage cuts. Again they were turned aside. Another swift lunge and Iain's sword drew a deeper gash along the other arm. Biting back the cry of pain the Norman gave a little ground, circling once more, warier now as he looked for an opening. Then he darted in again. This time Iain gave ground. Fitzurse smiled and went after him. Too late he saw the feint. The Scottish sword opened a gash along his ribs. Fitzurse snarled, clapping a hand to his side, feeling there the sticky warmth of blood. In fury and desperation he laid on anew, succeeding in driving the other man back by the sheer ferocity of the attack. Sparks leapt from the edges of the blades.

However, no matter how hard he tried he could not penetrate his enemy's defence and his sword met only steel or empty air. Another cut appeared on his left arm. He realised then that the Scot was playing with him, meaning to weaken him gradually, until he could step in and deliver the *coup de grâce*. Fitzurse knew a moment of panic. The wounds he had sustained were bleeding freely and the pain increasing. Sweat broke out on his forehead. He had fought many opponents but never one as fast or as skilled.

'Why do you not end it?' he demanded.

'I'm not ready to end it yet,' the Scot replied.

Fitzurse reeled away towards the edge of the circle, seeking blindly for some means of escape but was met with a ring of steel. Seeing there was nothing else for it, he turned and stumbled back towards his enemy. Iain let him come. The Norman laid on again, but his blows were wilder now and careless costing him a slash to the leg. He cried out as blood poured from the wound, staining the grass at his feet.

Ashlynn drew in a sharp breath, her gaze fixed on Iain's face. It was utterly remorseless, the face of a warrior whose hand wielded death, a face that fascinated and appalled. Beside her Ban never moved, riveted by the spectacle before them, understanding now exactly what he was watching.

It went on for some time until Fitzurse, bleeding from a dozen cuts, sank to his knees, exhausted, his expression filled with loathing.

'End it then, damn you.'

Ashlynn trembled, waiting for Iain to deal the death blow. It did not come. Instead he lowered his sword, regarding his enemy with contempt.

'I'll not take your worthless life,' he said then. 'I'll leave your fate to a higher authority.'

'What do you mean?'

'My king is well acquainted with your evil deeds already, and his views on those who violate the peace of his realm are well known. You're going to Dunfermline.' He turned away and gestured to Dougal and Fergus. 'Get him on a horse.'

Fitzurse paled, knowing the swift death he'd looked for would not be forthcoming. In its place was something far worse. The realisation of how much worse filled him with desperate fury. He struggled to his feet and lifting the sword rushed at his enemy's unguarded back.

Ashlynn screamed a warning. Iain spun round, sword raised to block the coming blow. As he did so Fitzurse's injured leg gave way, throwing him off balance and on to the thrusting point. The Norman froze in his tracks, hanging there, an expression of shock on his face, before both legs buckled and he fell.

Ashlynn looked on in shuddering disbelief. Then she ran towards her husband and a moment later was in his arms. He held her close and for the space of several heartbeats neither one spoke.

'I'll not pretend to be sorry that he's dead,' he said at last, 'but I truly intended to let Malcolm deal with him finally.'

'It wasn't your fault. Fitzurse was treacherous to the end.' Her voice caught on a sob. 'I thought he'd killed you.'

'But for your warning he might have done. I thank you, lass.'

'I can scarcely believe he's dead, that it's over now.'

'It's over. Today the ghosts of the past have been laid.' Even as he spoke the words he knew them for truth. The burden of hatred had been lifted along with all its corrosive power. Eloise could rest in peace for his promise to her was fulfilled, and he could move on. 'Fitzurse can harm us no more. Or anyone else for that matter.'

'I thank God for it, and for keeping you safe.'

'I thank Him too, lass.'

'If you had been slain today I would have died afterwards. If you were gone there would be no point in living, for without you I could never be truly alive.'

For a moment he was quite still, his heart full. The dark gaze burned into her own, intent, seeking the answer to an unspoken question. Ashlynn knew immediately what it was.

'I love you, Iain. More than my own life.'

'And I you, lass. When you were taken from me I finally understood how much. I have lived in dread since then lest history should repeat itself.' He drew a shuddering breath. 'But God was merciful this time.'

'Yes, He was.'

'It's a gift I value above all else. You are most precious to me, Ashlynn.'

'As you are to me, my lord.'

'My love and my wife,' he replied. Then he drew her close in a much more intimate embrace making further speech impossible.

Epilogue

◦◦◦∽◈∽◦◦◦

Ashlynn sat on a sun-warmed rock by the side of the burn and turned her face to the blue vault of the sky where a lark was singing. The liquid notes spilled joy on to the receiving earth and seeped into the soul like a healing benediction. For a while she followed the progress of the bird until it was no more than a dark dot on the edge of heaven. She smiled and brought her gaze back to earth, letting it range along the wooded slope of the glen, taking in the new green on every branch and twig, breathing the scent of grass and loam where splashes of yellow and white announced clumps of celandine and anemone. In the distant fields cattle grazed and new lambs frolicked. The land had thrown off the icy shackles of winter and everything around seemed to rejoice in the knowledge.

She was so engrossed in the scene that she failed to hear the soft hoof falls on the turf behind her, only becoming aware of the approaching horseman when his mount snorted. Startled from her reverie she looked round quickly and then smiled, getting to her feet. The dapple grey stallion stopped a few yards away, its rider surveying her keenly. Then he returned the smile.

'This is a most pleasant surprise.'

'Indeed it is. I did not expect you back from the village so soon, my lord.'

'My business there did not take as long as I feared it might.'

He brought his leg over the front of the saddle and dismounted, letting the rein fall so that the horse might graze. Then he came to join his wife, sliding an arm about her waist. 'I swear you get more beautiful each time I see you.'

'This is blatant flattery.'

'Not so.' He bent and kissed her soft mouth. ''Tis fully two hours since last I set eyes on you and I can avouch that your beauty has grown.'

Ashlynn laughed. 'My beauty, or your lust, my lord?'

'All right, my lust.' He seized hold of her with a teasing growl and, ignoring her startled shriek, took a much longer and more intimate kiss that sent the blood coursing through her veins. 'But what are you doing here, lass? Don't you know how dangerous it is to walk out alone?'

'It is too fine a day to be shut up indoors. Besides, there is no danger in walking alone in Glengarron. It is most strongly guarded.'

'Glengarron is especially dangerous,' he replied. 'Have you not heard about the reputation of its lord?'

'I have heard some rumours about that. Should I be worried?'

'At this moment you should be very worried.' He

swept her up and then took another lusty kiss. Breathless and laughing Ashlynn struggled in vain. The dark eyes gleamed. 'It's no use to try and escape, lass. You're in my power now and I'm minded to have my way with you.'

'Alas, the rumours are true then.'

His lips brushed her cheek and neck and throat sending a delightful shiver along her skin. 'Aye, they are, as you're about to discover.'

Ashlynn giggled. 'I beg you will be gentle, my lord.'

'Gentle? Why so?'

'Because I'm going to have a baby.'

The words stopped him in his tracks and all amusement faded. For a moment he stared at her, thunderstruck. 'A baby? When?'

'Next winter.'

'Ashlynn, are you sure?'

'Quite sure.'

A slow grin lit his face. 'That's wonderful!' Then another thought occurred to him and he regarded her with concern. 'But you should have told me before, lass. I wouldn't have been so rough. Have I hurt you?'

'No, you haven't hurt me.'

Feeling somewhat relieved he set her down gently, letting his gaze travel the length of her but could detect no sign of the child beneath the smooth surface of her gown. 'How long before it shows?'

'Not long. Another month perhaps.'

'How long have you known?'

'I have suspected for a while, but I wanted to be sure before I told you.'

He took her hand and raised it to his lips. Ashlynn regarded him askance.

'Nothing terrible will happen if you kiss me again, Iain.'

Nothing loath he accepted the invitation. Immediately he felt the familiar spark leap between them but he controlled it now, unwilling to do anything that might harm her or their child. And so the kiss was gentle and tender, conveying without words the thoughts of his heart. Then they sat together on the rock, enjoying the solitude and the sunshine and the secret knowledge they now shared.

'If our child is a son I would have him grow up to be a warrior like his father,' she said. 'If a daughter, then fair and wise.'

'Aye,' he replied, 'and with her mother's spirit.'

'I'm not sure that's such a good idea.'

'Not so. I would not have a milk-and-water maid in her place.'

'Whatever this child grows up to be, it will know its parents' love.'

His face grew serious and he nodded. 'Aye, lass, so it will.'

Having spent his youth finding out what fatherhood was not, he had a more than fair idea of what it should be. It was a role that, hitherto, he had only considered from a distance. Now it was about to become reality. The notion both scared and delighted him.

Unable to follow his thought Ashlynn eyed him quizzically.

'Will you mind very much if the child is a girl?'

Drawn back to the present he returned her gaze. 'No, lass. I won't mind as long as you and she are well.' He grinned. 'Besides, there is time aplenty to sire sons.'

She laughed. 'You sound very certain of that, my lord.'

'I am.' He bent and brushed her mouth with his. 'For I could never long resist the enchantment you have cast. I think the spell will not be broken while I live.'

The sun was past its zenith when they strolled back to the quietly grazing horse. Having lifted her on to the saddle he mounted and turned for home, keeping the grey to a gentle easy walk. Ashlynn relaxed against him, enjoying the warmth of his chest against her back, secure in the protective circle of his arm. Here, with him, in the glory of the spring sunlight the shadows of the past receded. All around them new life quickened like the child in her womb giving promise and hope for the future, a future that, not so long ago, she could never have dreamed would be hers.

Unable to follow her thoughts Iain bent and kissed her cheek. 'Happy?'

'Very happy. And you, my lord?'

'More than I could ever have hoped,' he said. And meant it.

* * * * *

MILLS & BOON
Historical

On sale 6th August 2010

Regency

RAKE BEYOND REDEMPTION
by Anne O'Brien

Alexander Ellerdine risks his life to rescue Marie-Claude
who's trapped by the tide. He's instantly captivated by her
dauntless spirit, but will she risk her heart on a rake who's
rumoured to be beyond redemption?

A THOROUGHLY COMPROMISED LADY
by Bronwyn Scott

Has Incomparable Dulci Wycroft finally met her match?
Viscount Jack Wainsbridge's dangerous work leaves no space
for love. Then he and Dulci are thrown together on a journey far
from Society's whispers – and free of all constraints…

Regency

BOUGHT: THE PENNILESS LADY
by Deborah Hale

Deceitful as Lady Artemis may be, embittered Hadrian
Northmore will marry her if he must! Hadrian thinks there's
been some mistake when his wife's disposition is sweet and
his hard-built defences begin to crumble…

MILLS & BOON

Historical

On sale 6th August 2010

IN THE MASTER'S BED
by Blythe Gifford

To live the life of independence she craved, Jane has
disguised herself as a young man! But she didn't foresee
her attraction to Duncan – and the delightful
sensations stirring in her very feminine body...

OUTLAW BRIDE
by Jenna Kernan

Bridget Callaghan is desperate to save her family stranded
in the Cascade Mountains. But the biggest danger is trusting
the only man who can help them – he's dark, dangerous
and condemned to hang!

TRIUMPH IN ARMS
by Jennifer Blake

Reine Cassard Pingre feels trapped: the only way to keep
her beloved home is to accept 'Falcon' Christien's bold
proposal of marriage. Reine cannot dissuade him
from wedding...and bedding...her!

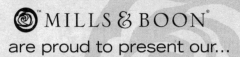

0710/01a

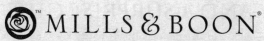

2 FREE BOOKS
AND A SURPRISE GIFT

We would like to take this opportunity to thank you for reading this Mills & Boon® book by offering you the chance to take TWO more specially selected books from the Historical series absolutely FREE! We're also making this offer to introduce you to the benefits of the Mills & Boon® Book Club™—

- **FREE home delivery**
- **FREE gifts and competitions**
- **FREE monthly Newsletter**
- **Exclusive Mills & Boon Book Club offers**
- **Books available before they're in the shops**

Accepting these FREE books and gift places you under no obligation to buy, you may cancel at any time, even after receiving your free books. Simply complete your details below and return the entire page to the address below. You don't even need a stamp!

YES Please send me 2 free Historical books and a surprise gift. I understand that unless you hear from me, I will receive 4 superb new books every month for just £3.79 each, postage and packing free. I am under no obligation to purchase any books and may cancel my subscription at any time. The free books and gift will be mine to keep in any case.

Ms/Mrs/Miss/Mr _____ Initials _____

_____

Surname _____

Address _____

_____

_____ Postcode _____

E-mail _____

Send this whole page to: Mills & Boon Book Club, Free Book Offer, FREEPOST NAT 10298, Richmond, TW9 1BR